ORBIT 13

ORBIT 13

Damon Knight, Ed.

A BERKLEY MEDALLION BOOK
PUBLISHED BY
BERKLEY PUBLISHING CORPORATION

Library of Congress Catalog Card Number: 66-15585

SBN 425-0 2698-1

*BERKLEY MEDALLION BOOKS are published by
Berkley Publishing Corporation
200 Madison Avenue
New York, N.Y. 10016*

BERKLEY MEDALLION BOOKS ® TM 757, 375

Printed in the United States of America

Berkley Medallion Edition, November 1974

CONTENTS

Kate Wilhelm

THE SCREAM

THE SEA HAD turned to copper; it rose and fell gently, the
motion starting so deep that no ripple broke the surface of the
slow swells. The sky was darkening to a deep blue-violet, with
rose streaks in the west and a high cirrocumulus formation in
the east that was a dazzling white mountain crowned with
brilliant reds and touches of green. No wind stirred. The ir-
regular dark strip that was Miami Beach separated the
metallic sea from the fiery sky. We were at anchor eight miles
offshore aboard the catamaran *Loretta*. She was a forty-foot,
single-masted, inboard motorboat.

Evinson wanted to go on in, but Trainor, whose boat it
was, said no. Too dangerous: sand, silt, wrecks, God knew
what we might hit. We waited until morning.

We had to go in at Biscayne Bay; the Bal Harbour inlet was
clogged with the remains of the bridge on old A1A. Trainor
put in at the Port of Miami. All the while J.P. kept taking his
water samples, not once glancing at the ruined city; Delia
kept a running check for radiation, and Bernard took pictures. Corrie and I tried to keep out of the way, and Evinson
didn't. The ancient catamaran was clumsy and Trainor was
kept busy until we were tied up, then he bowed sarcastically
to Evinson and went below.

Rusting ships were in the harbor, some of them on their
sides half in water, half out. Some of them seemed afloat, but
then we saw that without the constant dredging that had kept

7

the port open, silt and sand had entered, and the bottom was no more than ten to fifteen feet down. The water was very clear. Some catfish lay unmoving on the bottom, and a school of big-eyed mullet circled at the surface, the first marine life we had seen. The terns were diving here, and sandpipers ran with the waves. J.P.'s eyes were shining as he watched the birds. We all had been afraid that there would be no life of any kind.

Our plan was to reconnoiter the first day, try to find transportation: bicycles, which none of us had ridden before, skates, canoes, anything. Miami and the beaches covered a lot of miles, and we had a lot of work; without transportation the work would be less valuable—if it had any value to begin with.

Bernard and Delia went ahead to find a place to set up our base, and the rest of us started to unload the boat. In half an hour we were drenched with sweat. At first glance the city had seemed perfectly habitable, just empty of people, but as we carried the boxes to the hotel that Bernard had found, the ruins dominated the scene. Walls were down, streets vanished under sand and palmettoes and sea grapes. The hotel was five stories, the first floor covered with sand and junk: shells, driftwood, an aluminum oar eaten through with corrosion. Furniture was piled against walls haphazardly, like heaps of rotting compost. The water had risen and fallen more than once, rearranging floatables. It was hellishly hot, and the hotel stank of ocean and decay and dry rot and heat. No one talked much as we all worked, all but Trainor, who had worked to get us here, and now guzzled beer with his feet up. Evinson cursed him monotonously. We carried our stuff to the hotel, then to the second floor where we put mosquito netting at the windows of three connecting rooms that would be used jointly. We separated to select our private rooms and clear them and secure them against the mosquitoes that would appear by the millions as soon as the sun went down.

After a quick lunch of soy wafers and beer we went out singly to get the feel of the city and try to locate any transportation we could.

I started with a map in my hand, and the first thing I did was put it back inside my pack. Except for the general areas, the map was worthless. This had been a seawalled city, and the seawalls had gone: a little break here, a crack somewhere else, a trickle of water during high tide, a flood during a storm, the pressure building behind the walls, on the land side, and inevitably the surrender to the sea. The water had undermined the road system, and eaten away at foundations of buildings, and hurricane winds had done the rest. Some streets were completely filled in with rubble, others were pitted and undercut until shelves of concrete had shifted and slid and now rested crazily tilted. The white sand had claimed some streets so thoroughly that growth had had a chance to naturalize and there were strip-forests of palm trees, straggly bushes with pink and yellow flowers, and sea grapes. I saw a mangrove copse claiming the water's edge and stopped to stare at it for a long time, with curious thoughts flitting through my brain about the land and the sea in a survival struggle in which man was no more than an incidental observer, here, then gone. The afternoon storm broke abruptly and I took shelter in a building that seemed to have been a warehouse.

The stench of mold and decay drove me out again as soon as the storm abated. Outside, the sun had baked everything, the sun and rain sterilizing, neutralizing, keeping the mold at bay, but inside the cavernous buildings the soggy air was a culture for mold spores, and thirty years, forty, had not been long enough to deplete the rich source of nutrients. There was food available on the shelves, the shelves were food, the wood construction materials, the glues and grouts, the tiles and vinyls, the papers neatly filed, the folders that held them, pencils, everything finally was food for the mold.

I entered two more buildings, same thing, except that one of them had become a bat cave. They were the large fruit bats, not dangerous, and I knew they were not, but I left them the building without contest.

At the end of the first day we had three bicycles, and a flat-bottomed rowboat with two oars. I hadn't found anything of value. The boat was aluminum, and although badly corroded, it seemed intact enough. Trainor slouched in while J.P. was cooking dinner, and the rest of us were planning our excursions for the next day.

"You folks want boats? Found a storehouse full of them."

He joined us for dinner and drew a map showing the warehouse he had found. His freehand map was more reliable than the printed ones we had brought with us. I suspected that he was salvaging what he could for his own boat. Unless he was a fool that was what he was doing. When Evinson asked him what else he had seen that day, he simply shrugged.

"How's chances of a swim?" I asked Delia after we ate.

"No radiation. But you'd better wait for Corrie to run some analyses. Too much that we don't know about it to chance it yet."

"No swimming, damn it!" Evinson said sharply. "For God's sake, Sax." He issued orders rapidly for the next day, in effect telling everyone to do what he had come to do.

Strut and puff, you little bastard, I thought at him. No one protested.

The same ruins lay everywhere in the city. After the first hour it was simply boring. My bicycle was more awkward than going on foot, since I had to carry it over rubble as much as I got to ride it. I abandoned it finally. I found the Miami River and dutifully got a sample. It was the color of tea, very clear. I followed the river a long time, stopped for my lunch, and followed it some more. Ruins, sand, junk, palm trees. Heat. Silence. Especially silence. I was not aware of when I began to listen to the silence, but I caught myself walking cautiously, trying to be as quiet as the city, not to intrude in any way. The wind in the dry fronds was the only thing I heard. It stopped, then started again, and I jerked around. I went inside a building now and then, but they were worse than the ruined streets. Rusty toys, appliances, moldering furniture, or piles of dust where the termites had been, chairs that crumbled when I touched them, and the heat and silence.

I got bored with the river and turned in to what had been a garden park. Here the vegetation was different. A banyan tree had spread unchecked and filled more than a city block. A flock of blackbirds arose from it as I approached. The suddenness of their flight startled me and I whirled around, certain that someone was behind me. Nothing. Vines and bushes had grown wild in the park, and were competing with trees for space—a minijungle. There were thousands of parakeets, emerald green, darting, making a cacophony that was worse than the silence. I retraced my steps after a few minutes. There might have been water in there, but I didn't care. I circled the park and kept walking.

The feeling that I was being followed grew stronger, and I stopped as if to look more closely at a weed, listening for steps. Nothing. The wind in some pampas grass, the louder rustle of palm fronds, the return of the blackbirds. And in the distance the raucous cries of gulls. The feeling didn't go away, and I walked faster, and sweated harder.

I got out my kit and finished the last of the beer in the shade of a live oak with branches eighty feet long spreading out sideways in all directions. Whatever had poisoned Miami and reduced its population to zero hadn't affected the flora. The wind started, the daily storm. I sat in the doorway of a stinking apartment building and watched sheets of water race down the street. After the storm passed I decided to go back and try to get Corrie to bed with me. It never occurred to me to snuggle up to Delia, who seemed totally asexual. Delia and J.P., I thought.

Corrie was alone, and she said no curtly. She was as hot as I was and as tired. But she had a working lab set up, complete with microscopes and test tubes and flasks of things over Bunsen burners. She glanced contemptuously at the collecting bottle that I handed her. They knew about me, all of them.

"What did I do wrong?"

"Label it, please. Location, depth, source, time of day. Anything else you can think of that might be helpful."

Her tone said, and leave me alone because I have real work to do. She turned back to her microscope.

"So I'm not a hydrologist. I'm a pamphlet writer for Health, Education and Welfare."

"I know." She glanced at me again. "But why didn't they send a real hydrologist?"

"Because we don't have one."

She stood up and walked to the window netting and looked out. Her shirt was wet under her sleeves and down her back, her hair clung to her cheeks and the nape of her neck. "Why?" she whispered. "Why? Why? Why?"

"If they knew that we wouldn't be here."

She walked back to her chair and sat down again, drawing the microscope toward her once more.

"Is the bay all right?"

"Yes." She adjusted the focus and forgot about me. I left.

The warehouse where Trainor had found the boats was half a dozen blocks up the waterfront. I walked and sweated. Trainor had dragged some small boats outside, and I chose the smallest of them and took it down to the water. I rowed out into the bay, undressed and swam for half an hour; then I started to row, going no place in particular.

The water was marvelously calm, and I felt cooler and less tense after the swim. I stopped to dive a couple of times around a sunken yacht; it had been stripped. I stopped again, this time ashore at what looked like a copy of the Parthenon.

It had been a museum. The water lapped about the foundation; marble stairs and massive fountains indicated that it had been a grandiose thing. A statue had toppled and I considered it. A female form—vaguely female, anyway. Rounded, curving, voluptuous-looking, roughly hewn out of granite, it was touching somehow. The eye-hollows were facing out to sea, waiting, watching the water, waiting. The essence of woman as childbearer, woman as nourisher, woman as man's sexual necessity. Her flesh would be warm and yielding. She would be passive, accept his seed and let it come to life within her. Those great round arms would hold a child, let it suckle at the massive breasts. I wished I could stand the statue upright again. When it fell one of the arms had broken, it lay apart from the bulk of the work. I tried to lift it: too heavy. I ran my hand over the rough rock and I wanted to sit on the floor by the woman and talk to her, cry a little, rest my cheek against that breast. I began to feel suffocated suddenly and I turned and ran from the museum without looking for anything else. The sun was setting, the sky crimson and blue and green, incredible colors that looked like cheap art.

It was dark when I got back to headquarters. All the others were there already, even Trainor. Delia was cooking. I watched her as she added water to the dehydrated stew and stirred it over canned heat. She was angular, with firm muscles and hardly any breasts at all. Her hips were slim, boyish, her legs all muscle and bone. I wondered again about her sexuality. I had seen her studying Trainor speculatively once, but nothing had come of it, and I had seen almost the same expression on her face a time or two when she had been looking at Corrie.

I turned my attention to Corrie—a little better, but still not really woman, not as the statue had signified woman. Corrie was softer than Delia, her hips a bit rounder, her breasts bouncier, not much, but Delia's never moved at all. Corrie had more of a waistline. My thoughts were confusing to me, and I tried to think of something else, but that damn statue kept intruding. I should have talked to her, I found myself thinking. And, she would have looked at me with contempt. She would have looked at any of our men with contempt—except, possibly, Trainor.

I watched and listened to Trainor then, speaking with Bernard. Trainor was tall and broad-shouldered, his hair white, face browned by the sun, very lean and very muscular.

"Have you ever seen any wild animals as far north as the

cape?" Bernard asked, sketching. His fingers were swift and sure: That characterized him all the way, actually. He was soft-looking, but he moved with a sureness always. A dilettante artist, photographer, in his mid-thirties, rich enough not to work. There had been a mild affair with Corrie, but nothing serious. I didn't know why he was here.

"Deer," Trainor said in answer to his question. "There's a lot of things up in the brush. Foxes, rabbits, muskrats, possum."

"Anything big? I heard that lions were let loose, or escaped around West Palm Beach. Did they live, multiply?"

"Can't say."

"Heard there were panthers."

"Can't say."

"How about Indians? You must know if any of them are left in the swamps." Bernard's pencil stopped, but he didn't look at Trainor.

"Could be. Don't go inland much. No way to get inland, hard going by boat, hyacinths, thick enough to walk on. Too much stuff in the water everywhere. St. John's River used to be open, but not now."

"How about fish then? See any porpoises?"

"They come and go. Don't stay around long. Hear they're thick down around South America and in the Caribbean. Might be."

I watched Bernard for a long time. What was he after? And Trainor? I had a feeling that the seven people who had come to the city had seven different reasons, and that mine was the only simple one. Orders. When you work for the government and an undersecretary says go, you go. Why were the others here?

In bed later, I couldn't sleep. The odors all came back in triple strength after dark. I could feel the mold growing around me, on me, in my bedroll. The humidity was a weight on my chest. I finally got up again, drenched with sweat, my bed soaked through, and I went back to the second floor where I interrupted Delia and Bernard in a quiet conversation. I got a beer and sat down near the window, my back to them both. After a moment Delia yawned and got up.

At the doorway she paused and said, "Why don't you take him?"

I looked at her then. Bernard made a snorting sound and didn't answer. I turned back to the window. The silence was coming in along with the night-time humidity, and I realized that I had chosen my room on the wrong side of the building. The night air blew from the land to the sea. There was a faint breeze at the window. The oil lamp was feeble against the pressure of the darkness beyond the netting.

"Night," Delia said at the door, and I looked at her again, nodded, and she started through, then stopped. A high, uncanny, inhuman scream sounded once, from a long way off. It echoed through the empty city. The silence that followed it made me understand that what I had thought to be quiet before had not been stillness. Now the silence was profound, no insect, no rustling, no whir of small wings, nothing. Then the night sounds began to return. The three of us had remained frozen, now Bernard moved. He turned to Delia.

"I knew it," he said. "I knew!"

She was very pale. "What was it?" she cried shrilly.

"Panther. Either in the city or awfully close."

Panther? It might have been. I had no idea what a panther sounded like. The others were coming down again, Evinson in the lead, Corrie and J.P. close behind him. Corrie looked less frightened than Delia, but rattled and pale.

"For heaven's sake, Bernard!" J.P. said. "Was that you?"

"Don't you know?" Corrie cried. At the same time Delia said, "It was a panther."

"No! Don't be a fool!" Corrie said.

Evinson interrupted them both. "Everyone, just be quiet. It was some sort of bird. We've seen birds for three days now. Some of them make cries like that."

"No bird ever made a sound like that," Corrie said. Her voice was too high and excited.

"It was a panther," Bernard repeated. "I heard one before. In Mexico I heard one just like that, twenty years ago. I've never forgotten." He nodded toward the net-covered window. "Out there. Maybe in one of the city parks. Think what it means, Evinson. I was right! Wild life out there. Naturalized, probably." He took a breath. His hands were trembling, and he spoke with an intensity that was almost embarrassing. Corrie shook her head stubbornly, but Bernard went on. "I'm going to find it. Tomorrow. I'll take Sax with me, and our gear, and plan to stay out there for a day or two. We'll see if we can find a trace of it, get a shot. Proof of some kind."

Evinson started to protest. If it wasn't his plan, he hated it. "We need Sax to find water for us," he said. "It's too dangerous. We don't know what the beast is, it might attack at sight."

I was watching Bernard. His face tightened, became older, harsher. He was going. "Drop it, Evinson," I said. "They know about me. The only water I'll find is the river, which I already stumbled across, remember. And Bernard is right. If there's anything, we should go out and try to find it."

Evinson grumbled some more, but he couldn't really forbid it, since this was what the expedition was all about. Besides, he knew damn well there was no way on earth that he could enforce any silly edict. Sulkily he left us to plan our foray.

It was impossible to tell how the waterways had been laid out in many places. The water had spread, making marshes, and had changed its course, sometimes flowing down streets, again vanishing entirely, leaving dry beds as devoid of life as the Martian canals. Ruined concrete and sand lay there now. And the ruins went on and on. No frame houses remained; they had caved in, or had been blown down, or burned. A trailer court looked as if someone had taken one corner of the area and lifted it, tipping the chrome and gaudy colored cans to one side. Creepers and shrubs were making a hill of greenery over them. We rowed and carried the boat and our stuff all day, stopped for the storms, then found shelter in a school building when it grew dark. The mosquitoes were worse the farther we went; their whining drowned out all other noises; we were both a mass of swollen bites that itched without letup. We saw nothing bigger than a squirrel. Bernard thought he glimpsed a manatee once, but it disappeared in the water plants and didn't show again. I didn't see it. There were many birds.

We were rowing late in the afternoon of the second day when Bernard motioned me to stop. We drifted and I looked where he pointed. On the bank was a great grey heron, its head stretched upward in a strange but curiously graceful position. Its wings were spread slightly, and it looked like nothing so much as a ballerina, poised, holding out her tutu. With painful slowness it lifted one leg and flexed its toes, then took a dainty, almost mincing step. Bernard pointed again, and I saw the second bird, in the same pose, silent, following a ritual that had been choreographed incalculable ages ago. We watched the dance of the birds in silence, until without warning Bernard shouted in a hoarse, strange voice, "Get out of here! You fucking birds! Get out of here!" He hit the water with his oar, making an explosive noise, and continued to scream at them as they lifted in panicked flight and vanished into the growth behind them, trailing their long legs, ungainly now and no longer beautiful.

"Bastard," I muttered at him and started to row again. We were out of synch for a long time as he chopped at the water ineffectually.

We watched the rain later, not talking. We hadn't talked since seeing the birds' courtship dance. I had a sunburn that was painful and peeling; I was tired, and hungry for some real food. "Tomorrow morning we start back," I said. I didn't look at him. We were in a small house while the rain and wind howled and pounded and turned the world grey. Lightning flashed and thunder rocked us almost simultaneously. The house shook and I tensed, ready to run. Bernard laughed. He waited for the wind to let up before he spoke.

"Sax, we have until the end of the week and then back to Washington for you, back to New York for me. When do you think you'll ever get out of the city again?"

"If I get back to it, what makes you think I'll ever want out again?"

"You will. This trip will haunt you. You'll begin to think of those parakeets, the terns wheeling and diving for fish. You'll dream of swimming in clean water. You'll dream of the trees and the skies and the waves on the beach. And no matter how much you want to get it back, there won't be any way at all."

"There's a way if you want it bad enough."

"No way." He shook his head. "I tried. For years I tried. No way. Unless you're willing to walk crosscountry, and take the risks. No one ever makes it to anywhere, you know."

I knew he was right. In Health and Education you learn about things like public transportation: there isn't any. You learn about travel: there isn't any, not that's safe. The people who know how to salvage and make-do get more and more desperate for parts to use, more and more deadly in the ways they get those parts. Also, travel permits were about as plentiful as unicorns.

"You wanted to go back to Mexico?" I asked.

"Yeah. For twenty years I wanted to go back. The women there are different."

"You were younger. They were younger."

"No, it isn't just that. They were different. Something in the air. You could feel it, sniff it, almost see it. The smells were . . ." He stood up suddenly. "Anyway, I tried to get back, and this is as close as I could get. Maybe I'll go ahead and walk after all." He faced the west where the sky had cleared and the low sun looked three times as big as it should have.

"Look, Bernard, I could quote you statistics; that's my job, you know. But I won't. Just take my word for it. That's what I'm good at. What I read, I remember. The birth rate has dropped to two per thousand there. As of six years ago. It might be lower now. They're having a hell of a time with communications. And they had plague."

"I don't believe that."

"What? The birth rate?"

"Plague." He looked at me with a strange smile.

I didn't know what he was driving at. I was the one with access to government records, while he was just a photographer. "Right," I said. "People just died of nothing."

"It's a lie, Sax! A goddamn fucking lie! No plague!" He stopped as suddenly as he had started, and sat down. "Forget it, Sax. Just forget it."

"If it wasn't the plague, what?"

"I said to let it drop."

"What was it, Bernard? You're crazy, you know that? You're talking crazy."

"Yeah, I'm crazy." He was looking westward again.

During the night I wakened to hear him walking back and forth. I hoped that if he decided to start that night, he'd leave me the canoe. I went back to sleep. He was still there in the morning.

"Look, Sax, you go back. I'll come along in a day or two."

"Bernard, you can't live off nothing. There won't be any food after tomorrow. We'll both go back, stock up, and come out again. I couldn't go off and leave you. How would you get back?"

"When I was a boy," he said, "my father and mother were rather famous photographers. They taught me. We traveled all over the world. Getting pictures of all the vanishing species, for one last glorious book." I nodded. They had produced two of the most beautiful books I had ever seen. "Then something happened," he said, after a slight hesitation. "You know all about that, I guess. Your department. They went away and left me in Mexico, I wasn't a kid, you see, but I'd always been with them. Then I wasn't with them anymore. No note. No letter. Nothing. They searched for them, of course. Rich gringos aren't—weren't—allowed to simply vanish. Nothing. Before that my father had taken me into the hills, for a hunt. This time with guns. We shot—God, we shot everything that moved! Deer. Rabbits. Birds. A couple of snakes. There was a troop of monkeys. I remember them most of all. Seven monkeys. He took the left side and I took the right and we wiped them out. Just like that. They shrieked and screamed and tried to run away, and tried to shield each other, and we got every last one. Then we went back to my mother and the next day they were gone. I was fifteen. I stayed there for five years. Me and the girls of Mexico. They sent me home just before the border was closed. All North Americans out. I got permission to go back to New York, and for seventeen years I never left again. Until now. I won't go back again, Sax."

He leaned over and picked up a rifle. He had had it with his photographic equipment. "I have ammunition. I've had it for years. I'm pretty good with it: I'd demonstrate, but I don't want to waste the shell. Now, you just pick up your gear, and toss it in the boat, and get the hell out of here."

I suddenly remembered watching television as a child, when they had programs that went on around the clock—stories, movies. A man with a rifle stalking a deer. That's all I could remember of that program, but it was very clear and I didn't want to go away and let Bernard be that man. I stared at the rifle, until it began to rise and I was looking down the barrel of it.

"I'll kill you, Sax. I really will," he said, and I knew he would.

I turned and tossed my pack into the boat and then climbed in. "How will you get back, if you decide to come back?" I felt only bitterness. I was going back and he was going to be the man with the rifle.

"I'll find a way. If I'm not there by Friday, don't wait. Tell Evinson I said that, Sax."

"Bernard . . ." I let it hang there as I pushed off and started to paddle. There wasn't a thing that I could say to him.

I heard a shot about an hour later, then another in the afternoon, after that nothing. I got back to headquarters during the night. No one was up, so I raided the food and beer and went to bed. The next moring Evinson was livid with rage.

"He wouldn't have stayed like that! You left him! You did something to him, didn't you? You'll be tried, Sax. I'll see you in prison for this." Color flooded back into his face, leaving him looking as unnaturally flushed as he had been pale only a moment before. His hand trembled as he wiped his forehead that was flaky with peeling skin.

"Sax is telling the truth," Delia said. She had circles under her eyes and seemed depressed. "Bernard wanted me to go away with him to hunt. I refused. He needed someone to help him get as far away as possible."

Evinson turned his back on her. "You'll go back for him," he said to me, snapping the words. I shook my head. "I'll report you, Sax. I don't believe a word of what you've said. I'll report you. You did something, didn't you? All his work for this project! You go get him!"

"Oh, shut up." I turned to Corrie. "Anything new while I was gone?"

She looked tired too. Evinson must have applied the whip. "Not much. We've decided to take back samples of everything. We can't do much with the equipment we brought. Just not enough time. Not enough of us for the work."

"If you knew your business you could do it!" Evinson said. "Incompetents! All of you! This is treason! You know that, don't you? You're sabotaging this project. You don't want me to prove my theory. Obstacles every step of the way. That's all you've been good for. And now this! I'm warning you, Sax, if you don't bring Bernard back today, I'll press charges against you." His voice had been high-pitched always, but it became shriller and shriller until he sounded like a hysterical woman.

I spun to face him. "What theory, you crazy old man? There is no theory! There are a hundred theories. You think those records weren't sifted a thousand times before they were abandoned? Everything there was microfilmed and studied again and again and again. You think you can poke about in this muck and filth and come up with something that hasn't been noted and discarded a dozen times? They don't give a damn about your theories, you bloody fool! They hope that Delia can come up with a radiation study they can use. That Bernard will find wild life, plant life that will prove the pollution has abated here. That J.P. will report the marine life has reestablished itself. Who do you think will even read your theories about what happened here? Who gives a damn? All they want now is to try to save the rest." I was out of breath and more furious than I had been in years. I wanted to kill the bastard, and it didn't help at all to realize that it was Bernard that I really wanted to strangle. The man with the gun. Evinson backed away from me, and for the first time I saw that one of his hands had been bandaged.

Corrie caught my glance and shrugged. "Something bit him. He thinks I should be able to analyze his blood and come up with everything from what did it to a foolproof antidote. In fact, we have no idea what bit him."

"Isn't Trainor any help with something like that?"

"He might be if he were around. We haven't seen him since the night we heard the scream."

Evinson flung down his plastic cup. It bounced from the table to the door. He stamped out.

"It's bad," Corrie said. "He's feverish, and his hand is infected. I've done what I can. I just don't have anything to work with."

Delia picked up the cup and put it back on the table. "This whole thing is an abysmal failure," she said dully. "None of us is able to get any real work done. We don't know enough, or we don't have the right equipment, or enough manpower, or time. I don't even know why we're here."

"The Turkey Point plant?"

"I don't know a damn thing about it, except that it isn't hot. The people who built that plant knew more than we're being taught today." She bit her lip hard enough to leave marks on it. Her voice was steady when she went on. "It's like that in every field. We're losing everything that we had twenty-five years ago, thirty years ago. I'm one of the best, and I don't understand that plant."

I looked at Corrie and she nodded. "I haven't seen a transplant in my life. No one is doing them now. I read about dialysis, but no one knows how to do it. In my books there are techniques and procedures that are as alien as acupuncture. Evinson is furious with us, and with himself. He can't come up with anything that he couldn't have presented as theory without ever leaving the city. It's a failure, and he's afraid he'll be blamed personally."

We sat in silence for several minutes until J.P. entered. He looked completely normal. His bald head was very red; the rest of his skin had tanned to a deep brown. He looked like he was wearing a gaudy skullcap.

"You're back." Not a word about Bernard, or to ask what we had done, what we had seen. "Delia, you coming with me again today? I'd like to get started soon."

Delia laughed and stood up. "Sure, J.P. All the way." They left together.

"Is he getting anything done?"

"Who knows? He works sixteen hours a day doing something. I don't know what." Corrie drummed her fingers on the table, watching them. Then she said, "Was that a panther the other night, Davidson? Did you see a panther, or anything else?"

"Nothing. And I don't know what it was. I never heard a panther."

"I don't think it was. I think it was a human being."

"A woman?"

"Yes. In childbirth."

I stared at her until she met my gaze. She nodded. "I've heard it before. I am a doctor, you know. I specialized in obstetrics until the field became obsolete."

I found that I couldn't stop shaking my head. "You're as crazy as Bernard."

"No. That's what I came for, Davidson. There has to be life that's viable, out there in the Everglades. The Indians. They can stick it out, back in the swamps where they always lived. Probably nothing much has changed for them. Except that there's more game now. That has to be it."

"Have you talked to Evinson about this?"

"Yes, of course. He thinks it was Trainor who screamed. He thinks Trainor was killed by a snake, or something. After he got bitten himself, he became convinced of it."

"J.P.? Delia?"

"J.P. thinks it's a mystery. Since it has nothing to do with marine biology, he has no opinion, no interest. Delia thought Bernard was right, an animal, maybe a panther, maybe something else. She is afraid it's a mutated animal. She began to collect strange plants, and insects, things like that after you left. She even has a couple of fruit bats that she says are mutations."

I took a deep breath. "Corrie, why are we here? Why did the government send this expedition here?"

She shrugged. "What you told Evinson makes as much sense as anything else. The government didn't mount this expedition, you know. They simply permitted it. And sent an observer. It was Bernard's scheme from the start. He convinced Evinson that he would become famous through the proofs for his schoolboy theory. Bernard's money, Evinson's pull with those in power. And now we know why Bernard wanted to come. He's impotent, you know." She looked thoughtful, then smiled faintly at me. "A lot of impotent men feel the need to go out and shoot things, you know. And many, perhaps most men are impotent now, you know. Don't look like that. At least you're all right."

I backed away from that. "What about Evinson? Does he

believe a leak or an explosion brought all this about?"

"Bernard planted that in his mind," she said. "He doesn't really believe it now. But it leaves him with no alternative theory to fall back on. You can't tell anything by looking at these rotten buildings."

I shook my head. "I know that was the popular explanation, but they did investigate, you know. Didn't he get to any of the old reports? Why did he buy that particular theory?"

"All those reports are absolutely meaningless. Each new administration doctors them to fit its current platforms and promises." She shrugged again. "That's propaganda from another source, right? So what did happen, according to the official reports?"

"Plague, brought in by Haitian smugglers. And the water was going bad, salt intrusion destroyed the whole system. Four years of drought had aggravated everything. Then the biggest hurricane of the century hit and that was just too bloody much. Thirty thousand deaths. They never recovered."

She was shaking her head now. "You have the chronology all mixed up. First the drop in population, the exodus, then the plague. It was like that everywhere. First the population began to sag, and in industrialized nations that spelled disaster. Then flu strains that no one had ever seen before, and plague. There weren't enough doctors; plants had closed down because of a labor shortage. There was no defense. In the ten years before the epidemics, the population had dropped by twenty percent."

I didn't believe her, and she must have known it from my expression. She stood up. "I don't know what's in the water, Sax. It's crawling with things that I can't identify, but we pretend that they belong and that they're benign. And God help us, we're the ones teaching the new generation. Let's swim."

Lying on my back under the broiling sun, I tried again to replay the scene with my boss. Nothing came of it. He hadn't told me why he was sending me to Miami. Report back. On what? Everything you see and hear, everything they all do. For the record. Period.

Miami hadn't been the first city to be evacuated. It had been the largest up to that time. Throughout the Midwest, the far west, one town, one city after another had been left to the winds and rains and the transients. No one had thought it strange enough to investigate. The people were going to the big cities where they could find work. The young refused to work the land. Or agribusiness had bought them out. No mystery. Then larger cities had been emptied. But that was because of epidemics: plague, flu, hepatitis. Or because of government policies: busing or open housing; or the loss of government contracts for defense work. Always a logical explanation. Then Miami. And the revelation that population zero had been reached and passed. But that had to be because of the plagues. Nothing else made any sense at all. I looked at Corrie resentfully. She was dozing after our swim. Her body was gold-brown now, with highlights of red on her shoulders, her nose, her thighs. It was too easy to reject the official reasons, especially if you weren't responsible for coming up with alternative explanations.

"I think they sent you because they thought you would come back," Corrie said, without opening her eyes. "I think that's it." She rolled on her side and looked at me.

"You know with Trainor gone, maybe none of us will get back?" I said.

"If we hug the shore we should make it, except that we have no gas."

I looked blank, I suppose. She laughed. "No one told you? He took the gas when he left. Or the snake that killed him drank it. I think he found a boat that would get him to the Bahamas, and he went. I suppose that's why he came, to get enough gas to cruise the islands. That's why he insisted on getting down by sail, to save what gas Evinson had requisitioned for this trip. There's no one left on the islands, of course."

I had said it lightly, that we might not get back, but with no gas, it became a statement of fact. None of us could operate the sail, and the boat was too unwieldy to paddle. The first storm would capsize us, or we would run aground. "Didn't Trainor say anything about coming back?"

"He didn't even say anything about leaving." She closed her eyes and repeated. "There's no one there at all."

"Maybe," I said. But I didn't believe there was, either. Suddenly, looking at Corrie, I wanted her, and I reached for her arm. She drew away, startled. They said that sun-spot activity had caused a decrease in sexual activity. Sporadically, with some of us. I grabbed Corrie's arm hard and pulled her toward me. She didn't fight, but her face became strained, almost haggard.

"Wait until tomorrow, Davidson. Please. I'll ovulate tomorrow. Maybe you and I . . ." I saw the desperation then, and the fear—worse, terror. I saw the void in her eyes, pupils the size of pinpricks in the brilliant light, the irises the color of the endless water beyond us. I pushed her away and stood up.

Don't bring me your fear, I wanted to say. All my life I had been avoiding the fear and now she would thrust it upon me. I left her lying on the beach.

Evinson was sick that night. He vomited repeatedly, and toward dawn he became delirious.

J.P. and I took turns sitting with him because the women weren't strong enough to restrain him when he began to thrash about. He flung Corrie against the wall before we realized his strength and his dementia.

"He's dying, isn't he?" J.P. said, looking at him coolly. He was making a study of death, I thought.

"I don't know."

"He's dying. It might take a while, but this is the start of it." He looked at me fixedly for a long time. "None of us is going back, Sax. You realize that, don't you?"

"I don't know about the rest of you, but I'm going back. You're all a bunch of creepies, crazy as bedbugs, all of you. But I'm going back!"

"Don't yell." His voice remained mild, neutral, an androgynous voice without overtones of anything human at all.

I stamped from the room to get a beer, and when I got back, J.P. was writing in his notebook. He didn't look up again. Evinson got much worse, louder, more violent, then his strength began to ebb and he subsided, moaning fitfully now and then, murmuring unintelligibly. Corrie checked him from time to time. She changed the dressing on his hand; it was swollen to twice its normal size, the swelling extending to his shoulder. She looked at him as dispassionately as J.P. did.

"A few more hours," she said. "Do you want me to stay up with you?"

"What for?" I asked coldly. "I must say you're taking this well."

"Don't be sarcastic. What good would it do if I put on an act and wept for him?"

"You might care because he's a man who didn't deserve to die in this stinking city."

She shrugged. "I'll go on to bed. Call me if there's any change." At the doorway she turned and said, "I'll weep for myself, maybe even for you, Sax, but not for him. He knew what this would be like. We all did, except possibly you."

"You won't have to waste any tears for me. Go on to bed."

She left and I said to J.P., "You all hate him, don't you? Why?"

J.P. picked up his pen again, but he hesitated. "I hadn't thought of it as hating him," he said thoughtfully. "I just never wanted to be near him. He's been trying to climb onto the glory train for years. Special adviser to presidents about urban affairs, that sort of thing. Absolutely no good at it, but very good at politics. He made them all think there was still hope. He lied and knew he lied. They used to say those that can do; those that can't teach. Now the saying goes, those that can't become sociologists." He put his pen down again and began to worry at a hangnail. His hands were very long and narrow, brown, bony with prominent knuckles. "A real scientist despises the pseudo-scientist who passes. Something unclean about him, the fact that he could get permission for this when his part of it was certain to be negligible from the start."

"And yours was important from the start, I suppose?"

"For fifteen years I've wanted to get back into field research. Every year the funds dwindled more. People like me were put into classrooms, or let go. It really isn't fair to the students, you understand. I'm a rotten teacher. I hate them all without exception. I crammed and worked around the clock to get as good a background as I could, and when I was ready, I forced myself on Albert Lanier." He looked at me expectantly and I shook my head. Only later did I recall the name. Lanier had written many of the books on marine biology that were in the libraries. J.P. looked at me with contempt. "He was a great man and a greater scientist. During his last years when he was crippled with rheumatoid arthritis, I was his eyes, his legs, his hands. When he died all field research died with him. Until now."

"So you're qualified for this work."

"Yes, I'm qualified. More than that fool." He glanced at Evinson who was breathing very shallowly. "More than anyone here. If only my work is made known, this farce will be worth ten of him, of all of you."

"If?"

"If. Would any one of my own students know what I'm doing? My own students!" He bit the hangnail and a spot of blood appeared on his thumb. He started to scribble again.

At daybreak Evinson's fever started to climb, and it rose steadily until noon. We kept him in wet sheets, we fanned him, Corrie gave him cool enemas. Nothing helped. He died at one thirty. I was alone with him. Corrie and Delia were both asleep.

J.P. knew when he looked at my face. He nodded. I saw his pack then. "Where the hell are you going?"

"Down the coast. Maybe down the Keys, as far as I can get. I'd like to see if the coral is coming back again."

"We leave here Saturday morning at dawn. I don't give a damn who's here and who isn't. At dawn."

He smiled mockingly and shook his head. He didn't say good-bye to anyone, just heaved his pack onto his back and walked away.

I rummaged on the *Loretta* and found a long-handled, small-bladed shovel, and I buried Evinson high on the beach, above the high-water mark.

When I got back Corrie was up, eating a yellow fruit with a thick rind. I knocked it out of her hand reflexively. "Are you out of your mind! You know the local fruits might kill us." She had juice on her chin.

"I don't know anything anymore. That's a mango, and it's delicious. I've been eating the fruits for three days. A touch of diarrhea the first day, that's all." She spoke lightly, and didn't look at me. She began to cut another one.

"Evinson died. I buried him. J.P. left."

She didn't comment. The aromatic odor from the fruit seemed to fill the room. She handed me a slice and I threw it back at her.

Delia came down then looking better than she had in days. Her cheeks were pink and her eyes livelier than I had seen them. She looked at Corrie, and while she didn't smile, or do anything at all, I knew.

"Bitch," I said to Corrie bitterly. "Wait until tomorrow. Right. Bitch!"

"Take a walk, Sax," Delia said sharply.

"Let's not fight," Corrie said. "He's dead and J.P.'s gone." Delia shrugged and sat down at the table. Corrie handed her a piece of the mango. "Sax, you knew about me, about us. Whether or not you wanted to know, you did. Sometimes I tried to pretend that maybe I could conceive, but I won't. So forget it. What are you going to do?"

"Get the hell out of here. Go home."

"For what?" Delia asked. She tasted the slice of mango curiously, then bit into it. She frowned critically. "I like the oranges better."

"These grow on you," Corrie said. "I've developed an absolute craving for them in the past three days. You'll see."

"I don't know about you," I said furiously, "but I'm leaving Saturday. I have things to do that I like doing. I like to read. To see a show now and then. I have friends."

"Are you married? Do you live with a woman? Or a man?" Delia asked.

I looked at Corrie. "We're in trouble. It'll take the three of us to manage the boat to get back. We have to make plans."

"We aren't going back," Corrie said softly. "We're going to the Seminoles."

"Corrie, listen to me. I've been out farther than either of you. There's nothing. Ruins. Rot. Decay. No roads. Nothing. Even if they existed, you'd never find them."

"There's the remains of the road. Enough for us to follow west."

"Why didn't you try a little bribery with me?" I yelled at her. "Maybe I would have changed my mind and gone with you."

"I didn't want you, Sax. I didn't think the Seminoles would want to take in a white man."

I left them alone for the rest of the day. I checked the *Loretta* again, swam, fished, gloomed. That night I pretended that nothing had been said about Seminoles. We ate silently.

Outside was the blackness and the silence, and somewhere in the silence a scream waited. The silence seemed to be sifting in through the mosquito netting. The wind had stopped completely. The air was close and very hot inside the building. "I'm going out," I said as soon as I finished eating.

Delia's question played through my mind as I walked. Did I live with a woman? Or a man? I stopped at the edge of the water. There were no waves on the bay, no sound except a gentle water murmur. Of all the people I knew, I could think of only three that I would like to see again, two of them because I had lived with them in the past, and our relationships had been exciting, or at least not abrasive, while they had lasted. And when they were finished, the ending hadn't been shattering. Two women, both gone from my life completely. One man, a co-worker in my department. We did things together, bowled, swapped books, saw shows together. Not recently, I reminded myself. He had dropped out of sight.

A gust of wind shook me and I started back. A storm was coming up fast. The wind became erratic and strong, and as suddenly as the wind had started, the rain began. It was a deluge that blinded me, soaked me, and was ankle deep in the street almost instantly. Then, over the rain, I heard a roar that shook me through and through, that left me vibrating. A tornado, I knew, although I had never seen or heard one. The roar increased, like a plane bearing down on me. I threw myself flat, and the noise rocked the ground under me, and a building crashed to my left, then another, and another. It ended as abruptly as it had started.

I stumbled back to our building, shaking, chilled and very frightened. I was terrified that our building would be demolished, the women gone, dead, and that I would be alone with the silence and the black of the night.

Corrie opened the door on the first floor and I stumbled in. "Are you all right? It was a tornado, wasn't it?"

She and Delia were both afraid. That was reassuring. Maybe now they would be frightened enough to give up the nonsense about staying here. The storm abated and the silence returned. It didn't seem quite so ominous now.

"Corrie, don't you see how dangerous it would be to stay? There could be a hurricane. Storms every day. Come back with me."

"The cities will die, Sax. They'll run out of food. More epidemics. I can help the Seminoles."

Friday I got the *Loretta* ready for the return trip. I packed as much fruit as it would hold. Enough for three, I kept telling myself. Forbidden fruit. For three. I avoided Corrie and Delia as much as I could and they seemed to be keeping busy, but what they were doing I couldn't guess.

That night I came wide awake suddenly and sat up listening hard. Something had rattled or fallen. And now it was too quiet. It had been the outside door slamming, I realized, and jumped up from my bedroll and raced downstairs. No one was there, anywhere. They had left, taking with them Corrie's medical supplies, Delia's radiation kit, most of the food, most of the beer. I went outside, but it was hopeless. I hadn't expected this. I had thought they would try to talk me into going into the swamps with them, not that they would try it alone.

I cursed and threw things around, then another thought hit me. The *Loretta*! I ran to the dock in a frenzy of fear that they had scuttled her. But she was there, swaying and bobbing in the changing tide. I went aboard and decided not to leave her again. In the morning I saw that the sail was gone.

I stared at the mast and the empty deck. Why? Why for

God's sake had they taken the sail?

They'll be back, I kept thinking all morning. And, I'll kill them both. Gradually the thought changed. They would beg me to go with them inland, and I would say yes, and we would go into the first swamp and I would take their gear and leave them there. They would follow me out soon enough. They had needed the sail for a shelter, I thought dully. After noon I began to think that maybe I could go with them part of the way, just to help them out, prove to them that it was hopeless to go farther.

My fury returned, redoubled. All my life I had managed to live quietly, just doing my job, even though it was a stupid one, but getting paid and trying to live comfortably, keeping busy enough not to think. Keeping busy enough to keep the fear out. Because it was there all the time, pressing, just as the silence here pressed. It was a silent fear, but if it had had a voice, its voice would have been that scream we had heard. That was the voice of my fear. Loud, shrill, inhuman, hopeless. I felt clammy and chilled in the heat, and my stomach rejected the idea of food or drink.

Come back, I pleaded silently, willing the thought out, spreading the thought, trying to make contact with one of them. Come back for me. I'll go with you, do whatever you want to do. Please!

That passed. The storm came, and I shivered alone in the *Loretta* and listened to the wind and the pounding rain. I thought about my apartment, my work, the pamphlets I wrote. The last one I had worked on was titled: "Methods of Deep Ploughing of Alluvial Soils in Strip Farming in Order to Provide a Nutritionally Adequate Diet in a Meatless Society." Who was it for? Who would read past the title? No one, I answered. No one would read it. They were planning for a future that I couldn't even imagine.

The silence was more profound than ever that evening. I sat on deck until I could bear the mosquitoes no longer. Below, it was sweltering, and the silence had followed me in. I would start back at first light, I decided. I would have to take a smaller boat. A flat-bottomed boat. I could row it up the waterway, stay out of the ocean. I could haul it where the water was too shallow or full of debris.

The silence pressed against me, equally on all sides, a force that I could feel now. I would need something for protection from the sun. And boiled water. The beer was nearly gone. They hadn't left me much food, either. I could do without

food, but not water and maps. Maybe I could make a small
sail from discarded clothing. I planned and tried not to feel
the silence. I lectured myself on synesthesia—I had done a
pamphlet on the subject once. But the silence won. I began to
run up the dock, screaming at Corrie and Delia, cursing them,
screaming for them to come back. I stopped, exhausted
finally, and the echo finished and the silence was back. I
knew I wouldn't sleep; I built a fire and started to boil water.

I poured the water into the empty beer bottles and stacked
them back in their original boxes. More water started to boil,
and I dozed. In my near sleep, I heard the scream again. I
jumped up shaking. It had been inhumanly high, piercing, with
such agony and hopelessness that tears stood in my eyes. I
had dreamed it, I told myself. And I couldn't be certain if I
had or not.

Until dawn came I thought about the scream, and it seemed
to me a thing uttered by no living throat. It had been my own
scream, I thought, and I laughed out loud.

I loaded an aluminum rowboat the next day and rigged up
a sail that might or might not fall apart when the wind blew. I
made myself a poncho and a sun hat, and then, ready to go, I
sat in the boat and watched some terns diving. They never
had asked me what I had wanted to do, I thought bitterly.
Not one of them had asked me what I would have liked to do.

J.P. had complained about being forced into teaching,
while I would have traded everything I had for the chance to
write, to teach—but worthless things, like literature, art appreciation, composition. A pelican began to dive with the
terns, and several gulls appeared. They followed the pelican
down, and one sat on his head and tried to snatch the fish
from his mouth.

I thought again of all the pamphlets I had written, all the
thousands of pages I had read in order to condense them. All
wasted because in reducing them to so little, too much had
been left out. I started to row finally.

When I left the mouth of the bay, I turned the small boat
southward. The sea was very blue, the swells long and
peaceful. Cuba, I thought. That many people, some of them
had to be left. And they would need help. So much had been
lost already, and I had it, all those thousands of pages, hundreds of books, all up there in my head.

I saw again the undersecretary's white, dry, dead face, the
hurt there, the fear. He hadn't expected me to come back at

all, I realized. I wished I could tell Corrie.

The wind freshened. If not Cuba, then Central America, or even South America. I put up my little sail, and the wind caught it and puffed it, and I felt only a great contentment.

Grania Davis

YOUNG LOVE

HEADHI! I is so sugarsweet happy. Me and Jonsy is forever in love. For months, I couldn't think of nothing but Jonsy and his lovey-face. My queeny-pals was a-giggling and a-pooching me all the time, but I doedn't care. I knowed they was just jealous of my jolly-fine joy.

It were maybe ten months ago. A super-special day. Me and my queeny-pals, Mimi, Judy, and Sally gotted tickets to the beach, and we taked the rapid down super-early in the morning. It were a nice, bright, warmsy day, and it feeled jolly-fine to get away from the stuffy old commune for a bitsy.

Me and my queeny-pals hain't haved enough points for a outing for nearly two months before that, when we getted tickets for Golden Gate Park. But that were a real cold, blowy day.

So there we was, feeling super-spindly and wowsy. A-playing in the sand, and a-feeling of the sunny, and a-running in the shivery waves. And we was laughing and chittering, and smoking a little grassy. And Mimi alltimes so funny, when she feeling upper, she start mocking the commune-mommy:

"Come on now, queenies, line up for *bruncheon*. Do not push or *shove*. Do not take more food-a than you can *finish*. Wasters will get *demerits*. After bruncheon we will have bingo and checkers in the *aud*. Points for the *winners*. Demerits for *dragglers*."

When Mimi talk like the commune-mommy, it so hyster. We was all tearful with giggling, and getting sand in our mouths.

Soonly it were bruncheon time, and we was *starvy*. We dipped out the tokens what comed with our tickets, so we could get food-a at the beacheteria. We drawed straws, to see who haved to stand in liny to get it, and I losed. I groaned and chrised, but little doed I know it were my super-lucky day.

I glumphed along the beach with every's tokens, till I getted to the beacheteria, and there were a real *long* liny. I standed behind a old mommy and groaned and chrised somemore.

The singalong were playing "Riding on the Rapid" and "Old Man Moses." So I singed along, for awhile, while the liny creeped up. Then I looked around, behind me, and feeled like I just won 100 points in the aud, cause behind me were the most lovey-faced tommy I never seed.

He gleamed at me, and I gleamed back. And soonly we forgetted all about the singalong and the liny, and just standed there, gleaming and gleaming.

Finally he said, "Hi, queeny, what's you name?"

My heart quicked up and I said, "Silvy, what's yours?"

And he said, "Jonsy."

And then we gleamed somemore, while the singalong played "Old Man Moses."

And then he said, "Where does you live?"

And I said, "At the Powell Street queeny-commune. Where does you live?"

And he said, "Oh, not so farsy, at the Eddy Street tommy-commune."

And then we gleamed somemore.

And then he said, "Maybe I could come to your aud, sometime, on fun-night, and we could have some fun."

And I said, "That would be headhi. Ours fun-night are on Friday, that tomarrio. You could come then."

But then the glumphy old mommy up ahead sharped, "Hey, you youngs, you is interrupting the singalong." So we quit chittering, and singed "Old Man Moses," but we still gleamed and gleamed.

Finally, the old mommy getted her food-a, and then it were my turn. I putted in my tokens and taked out four platies, and seed it were turkey-a, which are one of my super-yumyum favorites. I waited for Jonsy to get his, and we walked out together, in the warmsy sun.

They was some propers outside, like usual, reading news-bills to any what would listen. Some was from the Mother Mary Commune, on Geary. And they was trying to get people to they Sunday lovelies. Other propers was from the Anti-Grass Group, and they was telling how grassy make the lungs all rotted, and how it should be against the law, like in the oldy days.

And they was somemore propers from the Real Food League, saying stuff about how food-a wreck brain cells and reflexes, so folks can't blink they eyes nomore.

But me and Jonsy was too deep in with each other to tune in on them. We jingled along, until we was nearly to my queeny-pals, and he said, "It were headhi chittering with you. Maybe we'll sees tomarrio."

And I said, "Jolly-fine."

And then he goed on to his tommy-pals. But I were thinking about him the whole day, and on the rapid, riding home, the singalong played "Old Man Moses," which maked my brain click right into before, and I singed so loud that my queeny-pals pooched me and giggled.

They clicked in that somesuch were weirdy with me, and wanted me to tell, but I just sitted at supper-time, chewing my stew-a and gleaming. But by sleepy-time, I couldn't seal it no more, so I telled. And Mimi mocked how the commune-mommy talked whenever any had a tommy guest, and that maked us all hyster in our room till lights-out.

We four was all so upped about it, the next day, we could hardly keep from hystering all through smart-time, which we do as in the morning. That day, we haved a cable-prog on how the Eskimos lived in the oldy days. Then the smarts-mommy readed us a newsy-bill what said how the white folks army were almost to Shanghai, which maked us clap and gleam. Then she turned on the singalong, what played "Hot Sunshine" and "Riding on the Rapid" and "Old Man Moses," and we all singed, though my brain were kind of buzzery.

At bruncheon, we haved bacon'eggs-a, what is very glum-phy and rubbery, and not yumyum at all. We all groaned and chrised and Mimi mocked the Real Food League propers:

"This stuff is *poison*. It is all maked of *chemicals*. It is not meaned for human *beings*. It will rot your brains and *reflexes*. Become real folks, demand real *food*!"

But the bruncheon-mommy heared her and said how we was lucky to be in a nicey queeny-commune, with lots to eat, instead of being a freaky what couldn't find no room in a commune and gots to sleep in the streets, and are always hungry and eating garbage. Then the bruncheon-mommy give us each a demerit, what maked us hyster unhappily.

After bruncheon are play-time, and cause the day were warmsy, we doed it on the sun-roof, instead of the gym. Me and my queeny-pals played bangmitten against four queenies from another room, but we was so buzzery, they winned easy, and the play-mommy gived them each two points.

Then comed supper-time, and it were rosbeef-a, what are yumyum, but thiseve, my heart were quicking so fast, I couldn't hardly eat. Would he really come? Doed he really like me, or were he just pooching?

Finally it were time. Fun-time. The best time of the week. I doed my hair in fine curlies, and Judy letted me use some blue pawpaint. And Sally letted me wear her bestest tunic of red shinycloth, what she getted last year from all her points. I haved to for sure promise to be super-careful and not spill no punch-a on it. And I putted on some julies and some leggies and my queeny-pals said I were the most headhi queeny they never seen.

It were real hyster down in the aud. All the queenies from the whole commune was there and also a lot haved invited they tommy-pals from other communes and some haved in-vited they parents to come from the family-communes. Me and my queeny-pals hain't invited our parents for a long time, though we keeped thinking to do it soonly. But no juice for that *now*.

I goed over to the door of the aud where folks was waiting to get in. The aud-mommy only letted invited folks in, to keep out freakies. Were he there? Were he there? My heart quicked along.

Yes, he were there! There he were! And he gleamed when

he seed me. And I gleamed right back. And after the aud-
mommy letted him in, we just standed there, gleaming for
awhile.

Then the aud-mommy telled us to sit down and they
showed a cartoon-prog what were real funny, about this
dumdum cat, trying to catch this brainsy mouse, in the oldy
days. And the mouse keeped on hitting the cat what gotted all
grunchy and mangly, and other weirdy things what maked us
hyster a lot.

And then we folded up the chairs, and all holded hands in a
circle, and we doed folk dancies, like London Bridges and
Here We Go Round the Rosy. But I couldn't hardly give them
no juice cause of Jonsy being right next to me and a-holding
of my hand, real tightsy, like no tommy never doed before,
with his fingers slidded right up, between mine, and now and
then a-squeezing and a-rubbing of them, so soonly my whole
hand and arm was buzzering and I could feel the little brown
curlies on his fingers, and rough places where his nails was
bited, and it feeled so warm and good, like a platy of hot
food-a.

And when the folk-dancy were done, and the aud-mommy
telled us to line up for punch-a and cake-a, he keeped ahold
of my hand, and still rubbing and squeezing, till I were near
hyster and the aud-mommy finally noticed and said we was to
quit, or I'd get demerits.

So we drinked our punch-a and eated our cake-a, and I
were supercare not to spillsy on Sally's shinycloth. And then
the singalong started and it were playing "Hot Sunshine" and
"Old Man Moses," which was jolly-fine.

And then the aud-mommy readed us a special newsy-bill
about how the white folks army were almost to Shanghai,
what maked us gleam. But then fun-night were *over*, and all
the guesties have to go away, what maked me feel superdown,
cept Jonsy gived my hand a quick, secret squeezy and
whispered, "I got tickets for the ballsy on Wednesday. You
wanna come?"

I getted so excity, I near hystered all over the shinycloth,
and I said, "I sure does! That would be super-upper. No tommy never taked me ta the ballsy before!"

Then the aud-mommy helped him with his coat, and he
gived my hand another squeezy and goed away. But I never
feeled so headhi in my life, and I decided I were never gonna

wash my hand again.

Oh, the week goed by so *superslow*. Smart-time, with cable-progs on how birdies used to grow in eggs, and how Eskimos used to live in the oldy days. And the singalong. And brun-cheons. Sometimes the food-a were yumyum, and sometimes it were glumphy. Play-time on the roof, or the gym, with bangmitten or pingypong. Then supper. Then game-time in the aud, with checkers or bingo, and the singalong, and then maybe a movie-prog with tommies and queenies holding hands and kissing, what maked me real hyster to think I doed that with Jonsy. And chittering with my queeny-pals. And lights-out.

Most times them things is jolly-fine. And I was glad I isn't one of them brainsy folks what thinks theys so upper, cause they gets to live in privapts, and eats real food sometimes and has privautos, and goes to privschools. They gots to spend all the day a-thinking and a-working and a-planning for the rest of us folks. They can't enjoy theyselves allatimes, like me. Even the commune mommies, what thinks theys so upper with they points and demerits and linies. Even them can't have as much fun, and doesn't get tickets out much moren me.

But this week I were wishing now I were a little brainsy, so I could think of something else cept *waiting to see Jonsy on Wednesday*, what were filling my whole brain.

But finally *Wednesday* comed, and I were near hyster the whole day, for fear he wouldn't come. But after supper, there he *were*, right at the door, and my heart roared like a rapid when I seed him. He showed the tickets to the door-mommy, so I could get a pass to go, and she helped me with my coat. Headhi! Two outings in one week! I hain't never beed on so many. While we was walking to the rapid, he taked my hand again. My *other* hand, this time. What maked me hyster to think that now I couldn't wash neither hand nomore. And Jonsy asked howcome I were hystering, but I wouldn't tell.

And then he started to tell me how he weren't brainsy enough for school, of course, but he were maybe enough brainsy to pass the test for the army, and then he could have a semipriv room and more tickets for outings, and stuff like that. And he were asking how I'd like to have a tommy-pal what were brainsy enough for the army.

And I said I wouldn't like it, cause he'd have to work hard

all a time, cleaning the streets and the rapid, and would maybe have to go to China.

But he said how most armytoms doesn't got to go to China, cause they's needed for all a jobbies here, what the robos can't do. The brainsy folks beed able to make robos to do most jobbies, but not ones where they has to move around by theyselves, like cleaning up, or watching folks like the mommies and daddies.

But Jonsy said how he thought it would be jolly-fine to walk around all day, doing something important, instead of staying in the stuffy old commune, with the commune-daddies telling him what to do.

And I said I doedn't like the commune-mommies, neither, but my queeny-pals was nice, and I sure hoped he doedn't got to go to China.

Then the rapid comed. And he taked my elbow to help me on. And I hystered to think I couldn't wash my elbow, neither. And there was two seats, what were a surprise, so we sitted down, and couldn't talk no more, cause of the singalong, what were playing "Riding on the Rapid," and "Old Man Moses." But Jonsy putted his arm around my shoulder, what maked me get all red and sweaty, cause I could feel his muscles, all hard and strong, and his hand all a-rubbing of my shoulder. And my cheek a-leaning against his warmsy chest. I could feel the scratchycloth of his shirt against my cheek, and could even smell the soap and sweat and shave cream and other tommy-do, all mixed up, and a special, sugarsweet smell what were just himself. And I were feeling like a movie-prog star, until the rapid-daddy noticed us and told us to quit it, or he'd take our numbers for demerits.

So we sitted up and gleamed through the singalong. And I figured I'd *have* to wash my cheek and shoulder, else I'd get all pimply like.

At the ballsy park was more folks than I never seed before. The propers all a time tell us why we gots to eat food-a instead of real food is cause there's so much folks. But I never believed there was *so* much till now. I couldn't count them in a week.

And they is all drinking beer-a and punch-a, and sitting on rows and rows and *rows* of benches, piled high like a mountain, and all going in a big circle, round a little park. And in the park is a bunch a tommies in white leggies, and they shoulders maked *huge*, with maybe pillows in they tunics, which was red or white, and like potties on they heads. And they is throwing around a little bit of a ball and they is running and a-kicking and a-punching and a-hitting of each other, and Jonsy said how each side are trying to steal the ballsy for theyself, and them as manages gets lots of points, but them as don't gets demerits. And that we was favoring the red tunics, but he didn't say why.

But then one of the white tunic tommies getted ahold of the ball, and started quicking along with it, up into the crowd, trying to get it out of the ballsy park. But some folks in they seats was trying to stop him and catch him and throw the ball back, while other folks was trying to stop *them*, and pretty soon there were a lot of fighting and yelling and folks was a-beating and a-stomping on each others.

And I getted kind of scaredy, but Jonsy laughed and said this were the funsy part and no one never getted too hurt, and besides it were headhi and pretty soon he were a-beating on some folks sitting near us, and they was a-beating back on him and I were hystering and trying to hide under the bench.

Then someone managed to throw the ball back into the park, and the tommies was fighting by theyselves, somemore. And folks was watching and petting they sore places. And then, someone getted the ball again and folks was fighting somemore. And then, no one knowed where the ball were and so folks was running all around and into the park and a-grabbing and a-beating of each other and they was yelling and screaming and it doedn't seem so funsy to me. And Jonsy were gone someplace, a-fighting with the rest. And some old daddy falled back and stumbled over my legs, which I couldn't get all a way under the bench, and it were real cold and dirty under, so I started to hyster real loud and lots of other folks was hystering too.

And then a loud buzzerbell ringed and a voice said, from the singalong, *"The reds has taken the ballsy. I repeats, the reds has taken the ballsy. Go back to your benches, everyone. The reds has taken the ballsy. The game is over. Go back to your benches. The reds has taken the ballsy."*

And so on, while folks was sitting down again. And some was hystering happy, and some was unhappy cause they was all mangly or cause the reds winned all the points.

And I were worrying about Jonsy finding me again, but

then I seed his lovey-face and it were all grunchy and blubby, and his clothes was all mangly, but he were all upper cause his side winned. And he helped me out from under the bench and said, "Weren't that jolly-fine?"

And I said, "Headhi," cause I were so glad to see him again.

And he said, "Its jolly-fine you thinks so, cause lots queenies too scaredy of the ballsy." And he gived my hand another squeeze.

For sure hearing him say that maked me feel sugar-sweet, and I doedn't even care that my tunic and leggies was all torn and dirty and there were a grunchy on my ankle.

On the way back to the rapid, Jonsy putted his arm around my shoulder again, real super-tight, and his lovey-body were even warmer now cause of all the fighting and sweating, and he were breathing hard.

The rapid was super-crowded, cause of every going home from the ballsy. Folks was a-pushing and a-shoving, and lots was still hystering from behing hurt or cause they side had loosed. But the rapid-daddy said to quiet down, or we'd all get demerits. And there was no seats and we was packed standing, tight as could be, but we doedn't mind, cause it gived Jonsy a chance to hug me hard.

Then a weirdy thing happened. The singalong were playing "Old Man Moses," and it getted to the place where it says, "He climbed up the mountain." And the singalong getted *stuck* there, and it keeped singing, "He climbed up the mountain, he climbed up the mountain."

And for a while, no one gived it no juice, and we just keeped singing. "He climbed up the mountain, he climbed up the mountain."

And then some brainsy folks noticed and they starts to hyster and yell that the rapid weren't going nowhere and were stuck in the tunnel, and that howcome the singalong were stuck.

And other folks was hystering again, too, but the rapid-daddy yelled real loud that he would take our numbers for demerits, sure, if we doedn't quit.

So soonly all was back to singing, "He climbed up the mountain, he climbed up the mountain, he climbed up the mountain, he climbed up the mountain."

And we keeped on singing it for a super-long time, and

most folks was kind of downer about it, but not me and Jon-sy. We just gleamed and gleamed at each other, and no one noticed how he haved both his arms around me, real tight.

And then, finally, the rapid gived a big jerk, and moved along again. And we getted to sing the next words of the song, "To chitter with Godsy, what gived him all the rules, so we wouldn't get demerits." And so on.

And the rapid-daddy gived us all passes for being late. When we getted off at the Powell Street stop, there were a tommy proper from the Real Food League. He were reading a newsy-bill about how eating food-a makes folks dumdum and ruins they reflexes so they eyes don't blink right, and they can't make babies, and sometimes they forgets how to breathe! This were making me feel real downer, but then Jon-sy start to chitter with him.

"Howcome you knows this?" he asked the proper.

"Cause I is a brainsy, and gets to hear about it in school, and I doesn't like to see folks brains getting rotted."

"Well, what can we eat if we doesn't eat food-a?"

"We can eat real food, like in the oldy days."

"Where would we get the real food?"

"We gots to grow it in the parks."

"But how would we get to the parks without tickets, and how would folks know how to do the growing?"

"We gotta learn how again!"

"But how we gonna do that? And what is we gonna eat in the meantime?"

"I guess we'd eat food-a."

"Well, that what I's doing right now, so howcome I should do all this bothering? I doesn't think you is very brainsy at all!"

And then the proper getted real mad, and telled Jonsy he were dumdum, and his brain were already rotted. And then Jonsy gived him a big grunchy in the face and said his brain were rotted, too. And then we runned away real fast, before someone seed us, and gotted us demerits for fighting. And I telled Jonsy he were the most brainsy tommy I never meeted.

And he said, "Yeah, that's howcome I wanna get in the ar-my, cause I is too brainsy to sit around the commune all a time."

And I said how I were sure he could pass the test. We seed somemore propers, from the Mother Mary commune, but we was too dozy to chitter with them. And we seed lots of freakies, laying around in the street, sleeping. I never beed out so late to see it before, even though the commune-mommy all a time tell us how we's so lucky our parents getted enough points to have us in a commune when we growed up, and how there aren't room for lots of folks what gots to sleep in the streets, and gots to stand in long linies for tiny bits of food-a with no flavor at all!

Some of them freakies waked up and tried to grab us, asking if we haved any food-a to give them, or any grass. But we telled them "No," and they goed away, cause they knowed it were true. But a couple of tommy freaks tried to pooch me, in a nasty way, and I were glad Jonsy were there, cause he gived them a kick, and they goed away.

It were after lights-out when we getted back to the commune, and we haved to bang super-loud at the door. While we was waiting to get letted in, Jonsy putted his both arms round me and pulled me super-close to him and kissed my curlies and said, "You is a sugarsweet queeny."

I thinked my head would buzz to bits with happy. When the commune-mommy comed to the door, she started to sharp, but I doedn't give her no juice. I just showed her the late pass from the rapid-daddy, and goed up to bed. But even though I were super-tired from the headhi day, I keeped clicking back to Jonsy, and I couldn't drowsy, the whole night through.

The next day, I were drowsing at smart-time, and missed most of the cable-prog on how Eskimos lived in the oldy days. The smarts-mommy said if I doedn't quit, she'd send me to the nurse-mommy for a shot. That maked me hyster, unhappily. Folks mostly doesn't get sick now, like they doed in the oldy days, cause of all the vitas and trancs and antibods whats in the food-a. But sometimes the nurse-mommy gots to take care of folks grunchies, and also to give them a shot if they won't behave. So I tried harder to stay wakesy.

Anyhow, the next few weeks was mostly usual. Smart-time bruncheon, play-time, supper, game-time and pooching and chittering with my queeny-pals. The only thing that weren't usual were me, cause of all the time clicking into Jonsy. And fun-night, the best night of the week, and the only time I could see his lovey-face.

But it were hard now to give juice to the singalong, or the

folksy, or the movie-prog, or the cake-a and punch-a, and all the other fun-night-do. Mostly we was busy trying to sit in a sneaky way, to hold hands without the aud-mommy seeing, or pretending to bump into each other, so he could give me a hug, or even a little kissy on the curlies, or to chitter together for a couple of minutes.

My queeny-pals noticed, and pooched me a lot, but I knowed they wouldn't tell. Not even Mimi, whats so brainsy they is letting her take the test to be a commune-mommy. Nor even Judy, what were going to the Mother Mary lovelies a lot lately. And were all the time telling us to leave off smoking grass, and watching movie-progs and thinking of tommies, and learn to get upper from loving Jesus.

Judy were even thinking to put her name on the waity-list to *live* at the Mother Mary commune, what would be weirdy for us, cause we'd have someone new in our room. Maybe a youngling, fresh from her parents room, what would be all sobby, or, worse yet, a freaky from the street, what would be all smelly and dumdum and steal our pretties.

But anyhow, me and Jonsy was wishing and *wishing* how we could just be by ourselves, to chitter and touch and hug and kiss and, well, you *know*, queeny and tommy things, like in the movie-progs. And I were wondering if Jonsy were wishing the same thing. And I were meaning and chrising alot about how we never gets to do what we wants, and my queeny-pals was saying how freakies gets to do whatever *they* wants, with no mommies watching them, and I should be proper grateful. But I knowed they was just jealous.

Also, I were getting lots of demerits, from not giving enough attention, and I knowed I wouldn't have enough points for no new pretties this year, what maked me glumph even more.

Then, one Friday night, the most sugarsweet thing in the whole world happened. Jonsy comed for fun-night, like regular. But I could tell, right away, he were headhi about something. First I thinked he maybe haved too much grass, or tickets for a outing. But it were even upper than that.

Minute he could, he whispered in my ear, "I passed the test for the army!"

"Oh, Jonsy," I hystered. The aud-mommy sharped me with her eyes. "You'll be able to get more tickets for outings," I said.

"Yeah, but there moren that," he said, "soonly, I'll go to the army school, and learn how to clean the streets real good.

Then I'll be ducted. And then, I can get me on the waity-list
for a semipriv room at the army commune, *or*, Silvy, I can get
me on the waity-list for a room at the army family-commune.
We could get *married*, and jingle together every night, and
chitter and hug and . . . and all kinds of jolly-fine things, just
like the movie-progs. We could have a wedding in the aud,
and maybe even a honey-trip, and stay headhi all the time!"

"Oh, Jonsy," I said, and I hystered so hard I couldn't stop,
even when the singalong played "Old Man Moses," so I getted
five demerits, but who cared, cause I were the upperest
queeny in the aud.

The next week, at fun-night, the aud-mommy read us a
newsy-bill about how they isn't so much babies, nomore,
cause of stricter controls, and so they will be less freakies
sleeping in the streets in twenty years or so. And also how the
white folks army were almost to Shanghai. And while all was
gleaming and cheering, Jonsy whispered to me how there
would maybe be a room in the army family commune in
maybe seven or eight months. And how we could get tickets
for a *two-day* honey-trip in Yosemite Park, what are further
away than any of us never been. And how a armytom can
have punch-a and cake-a at they wedding, and they parents
and pals can come and see. And lucky, all was cheering so
loud from the newsy-bill, they doedn't hear me hyster.

Seven or eight months! It feeled like seven or eight years. I
thinked I were dying from waiting for that sugar-sweet day
when me and Jonsy would be married folks and could do
whatever we wanted.

In the meantime, every were usual. Smart-time, bruncheon,
play-time, supper, game-time, lights-out. Just like always.

Only a couple differy things happened in that time. Like
Mimi failed the test to be a commune-mommy, and were very
sobby for awhile.

Another thing what happened, were one time, all the food-a
in this whole part of the city doedn't get sent to they communes. And we sitted two whole days, in the aud, without
nothing to eat. And they keeped telling us how it were OK,
and the food-a would be here soonly, and they keeped the
singalong and movie-progs on real loud. But we getted real
starvy, and started to hyster, and finally we was all hystering
so loud, you couldn't hardly hear "Old Man Moses" going.
Finally the mommies telled us they didn't know howcome and
we was all to do linies, cause we was going *outside*, to the

depot where the freakies gets they food-a.

And we walked a long way. Longer than I never walked before. And we seed lots of broken-up buildings, and lots of other communes. And they folks was also marching out to the depot. And soonly they was a super-big crowd of folks, all over the street, and they was pushing and shoving, what aren't usual allowed, and I wondered howcome folks wasn't getting demerits. But then I seed how the mommies and daddies was also pushing and shoving cause they was starvy, too.

And soonly, they was so much folks on the street, that you couldn't keep no more linies, and I couldn't find my own queenies nomore, and I were in a super crowd of strange folks, all pushing real hard to try and get to depot, but none knowed where it was, and so some was pushing one way, and some was pushing another.

And then one old mommy getted pushed down, and no folks would let her get up and she were yelling and screaming, and other folks was being pushed on top of her. And pretty soon, she were getting all grunchy and mangly. And this were happening to other folks, too. And all was hystering super-loud, cause of being starvy and scaredy, and not knowing the way to the depot.

And then some big privautos was coming along the streets with singalong speakers, and super-daddies was yelling, *"Go back to your communes. Food-a will be sent to your communes. Go back to your communes. Food-a will be sent to your communes. Go back to your communes. Food-a will be sent to your communes."*

So then, folks started trying to find the way back to they communes. But I doedn't know the way back and were hystering, super-loud. And then, a smelly freaky queen grabbed my arm, and said if I were loosed she would help me find my commune, but I haved to give her something. So I gived her my ear julies. She taken them, and runned away into the crowd. And I hystered even louder.

But then I seed a Mother Mary commune, and I thinked one of they propers could tell me the way back, so I goed inside, and they haved they own singalong, about Jesus and such, and good smellies in the air. And I sitted down, and singed for a while. But then I remembered how I was starvy and loosed, so I started to hyster. And then, the commune-daddy comed and said he would tell me the way home if I letted him look inside my leggies. So I doed that, and he telled me the way home.

When I finally getted back, lots was sitting in the aud, like before, singing "Hot Sunshine." But some haved manglies and grunchies and they tunics and leggies was torn. And some was still loosed. I sitted down and singed, but were feeling awful buzzery from being so starvy.

But later on, a privauto comed to the door, and gived the mommy a big box of food-a. It weren't flavoured, and looked kind of like a cleaning sponge, but we was glad to get it, and feeled a whole lot better, after.

Except for some of the queenies, what getted such bad manglies that they haved to go the the nurse-mommy. And three of them never comed back. And also, some of the queenies getted so losed in the crowd that they never comed back neither. So we getted some new queenies to fill they places. Lucky they was all sobby young ones from they parents communes, and none was smelly freakies.

The only other differy thing what happened in them waiting months were Jonsy getted tickets to the museum, what I never beed to before, and were very excity to go.

All the way to the rapid, he holded my hand real tight and telled me about army school, and how he get to walk around in the streets all day, with a big bag on his shoulder and a broom and a stick with a point on the end, to pick up garbage. And he said how interesting it were seeing all the strange communes and folks, and stuff, and how he getted a super-tiny singalong to put in his ear, so he wouldn't get bored.

And he telled me how jolly-good it would be when we's married, with a room by weselves, every night. And our honey-trip, and maybe a outing every month, and maybe we could save points for a vacation trip someday. And how we'd get a baby, someday, just like the movie-progs, a real cute one, and we'd save points so it could go live in a queeny or tommy commune when it were twelve years old. And so on, till I nearly bursted with thrill.

And then, while we was waiting for the rapid, he putted his arms around me, super-tight, and gived me a rubby kiss, right on the mouth, and petted my back, real shivery like, and maked me feel all burny hot, and full of love-do.

The museum were jolly-fine. It were full of stuffed-up animals, showing how they used to live in the oldy days. Lions and tigers in the jungly, looking real scary. And birdies in trees with they eggies. And super-giant dinosaurs. And elephants and fishies and doggies and catties, what used to live

right in communes with folks, and even super-teeny animals
called buggies.

They was also stuffed-up folks what used to live in the oldy
days. Eskimos, what I knowed right off, cause I once
seed a cable-prog about them. And Americans and Chinese,
and so on. All of them with funny, super teeny communes
what was called houses, and with trees all around, like it were
Golden Gate Park, or something.

In the museum aud, we seed a scaredy film about all the
awful things the red folks army do, and how they *eats* folks,
and stuff. And we all gleamed a whole lot when the aud-
daddy told us not to worry, cause the white folks army were
almost to Shanghai. And then they gived us punch-a and
cake-a and played "Riding on the Rapid" and "Hot Sunshine"
on the singalong.

When we walked back to the rapid, Jonsy told me how he
were glad to be in the army and how he wouldn't never let no
red folks eat me. And he putted his around me again, and
gived me another super-long and super-hard kiss. And I kissed
him back, sugarsweet hard as I could.

Well, finally, after I couldn't hardly stand it no more, Jonsy
told me the waiting were over. We could get our room in the
family commune. But first we'd get married, real good.

So the next day, I telled my counselor-mommy, and she
were real glad I finded such a brainsy tommy, whats in the army, and getted tickets for a honey-trip in Yosemite, and all.
And she said how we could get married next fun-night, and I
could invite my parents.

I were glad about that, cause I hain't chittered with my
parents in months, but when I phoned the Geary Street
family commune, where they lived, the daddy said how Mr.
and Mrs. Andrews was still losed from the day when all a
folks tried to get to the food-a depot, but if they getted finded
again, he would tell them about my wedding. I hystered a little, but my counselor-mommy said they probably finded
someplace else to live, or something, and I getted to choose
chocolate or vanilla cake-a for my wedding, so I choosed
chocolate, what are yumyum.

On that night, I weared my best tunic and julies and leggies
and even some head paint, and doed curlies up real fine. Jonsy comed with his three pals, and were wearing his new army
tunic and leggies of bright green, what looked headhi. And his
face and head, and even his eyebrowios was shaved. He
looked so strong and handsome, I were stuffed up with love-

do from the sight.

The fun-night were just like usual, and I could hardly sit still, but then, just before the movie-prog, the aud-mommy getted up and said, "I got a special surprise for *you*. Our queeny-pal, Silvy, is gonna marry her tommy, *Jonsy*. And we got chocolate cake-a and cherry punch-a for a *treat*. Let's all sing the special wedding *song*!"

So they all singed,

> "Happy wedding to you
> Happy wedding to you
> Happy wedding, dear Silvy and Jonsy,
> Happy wedding to you."

And then the aud-mommy said, "You is now man and wife."

And then we blowed out the candle on the cake-a, and Jonsy gived me a sugarsweet kiss, what maked me hyster to think every was looking.

And then they showed a excity movie-prog about this tom in the oldy days, with a mask, called the Long Ranger, what killed baddy freakies. And Jonsy putted his arm around me for the whole thing.

When it were time for him to go home, he gived me another big kiss, and said, "I'll come and get you early tomarrio, for the honey-trip to Yosemite." And kissed me again, and the aud-mommy doedn't even tell him to quit, cause we was married folks now, and could do whatever we wanted. I were so buzzery that night, I couldn't drowse at all.

The next morning, right after bruncheon, I putted all my privy things in a bag, and he comed to get me. I said lots of hystery goodbyes to my queeny pals, and even to the mommies, what I wouldn't never see no more.

Jonsy helped me carry my bag. He said most all his privy things was already in our room at the family commune. Our *own* room! I wouldn't see it till the next day, though, after our honey-trip.

We was going to take the rapid all the way to Yosemite, what takes nearly three hours! Yosemite are a super-big park. It got a mountain and a waterfall and lots of trees. And they is stuffed-up birdies living in the trees, just like the oldy days. And the stuffed-up birdies gots little singalongs inside them, cause oldy day birdies used to sing. But the stuffed-up birdies is better, cause they sing songs with words, what is more fun for folks to join in.

Inside Yosemite are a big family commune, where folks from all northy Cal comes for they honey-trip, or, if they saves enough points, for they vacations.

The rapid ride were super-long. We was lucky to get some seats, after a hour. We was underground, of course, and couldn't see no scenery. But Jonsy said he thinked it were pretty much the same, all the way to Yosemite. Streets and communes and lots of broken-down stuff and queenies and tommies and parents and freakies. Lucky the singalong were playing. "Hot Sunshine" and "Old Man Moses" and "Riding on the Rapid," so we doedn't get bored, and besides, Jonsy holded me close, all the way.

It were nearly dark when we getted there. But between the rapid stop and the commune was two trees, with the stuffed-up birdies singing "Hot Sunshine." They was also some Real Food League propers, saying how our reflexes was getting rotten, but we doedn't give them no juice.

We gived our tickets to the commune-daddy, what said we should go have supper. The communiteria were the biggest I never seed, with lots of strange folks chittering and laughing and hystering, happily. There were turkey-a for supper, what are my yumyum favorite. And after there were some bingo and singing, and then the daddy telled us all it were bed-time, what maked my hyster to think of.

So we goed looking for our privroom. The first time I never been in one! We gotted to climb a bunch of stairs and go down a couple of halls, and keeped getting losed, but finally we finded it.

The room were little, but jolly-fine. It haved only two bunk-beds, instead of four, like my oldy room. And it haved a chair to sit on, and a pitcher of water-a and two cups. And it were right near the pissy. It doedn't have no window, but I doedn't care, cause I just wanted to look at my Jonsy.

Then we was both feeling a little buzzery and shy, and standed there, chittering and hystering a little. And finally, Jonsy said we should turn our backs and put our night tunics on. So we doed that, but it maked us hyster a whole lot, cause I never seed no tommy in his night tunic, and he never seed no queeny in one, neither.

Then he taked my hand, and we both sitted down on the lower bunk together. And he started to kiss me and hug me, and pat my back and my curlies and all kinds of other places, and I were kissing him and petting him, too, and it were just like a movie-prog.

Then he said, "I loves you, Silvy."

And I said, "I loves you super-much, and I feels headhi about us being married."

And he said, "I feels headhi, too. Just like a movie-prog."

And I said, "Me, too."

And he said, "Tomarrio, before we has to go back, we can take a walky, and we'll see the trees, and the waterfall, and the mountain, and we'll singalong with the birdies, and then we'll go back to our own family commune and be together, just like now, doing whatever we want."

And I said, "That's the most sugarsweet thing in the world."

And then the speaker in the wall said, *"It's lights out, go to your own bunk. No more chittering. It's lights out. Go to your own bunk. No more chittering,"* and so on.

So then he said, "Well, we both haved a longy day, and better go dozy." So he climbed into the upper bunk: And I curled up, under the blanket of the lower bunk, what were super-comfy.

And he whispered, "Good night, lovey Silvy."

And I whispered back, "Good night, lovey Jonsy."

And then we both hystered to think we was chittering after lights-out, and was getting to sleep in the same room, together, like real married folks.

Then I heard him breathing and snory, like, cause he were dozing, and even though I were headhi and buzzery, I started to feel dozy also. And super-glad, cause I were the luckiest queeny I knowed, and a real married folk, with the best tommy in the world, and tomarrio I could hear the stuffed-up birdies sing.

R. A. Lafferty

AND NAME MY NAME

1

> It was said our talk was gone or rare
> And things with us were ill,
> But we're seven apes from everywhere
> A-walking up a hill.

THEY CAME to those Kurdish highlands by ways that surely were not the best in the world. They came with a touch of furtiveness. It was almost as if they wished to come invisibly. It had been that way the other times also, with the other groups.

There were seven creatures in most of the groups coming, and there were seven in this group: two from the Indies, two from Greater Africa, two from Smaller Africa (sometimes called Europe), one from Little Asia. There was no rule about this, but there was always variety in the groups.

"I never believed that the last one was truly valid," said Joe Sunrise. He was the one from Little Asia: he was big and brindled. "Yes, I still regard the last one as an interloper. Oh, he did show greater power than ourselves. He set us back into a certain place, and since that time we don't talk very much or very well. We don't do any of the things as well as we did before. I suppose he is master of us, for a little while, and in a skimpy way. I believe, though, that that 'little while' is finished today. I believe that he will be shown as no more than a sad aberration of ourselves, as a step backwards or at least sideways.

"But it will be a true stage of the sequence today, as it was in our own primary day, as it was when we named the world and all its fauna, when we set it into its hierarchy."

"It comes to me from the old grapevine," said Mary Rainwood, the blondish or reddish female from the Indies, "that the Day of the Whales was a big one. For showiness it topped

51

even our own takeover. The account of it is carved in rocks in whale talk, in rocks that are over a mile deep under a distant ocean: It is an account that no more than seven whales can still read. But there are several giant squids who can read it also, and squids are notoriously loose-mouthed. Things like that are told around.

"There are others that stand out in the old memories, though they may not have happened quite as remembered. And then there were the less memorable ones: the Day of the Hyenas, for instance; or that of the present ruler (so like and yet so unlike ourselves) whose term is ending now. I for one am glad to see this one end."

"There is an air of elegance about the New One," said Kingman Savanna, the malĕ delegate from Greater Africa. "He also is said, in a different sense from the one who now topples from the summit, to be both very like and very unlike ourselves. The New One hasn't been seen yet, but one of real elegance will be foreknown. Ah, but we also were elegant in our short time! So, I am told, were the Elephants. There was also something special about the Day of the Dolphins. But about this passing interloper there has not been much special."

"What if this new event and coming blocks us out still more?" Linger Quick-One asked in worry. "What if it leaves us with still less speech and art? What can we do about our own diminishment?"

"We can grin a little," Joe Sunrise said with a certain defiance. "We can gnash our teeth. We can console ourselves with the thought that *he* will be diminished still more."

"He? Who?" Kingman asked.

"The Interloper: he under whom we have lived for this latter twisted and foreshortened era. The Days of the Interlopers are always short-lived, and when their day is finished they tend to lose their distinction and to merge with the lords of the day before."

"They with us? Ugh!" Mary Rainwood voiced it.

There were seven persons or creatures going in this band, and Joe Sunrise of Little Asia seemed to be the accepted leader. They walked slowly but steadily, seeming to be in some pain, as if they were not used to wearing shoes or robes. But they were well shod and well wrapped; they were wrapped entirely in white or gray robes such as the desert people wore, such as fewer of the highland people wore. They were hooded, they were girt, they bore packs and bundles. They were as if handless within their great gray gloves; they were almost faceless within their hoods and wrappings.

But two things could not be hidden if one peered closely at them: the large, brown, alert, observing eyes (these eyes had been passively observing now for ten thousand generations); and their total hairiness wherever the least bit of face or form gave itself away.

Well, they had a place to go and they were going there, but they had a great uneasiness about it all. These seven, by the way, out of all the members of their several species remaining on Earth, still retained speech and the abstracting thought that goes with it. And on what dark day had these gifts been lost by all the rest of their closest kindred?

And such was the case with almost all of the so-different groups moving toward the meeting place. Such was the case with the elands and the antelopes, with the hogs and the hippos, with the asses and the zebras, with the eagles and the cranes, with the alligators and the gavials, with the dolphins and with the sharks. They were small elites representing large multitudes, and they retained certain attributes of elites that the multitudes had lost.

> Came Polar Bears on bergs past Crete,
> And Mammoths seen by Man,
> And Crocodiles on tortured feet,
> And Whales in Kurdistan.

There had been all through the Near East, and then all through the world, a general hilarity and an air of hoax about the reports of the "Invisible Animals." There were, of course, the bears that walked and talked like men and were reported as coming out of the Russias. One of these bears, so the joke went, entered a barroom in Istanbul. The bear was nattily dressed, smoked a cigar, laid a hundred-lira note on the bar and ordered a rum and cola.

The barman didn't know what to do, so he went back to the office and asked the boss.

"Serve the bear," the boss said, "only don't give him ninety lira change. Give him ten lira only. We will make the prodigies pay for being prodigies."

The barman went and did this, and the bear drank his drink in silence.

"We don't get many bears in here," the barman finally said when the silence had gotten on his nerves.

"At ninety lira a throw I can understand why not," the bear said.

There were hundreds of these talking-animal jokes in those days. But they had a quality different from most jokes: they were all true exactly as told.

Then there were the invisible African elephants (how can an African elephant possibly be invisible in clear daylight and open landscape?) coming up across the Sinai wastelands and going on for a great distance across the Syrian Desert. They were seven very large African elephants and they spoke courteously to all who stood and gaped as they passed. They were the only African elephants in the world with the gift of speech: the others had lost it long ago. No one would admit seeing these out-of-place elephants, of course. That would be the same as admitting that one was crazy.

There were the great crocodiles traveling in labor and pain over the long dry places. There were the zebras and giraffes snuffling along out of Greater Africa, and the black-maned and the tawny-maned lions. There were the ostriches and the Cape buffalo and the huge boa snakes (the Day of the Snake had been a very long time ago). There were not large groups of any of these, five or seven, or sometimes nine. All were rather superior individuals of their species: all had the gift of speech and reason. All had a certain rakishness and wry humor in their mien, and yet all went under that curious compulsion that is the younger brother of fear.

No person would admit seeing any of these "invisible animals," but many persons told, with a peculiar nervousness, of *other* persons claiming to have seen them. There was somebody telling of somebody seeing a band of Irish elk: no matter that the species was supposedly extinct for several hundred years; reportorial jokers would never be extinct. And it is true that these very few elk said that they were the very last of their species.

Many persons were said to have seen two floating islands going past Cyprus in the Eastern Mediterranean. One of these floating islands was loaded with various animals from South America; the other was filled and painfully crowded with sundry animals from the North American continent. At least half of these animals had been believed to be extinct. Some of them must have kept themselves well hidden for centuries to be able to appear now even as "invisible animals."

But even odder things were coming across the plains of India and Iran. They were hopping and leaping animals. Actually their motion, when they were at full speed, was like that of the hindquarters of a galloping horse, a horse that has no forequarters. These were the big kangaroos and the smaller wallabies and such. But what were they doing here? With them were many other creatures from Australia and New Zealand and Tasmania and the Impossible Islands.

Ah well, then what about the polar bears riding on a small iceberg that floated past Crete and on toward Little Asia? There were seals riding on this also, and sea lions were sporting in the lee of it. Oddest of odd, there was a light but continuous snowstorm over this berg and the circle of graying frothing water around it, and over no other place.

But whales in the Kurdish Highlands? What? What? Yes, the rivers had been very high that year. They had cut new channels here and there and left parts of their old channels in the form of a series of lakes. But whales in the Highlands! It's true that nobody told about it without winking. And yet it was told about.

And how's about the angel out of heaven who walked and stood in those high plains and who seemed to be in some sort of pleasant trouble? It's true that he *said* he was not an angel. He said he was a man only and was named Man. It is true that he looked like a man and not an angel (nobody knowing what an angel looked like). He looked like a man, a man of a very superior sort. But even this is a presumptive statement, since no one had admitted seeing him at all personally.

Even so, whales in the Highlands, and a new special man named Man! And a thousand other prodigies. Could it all be the report of jokers?

3

> To us, the bright, the magic set,
> The world is but a crumb.
> If *we* be not the People yet,
> When *will* the People come?

But there were seven other very special humans met together in that same part of the world—met together, perhaps, by a sort of contrived accident. Nobody could deny that they were human; and yet one of the things they were discussing was the report that their humanity might be denied that very day or the following day.

They had met in a private clubroom of the International Hotel in Mosul. They were making ready for a journey beyond Mosul. Which way beyond Mosul? Well, that was the thing they were discussing with some puzzlement on their own part. It would not be North or South or East or West or Up or Down from Mosul. It would just be beyond, a little bit beyond Mosul town.

The seven special humans were Antole Keshish, a Turkish-Greek-Armenian intellectual of easy urbanity; Helen Rubric, the great lady and puzzle forever; Toy Tonk, a Eurasian girl who constructed philosophies that were like flower arrangements; Hatari Nahub, that charismatic Negro man who transcended continents and cultures; Lisa Baron of the light-haired and light-eyed peoples, and she was light-minded and light-tongued beyond the others; Charley Mikakeh, who was six kinds of American Indian, with a few touches of French, Irish, dark Dutch, and Jew in him; Jorge Segundo, who was all the Latins in the world in one man, but in whom the old Roman predominated (there was once a wise man who said that we tended to forget that the old Romans were Italians, to believe that they were Englishmen, but they weren't).

These seven had brilliance dripping off them like liquid jewels, an image which we cannot express rightly in words, not even their own fragmentary words.

How these seven had been selected for a mission that they understood hardly at all is a puzzle. But they had gathered here from all over the world without a word of instruction or suggestion from anyone. It was only a sort of psycho-biological urge that had told them to come exactly here, exactly now.

"We are met here and we hardly know why," said Jorge Segundo. "We know each other not at all personally and only slightly by reputation. We are called here, but who is the caller? We come like lemmings."

"The lemmings came today," said Toy Tonk, "but only seven of them, and they not at all in a panic. Nor are we, though perhaps we should be. This is perhaps the 'Childhood's End' as foretold by the Clarke in the century past. Will this now be 'The Second Age of Man'? And will ourselves seem children in comparison to the man (so far he is reported as singular in all ways) who comes?"

"This is perhaps the new morning, the epiphany of one more of the 'Nine Billion Names of God' as phrased by the same Clarke, and we will either be ourselves magnified, or we will be reduced to something less than children," Lisa Baron said lightly. "But we do not know that anything is happening."

"I stood and talked to a camel this afternoon," said Charley Mikakeh, "and you say that nothing is happening? 'What do you make of all the new and strange animals passing through?' the camel asked me. 'It's a puzzler, is it not? And what do you make of myself talking? I and the very few others of my species have not done that for a very long time, not since the mushrooms still had prepuces as a normal thing, and yourself began to walk upright. It's an odd thing, ape, is it not?' 'I am man and not ape,' I told the camel, somewhat stiffly, I'm afraid. But the very fact that there was this conversation with a camel indicates that something is happening."

"Perhaps only inside your own head, Charley," Anatole jibed. "I have had conversation with a variety of animal species myself today. All say that it is unusual with them; not at all common for their species to be able to talk. Yet I find it less strange than that we seven, previously unknown to each other, should be gathered here and talking together."

"Oh, we are the seven magic people," Hatari said rationally, though he now had a not quite rational look in his eyes. "Every age of the world (and I believe that our own has been the penultimate age) has its seven magic people who came together by psychic magnet at a hinge time. We are the spokesmen for the rest. But if we are the spokesmen, what will we say, and to whom?"

"If we be people indeed (and we never doubted it till this day) then we will speak it to our own variant (this mysterious shining man), and it will be given to us in that moment what we should say," Helen Rubric was murmuring with her eyes half-closed. "But I am very edgy about all this, and I believe that we are really coming to the edge. There is something wrong with the setting and the set."

"What do you say, Helen?" Jorge asked. "What is wrong with the set?"

"The set is off; it is gone wrong. Both the picture and the sound seem doubled, Jorge."

"Cannot it be fixed? But what am I talking about? I do feel

for a moment that we are no more than animated cartoons on a screen. But this isn't a TV set; it is something larger."

"This set is the whole-world set, Jorge," Helen Rubric muttered. "And it has gone too far wrong to be fixed by ourselves. It may be fixed by this new fixer who comes. But I feel that we ourselves are diminished and demoted, that we are put into a shadowy box now and confined to a narrow corner.

"I gazed upon my own double today and talked with her. She said that her name was Mary Rainwood. She seemed to take a saddened and sisterly view of me. She is an animal of the species orangutan; and if we are sisters under the skin, then hers is much the thicker and hairier skin; I might say that hers is the harder skin to get under. I know her species, but of what species am I an animal?

"It was odd that she was able to speak. She says that it only happens in the last seven days of an age. It seems equally odd that I am able to speak, and I really wonder whether I have been doing it for more than seven days. I believe that our own era has been a very short one and a deponent one."

It was something like a ski lodge there in that private club room of the International Hotel of Mosul. Very cozy there by the open fire at night after a strenuous day on the snow slopes. What open fire? What snow slopes? That was all illusion.

It was more like a cave they were in. Open fire or not, there was a flickering and a shadowing on the cave walls. And the talk among them became more and more shadowy on that last night of the age.

It was morning then. It hadn't been such a long evening and night, only a few hours. It hadn't been such a long age, no more than thirty or forty thousand years. They went out in that morning to a place a little bit beyond Mosul. Seven magic persons on either the last or the first morning of their magic.

4

> Yours: nervous sort of apish lives,
> Derivative the while:
> And, somehow, ferroconcrete hives
> Have not a lot of style.

The shining man hadn't arrived from anywhere. All ways of coming had been watched by some or other of the creatures. And yet he was there now on the crown of the animated hill. He was very much as all the creatures had supposed he would be, before they had seen him at all: not really shining, not of imposing stature, with an inexperienced and almost foolish look on his face, not complex, not at all magic; competent, though, and filled with an uneasy sort of grace.

He was not nervous. Nervousness, of course, was not possible for such an excellent one as he was. But he was in some pain, for he was already in light travail.

The animated hill was merely a wide low hill (higher, though, than the high hills around it) covered with creatures. They were in tiers and files and arrays; they were in congregations and assemblies and constellations. Creatures almost beyond counting, enough seemingly to cover the earth, and they did very nearly cover the wide hill.

The man appointed and named them, speaking to them with an easy dominance, and then sending them away again, species after species, speechless again for another era, yet having their assigned places and tasks for a new age of the world.

Earthworms, beetles, damselflies, honeybees, locusts, cicadas, came and went. They had slightly new assignments now in a world which would be at least slightly different. Shrikes and eagles and doves and storks came through the crowded air. The spoke; sometimes they argued; they were convinced, or they accepted their assignments without being convinced. But they winged away again, speechless now once more, but far from soundless.

Time became diffused and multiplex, for the man imposed and directed thousands of species while the sun hardly moved. Space also was extradimensional, for the wide low hill could not have served as staging space for so many species in the normal order of things.

"We will be the last ones," Lisa Baron said to her magical companions. "As we are the highest species, the lords of the world, so we will have the final instruction and appreciation. Ourselves, the first age of mankind, will receive confirmation and approval from this aberrant creature who (however unlikely he seems) ushers in the second age of mankind. I beg you all, confer with him straightfaced and in all seriousness. Consider that his office is more important than himself. We are the giants and he is the dwarf, but he is higher than ourselves, for he is appointed to stand on our shoulders."

"We will not be the last ones," said Jorge Segundo. "Can you not see that all these confrontations and instructions are simultaneous? And yet we wait. It is as if he notices all the others and not ourselves; he is probably jealous of our basic stature. But do you not see that even the trees and grasses come and go, speaking with him in their moment, and then going away speechless again to their own places. It is the un-naturing of the ecology that happens now, the preter-naturalizing of the ecological balance. The natural world was always out of balance. There could not be a balanced ecology before or without man. Well, but why did we not bring the balance in our own time? Are we not men?"

The whales went away, greatly pleased and greatly relieved about something. And yet, all that the man had done was bless them and say, "Your name is whale."

There were long conversations with some of the species, and the man was forced to become eloquent with these. But the long confrontations did not use up great quantities of time. All these things were telescoped and simultaneous.

"Your name is lion, . . . Your name is buffalo, . . . Your name is donkey," the man was saying. The man was tired now and in more than light travail. But he continued to name and assign the creatures. There was much discussion and instruction in each case but they did not consume much time. "Your name is swine," for instance, was a total statement that contained all that discussion and instruction. The palaver was like a scaffold that is disassembled and taken down when the building is completed. "Your name is carp-fish" was such a completed structure, with very much of stress and synthesis having gone into it.

"Your name is ape," the man said, smiling in his pain.

"No, no, no, we are men," shouted Joe Sunrise, that big and brindled ape from Little Asia. "We are not ape. It is the miserable half-creature there who called us ape. Can he be right about anything?"

"Not of himself, and surely not about himself," the man said. "But he hadn't this knowledge of himself. He is only an air and a noise. Remember that you yourself had the day when you named the names: you named lion and buffalo and mammoth and others. This half-thing also had his shorter day. It may have sounded as though he said, and perhaps he did say, 'Your name is ape.' I do say it. 'Your name is ape.' Now go and fill your niche."

There was much more to it, as there was to every confrontation, yet it consumed little time. There was lamentation from Mary Rainwood and Kingman Savanna and Linger Quick-One and others of their group. There were hairy visages and huge brown eyes shining with tears. But the apes were convinced and almost at peace when they finally accepted it and went away, speechless again but not noiseless, shedding their robes and wrappings and going hairy. They were confirmed as apes now, and they would be more fulfilled apes than they had been before.

It seemed that there was only one group left. Really, it had seemed to every group that it was the last one left; and yet, every group had heard the naming of every other group, for it was all simultaneous.

"Well, come, come, my good man," Anatole Keshish said to the man, and he clapped his hands for attention. "Now that you have disposed of the animals (and you did do it neatly, even though you were a little too wordy about it sometimes), it is time that we had our talk. We will clue you in on the world situation. Then we will be willing to listen to your special mission and message. I believe that we have been waiting for the message a long while, though frankly we expected it to be brought by a more imposing messenger."

"You haven't any name," the man said almost with bluntness. "Your particular species vanishes now as a separate thing. It has never been a real species. It hasn't either body or spirit: only air and noise. Several of the creatures were correct in calling you the interlopers, the half-creatures. Be submerged now! Be nothing!"

"No, no, no, we are men," Jorge Segundo cried out, very much as the brindled ape Joe Sunrise had cried out the same words. "We are the lords of creation. Ours is the world civilization. We are the First Age of Mankind."

"You were the Second Age of Apedom," the man said, "and an abridged and defective age it has been. I intuit that there have been other such unsatisfactory half-ages or no-ages. Ah, and I am responsible for getting rid of the clutter you have left."

The magic had suddenly gone out of the seven persons or erstwhile persons. Pieces of it that had fallen off them seemed to shine like jellyfish on the ground.

"We have fission, we have space travel," Hatari Nahub protested. "We have great cities and structures of every sort."

"I intuit all this," the man said. "You are a hiving species, but your hives and structures do not have the style of those of the bower-birds or the honeybees or the African termites. I have wondered a little though, how you build up these ferroconcrete hives that you call cities. Do you accrete them by deposits of you regurgitations or your excrement after you have eaten limestone and iron ore? It's a grotesque way, but the blind and instinctive actions of such hive creatures as yourselves always seem grotesque to thinking creatures such as myself. Such mindlessness, such waste in all that you do! The ferroconcrete and wood and stone and chrome hive-colonies that you construct for the billions of inmates, they are more strange, more mindless, of less use than would be so many great anthills. Go now, you mindless hiving folk. You tire me."

"But we have civilization; we have the electromagnetic complex and the nuclear complex," Charley Mikakeh challenged.

"And the firefly has a light in his tail," the man said. "Go. Your short day is done."

"But we have all the arts," Toy Tonk claimed, and she was very near the art of tears.

"Can you sing like the mockingbird or posture like the peacock?" the man asked. "What arts do you have? Go now."

(This was not really a long argument. The crows had argued much longer, and just for the jabbering fun of it. Besides, this was happening at the same time that all the other decisions were being given.)

"We will not go. You have not named us yet," Helen Rubric spoke.

"It will be better if I do not speak your name," the man said. "You will shrivel enough without. Go back to your hive cities and decay in their decay. Your speech now becomes gibberish and you begin your swift decline."

"Why, I know who you are now," Lisa Baron exclaimed. "You are the Genesis Myth. In fact you are the Partheno-Genesis Myth. Is it not strange that no language has a masculine form of 'parthen,' and yet it appears to be the oldest. Now I know why the myth is in pain. From your side, will it be? I am a doctor, among other things. May I assist?"

"No," the man said. "You may not. And know you something else, female of the unnamed species: every myth comes true when enough time has run. There was a great myth about the earthworm once. There was even a sort of myth about yourselves. And you, creature, have a little more than the rest of your kindred. It seems a shame that you have already come and gone before the scene itself begins."

"We have not gone, we will not go," Anatole Keshish insisted. "Everyone is of some use. What can we offer?" Then his tongue lost its cunning forever.

"You can offer only your submission and retrogression," the man said.

"Ah, but tell us finally, what is our real name?" Hatari Nahub asked. Those were the last true words he ever spoke.

"Your name is ape," the man said. "Really your name is 'secondary ape.' "

There were fair and dark visages, and blue and gray and brown eyes shining with tears. The seven followed the other seven away, speechless forever, shedding their robes and wrappings, knowing that the blight was already upon their already obsolete world-hives, knowing that their minds and talents were dimmed, and then not really knowing anything, ever again.

Edward Bryant

GOING WEST

HIS NAME was Lindsey.

They (mother, stepbrother, older sister) reared him on a farm in upstate New York. Raised from the potent germ plasm of a father lately dead in Cambodia, Lindsey endured a generally happy childhood. The stepbrother, product of an earlier marriage, served as a surrogate father until he was killed pulling a service-station holdup in Rochester. Eleven at the time, Lindsey cried in his mother's arms, then returned to the woods behind the house to play with his soldiers.

In his infancy: Lindsey's mother read some arcane predecessor of Dr. Spock and decided not to make the same mistake she had perpetuated through her first two children; she made a point of never holding Lindsey more than a minute, and then never rocking him. When it was too late, she read in the medical section of *Time* that physical contact is essential for the development of a child's motor skills. She wondered, then shrugged off the knowledge. Lindsey grew older in a frangible world, wondering why he alone stumbled over obstacles others easily avoided.

In his childhood: Naturally shy, Lindsey found himself increasingly alone and lonely when he started town school. His stepbrother neglected to teach him how to play baseball or fight. His sister never taught him to dance. Lindsey inhabited the periphery of his peers' world, and he felt the pain.

64

Every recess Lindsey went to the school bus parking lot. He played alone among the buses, their high, yellow flanks reminding him of animals. He gradually discovered the buses' names and personalities.

Crosstown busing for integration came to Lindsey's city. One night someone dynamited one of the buses at his school. When he saw the burned-out wreckage in the morning, Lindsey collapsed. The school nurse took him home and he spent the next week in bed with a high fever. The doctor diagnosed the cause as a virus.

When Lindsey returned to school, the bus parking lot was surrounded by a chain-link fence twice as high as he. All recess he looked through the mesh; the school buses returned his gaze from forlorn headlights.

In his youth: Lindsey won a Regent's scholarship and went off to college to become a certified public accountant. It was actually his mother's idea. Lindsey lived with three roommates in a sterile new apartment building across the street from campus. He bought a tenspeed Schwinn and kept it chained to the outside stairs. After a month, Lindsey realized that someone was spitting on the seat of his bicycle.

His roommates suggested he was paranoid.

Lindsey grew to dread returning from class to discover the iridescent spittle on his bicycle. He carried a handkerchief used only to wipe off the seat. Lindsey stayed home from classes one entire morning, hoping to catch the phantom expectorator. Nothing happened until noon, when Lindsey left the window and went into the bathroom to relieve a painful bladder. When he returned, he checked the bike. Someone had spat on the seat.

A month later someone cut the locking chain with boltcutters and stole the bicycle.

"You see," said Lindsey to his roommates. *"You see!"*

Stripes; they zip-zipped past the left side of his car, disappearing somewhere close under the front fender, then reappearing in the rear-view mirror, to recede into a vanishing perspective. Lindsey counted endlessly in his mind, all the way across Nebraska, about five hundred miles. Six feet of white stripe, six of black asphalt, six of white again, past Omaha and Lincoln, Grand Island and Hershey, North Platte. One day earlier it had been Newark and Allentown,

McKeesport and Columbus. Stripes and stripes, cut along a hypnotic dotted line from coast to coast.

Out of habit, Lindsey turned on the radio. Interference from the power towers beside the highway dismembered the music, saw blade biting obliquely into wet wood.

It was early morning and enough sun up behind him so he could turn off the headlights. Lindsey inventoried stripes, but over ten the numbers became meaningless. "Zip, zippety zip," he mumbled, counting the stripes individually as they slipped under and into the rear-view mirror. The great attraction of the stripes was their utter lack of variation. Thousands upon thousands during the night, and only a dozen seemed to have been deformed. He wasn't sure he had been fully awake all the time.

Signs swept past, but Lindsey couldn't integrate letters with meanings until he was jarred into alertness by a day-glo cowboy. HOWDY, PODNUH, read the sign. FOOD SIX MILES. Lindsey looked at the fuel gauge.

"Hay and water," said Lindsey. "Curry him down, isn't that right?"

"What?" said the filling station boy. "Fill her up?"

"Right, podnuh," said Lindsey, walking off toward the sign FOOD. He leaned against the steel jamb of the door for a moment and took a deep breath. The clean prairie air scored his mind with a terrible clarity; Lindsey reeled. A Minnesota tourist couple seated at a table by the window thought he was drunk and ignored him.

Lindsey grinned and assumed a sober posture. The Minnesotans studied their plates of steaming buffalo sausage. The chill rigidity of the jamb passed into Lindsey's fingers and down his backbone; he entered the restaurant.

The skeg: I'm Lindsey, he thought, looking around the dining room for an empty booth. Not Lindsay or Lindsy. Certainly not Veach. Veach was a fag who entered the office mornings with a flourish of violet—scent and shirts. Veach's face, framed in the doorway of Lindsey's office, said, "Hey Lindy, come home with me tonight and meet the wife?" Ritual, almost daily joke for two years. Lindsey said automatically into his ledger, "No thanks, not tonight. Mona's having friends over." For the first months Veach had frightened him. Veach took note and was amused.

Not Lindsay or Lindsay, old or young. The older Lindsay had founded the firm just after one of the Great Wars. There was never a question to whom he was referring—Lindsay or Lindsey. A Harvard man, unselfconscious aristocrat, his pronunciation always came down hard on the *a*. He tolerated Veach out of a perverse democratic fascination, and he thought Lindsey was a good solid worker.

The son Lindsay had attended the University of Southern California. He slurred his words, and his meanings all came from contextual clues. He would rather have been someone other than a CPA.

Lindsay, Lindsay, Linsey, and Veach. A firm firm, thought Lindsey, which is losing its grip. Veach always knew the difference between the Lindsays and the Lindsey; but Veach was—

"Guhmorninmistuhwhatcherwant?" like a garbled readout from the office terminal.

"Mona," Veach learned to say. "Who the hell's Mona?"

Persistent, the waitress hovered impatiently at Lindsey's elbow. "Black coffee," he said.

"Nothin' else?"

It's too quiet in this apartment. The stereo is up and the street buffets the windows, but it's too silent. All sound sinks into the green-flowered wallpaper.

If there were movement, if there were warmth . . .

If she were in the kitchen, fixing breakfast.

If . . .

There is movement and there is warmth.

She is in the kitchen fixing breakfast.

Sure you don't mind?

Of course not. I love making your breakfast.

Never mind; come here. I don't want breakfast. Only you.

"You all right?" The waitress looked at him suspiciously.

"Just coffee," said Lindsey. "Leave the pot." The waitress left.

The coffee was hot and caustic. Lindsey patiently cooled it with his spoon, a steel hull constantly filling and sinking and carrying him to cooler depths. The two men in the next booth were talking, and Lindsey listened.

"Look at the headlines," one declared, crackling the newspaper. "New York Man Sought in Nebraska." He traversed the page with his finger. "Supposed Psychopath Sighted Near Omaha."

They both studied the photograph.

Lindsey slouched low in his seat.

"What did he do?" said the nearer man in the next booth.

"Assault," said the man with the paper. "Beat up a doctor."

Lindsey surfaced from dreams raggedly, limbs jerking in small spasms. He awoke and Mona would be close, very warm and reassuring. Her stroking fingers calmed him. Her voice soothed, cradled him until he could sleep peacefully. No dreams then, not until morning when he awoke to dirty sunlight in the city.

The waitress slapped down the lime-green check. Lindsey reached for his wallet. "Pay the cashier."

On his way out of the restaurant, Lindsey slipped a quarter into a vending machine and took out a copy of the newspaper. One headline read, NEW YORK AIR ALERT IN EIGHTH DAY. The other read, NO AGREEMENT IN YUCATAN. The front page photo was of the president of Mexico. Lindsey dropped the paper in the KEEP AMERICA CLEANER receptacle.

Again the stripes zip-zipped past, all the way across arid Wyoming. Lindsey surrendered to their peaceful procession. A hum rose loud and louder in his ears until it drowned the motor and road noise. The road ahead constricted to a view seen through a tunnel. Lindsey took another of the red pills his doctor had prescribed for appetite-suppression during college. It stuck in his throat and he had to swallow repeatedly.

Across the Utah border there were white airplane silhouettes painted on the pavement. With his limited knowledge of the Mormon culture, Lindsey assumed they were stylized seagulls. A public service billboard informed him that the road was under radar surveillance from aircraft. Lindsey reduced the ancient Camaro's speed to five miles above the speed limit.

Just before sunset on the salt flats, Lindsey invented a new game. He focused his left eye on the line of stripes coming toward him from the west. He focused his right eye on the rear-view mirror where the stripes receded into the distance. A dozen times his peripheral vision barely saved him from death. Twelve angry drivers drove toward Salt Lake, shouting silent curses back across the desert.

"You idiot, you wanna get killed?"

There was a need for running. They were driving him crazy.

Go west, young man. So he went west.

In Wendover, on the Nevada state line, Lindsey discovered he had taken the wrong turn for Los Angeles.

"You wanted Interstate Fifteen," said the wrinkled man, handing Lindsey a Chevron roadmap. "You're headed for San Francisco."

"So I'm lost," Lindsey admitted. "Help me."

They spread the map on the service-station counter above the gum and candy. "Bear south on U.S. Alternate Fifty. 'Bout a hundred miles it runs into U.S. Ninety-three. That puts you right into Vegas and then it's freeway all the way to LA. All downhill."

"Thanks," said Lindsey, folding the map along the wrong creases.

"You better get some rest."

"I'm fine," said Lindsey, "but I'm late."

The service-station man called across the tarmac, "You remind me of that white rabbit in that kids' book—sayin' 'I'm late, I'm late, for a very important date.' You got something important?"

"A very important date," said Lindsey. He looked at his watch. It had stopped at three twenty; he had forgotten to wind it.

"What?" said the service-station man.

"I'm late," said Lindsey, looking back at him blankly.

Left turn, right turn, Lindsey stopped his car at the junction and slumped forward, resting his forehead on the wheel. Choices—San Francisco and Los Angeles both meant California. San Francisco . . . something about fog and damp. He was too tired to consider more than simplicities; there was something mythic about Los Angeles. Hating decisions, he surged blindly into the intersection.

For the first time he drove along two-lane black-top. The constant white dashes were now supplemented on curves and hills by continuous yellow stripes. Lindsey marked the addition.

He encountered little traffic on the Nevada highway, yet the road was strewn with dead animals: rabbits, porcupines, even an occasional badger. Once he had to swerve to avoid something so massive it could only have been a dead cow. He opened his window to the cold night air and after many miles realized that the scent coming into the car was the odor of corruption.

Seventy miles south of Wendover he pulled off the road. He urinated in the barrow pit beneath the cold sky and stars. The desert tried to retain him. Lindsey thought of the highway department crew finding his frozen body in the morning, standing spraddle-legged and stiff, jutting a yellow rainbow into the east. When he got back into the car it was like slamming a refrigerator door. Lindsey turned the heater controls all the way up and the car began to smell of dust.

At a truckstop south of Ely, he stopped briefly for gasoline. As Lindsey pulled out of the service area, he passed a hitchhiker. The man waited on the shoulder of the highway beneath a mercury lamp and extended a tentative thumb. Lindsey's foot hesitated on the accelerator. He looked through the window at the hitchhiker; the man looked back from shadowed, invisible eyes. The hitchhiker was tall and thin, with a dark tapered beard. He was wrapped in heavy, shabby clothing, and carried a canvas rucksack slung over one shoulder.

There was something naggingly familiar about the hitchhiker. Was he— Sorry, thought Lindsey, and drove away so fast that gravel scattered from the Camaro's rear tires. Pebbles leaped and ticked around the hitchhiker's feet.

Veach appeared unexpectedly on the passenger's side of the seat. He looked across at Lindsey with a Cheshire grin. "Hey Lindy, come home with me tonight and meet the wife."

What wife, thought Lindsey. Some nice boy you picked up on Forty-second? He instantly regretted the thought and felt ashamed; Veach had more taste. "No thanks, not tonight. Mona's having friends over."

"Mona," said Veach. "Who the hell's Mona? Lindy, baby, you ought to see a shrink."

I love her, thought Lindsey.

"It won't kill you," Veach said, taking a cigarette from a gold case and tapping it against the dashboard.

"What?" Lindsey said vaguely.

Veach was disgusted. "You're not listening."

"I am. Why should I see a psychiatrist?"

"Are you unhappy?"

Lindsey admitted he was.

"Shrinks help. Trust me."

"Psychiatrists fool around with things that aren't their business."

"That's their business," said Veach.

Later: the elder Lindsay, implacable. "You're a good, solid man, Lindsey. An asset to the firm."

"Thank you, sir."

"But I think perhaps you are upset. Lately your work has

been uneven."

"I'm sorry, sir."

"I want you to take some time off. Maybe . . . seek some professional help."

"I'm fine, sir. I'd rather not."

"I'd rather you did, boy."

"Sir . . ."

"Mr. Veach can recommend an extremely competent man."

Sometime during the night, the sky above the hills to the southwest began to lighten. In an hour it became a white glow. Another hour: Las Vegas. Lindsey had never been to Las Vegas—he had never before been west of Pittsburgh—yet he had heard . . . The coins in his right trousers pocket pressed against his thigh. Lindsey unconsciously touched the wallet in his jacket. He realized it was too easy a dream and instantly denied it, laughing.

Lindsey took the freeway bypass to the west. On his left, the carnival glared and blared, merging his night with others from long before. Neon incandescence, flashing:

CAESAR'S PALACE
TILT-A-WHIRL
THE NUGGET
FREAK SHOW
DUNES HOTEL
COTTON CANDY

Dizzy, Lindsey hunched forward over the wheel and concentrated on the stripes. He heard a chorus of "In the Good Old Summer Time," as though played by a distant calliope, the sound teasingly distorted by wind. He twisted the knob of the radio, but the radio was already off.

The sound, he realized, was distorted by time.

A sign of soft, reassuring green swept by on the right:

LOS ANGELES 280 MILES

It was an anchor of tangibility; a promise he could grasp.

"Where's the ashtray in this thing," said Veach.

"Under the radio."

"How was the session with the shrink?"

"That's, uh—"

"None of my business, right?"

"The psychiatrist was quite pleasant."

"Crap," said Veach, "you hated it, right?"

"I didn't hate it, no."

Veach exhaled a cloud of smoke. "Don't obscure your hostilities, chickie. Did you tell him about Mona?"

"He didn't ask."

"Stop and let me out," said Veach. "I can get further with a desert cactus."

As the road began to climb into the Sierras, Lindsey checked the fuel gauge. The needle rested well below *E*, so he exited at a station where the floodlit signs assured him ALL NIGHT, LOWEST PRICES, LIVE GILA MONSTERS, and CACTUS CANDY. The attendant told him the live gila monsters were asleep in their pens, not to be disturbed until morning.

On the access road to the highway, Lindsey passed a hitchhiker again. *The* hitchhiker. Lindsey stared as the hitchhiker put out his thumb. Unaccountably terrified, Lindsey swung wide into the left lane to avoid him and pressed the accelerator to the floor. He looked back in the mirror; there was only darkness.

Lindsey joined the westbound freeway and felt his panic subside. There was nothing frightening about a recurring hitchhiker. It was an anomaly, but nothing sinister. Lindsey concentrated on keeping his lane as the highway wound farther up the Sierra slope. At times traffic from the opposite direction swept down around the curves toward him, headlights strobbing between posts of the divider fence.

He wondered about the time. The luminous dial of his watch read three twenty. A uniformed man at the agricultural check station across the California border gave Lindsey the correct time.

"I have time and money enough to see a psychiatrist," said Lindsey, "but not the inclination. What for? I know how things are."

Do you have any citrus fruits, vegetables, or other plants?

Yes I have no bananas, Lindsey indicated. He had heard his mother say that.

Don't give me a hard time, buddy.

Time, that's all I want.

"You'll love him," said Veach. "His name is Dr. Van der Mark. He's a pussycat."

Coasting down the long grade into Barstow, Lindsey looked into the mirror and once again saw a glow. This time it was morning. A reddish sun edged above the mountains and the Mojave instantly turned incinerator. Having no air conditioner, Lindsey rolled his window down and suffered.

Dr. Van der Mark (Veach explained) spent a number of years interned by the Japanese in New Guinea. The experience gave him a profound insight into mankind; a great compassion for humanity. Only a child then, at war's end he determined to become a psychiatrist.

Lindsey wondered aloud why his experience in the Japanese internment camp hadn't caused Van der Mark to become a misanthrope.

Maybe he's crazy, Veach suggested.

So why should I waste my money on a crazy person?

Because he's a pussycat.

"I will want to see you again in one week," said Dr. Van der Mark. His voice was precise. He smiled only slightly, allowing his lips little freedom to disturb the meticulously tended Vandyke.

Lindsey silently collected his hat and coat.

"Next week I should like an introduction to Mona."

"Did Veach—"

"That would be unprofessional," said Van der Mark.

"Then how—"

Van der Mark carefully touched his Vandyke with one finger. "You talk; I listen."

The air temperature rose, all the way from Barstow into San Bernardino, where Los Angeles actually seemed to begin. Berdoo—Lindsey dinsinterred the word from a youthful memory of a motorcycle film. Berdoo was palms and lanai apartment buildings, light-to-medium industry spread along the freeway, and air that made Lindsey think of home. His lungs began to smart, his eyes to water. From time to time he glanced sidewise at the roadmap on the seat. The processional rolled past: Riverside, Ontario, Pomona, West Covina. He repeated the place-names, a potent incantation.

Lindsey felt a tangible relaxation, barely short of unconsciousness. The long drive was nearly ended; he was Here. But where was that? His reach and grasp were suddenly equivalent.

"Oh my God, oh my God," said Lindsey. He wanted to pull over on the side of the highway and be sick or fall asleep, or both. He craned his neck stared out the windows and into the mirrors. There was no way. Lindsey's Camaro was in the fourth lane from the right of six lanes westbound. Traffic chains of multicolored links bound him on both sides. Lindsey flashed his turn signals first one way, then the other. He pressed on the horn.

Some of the other drivers ignored Lindsey; some cursed him; some laughed.

Veach reached for the lighter. "Well, Lindy, you're here." He paused to light his cigarette. "Are you just going to drive indefinitely west in this lane?"

Lindsey looked helplessly across the hood of his car. Traffic in the lane immediately to his left was moving slightly faster than he; cars in the right lane were traveling slower.

"It may take an hour or two," said Veach, "but you'll run out of gas. Here you'll be. Helpless and surrounded."

"I'll make it," said Lindsey. "I'm here. Just give me time."

"No time, bunny."

Signs abounded on either side of the freeway and overhead: guidance for the lame and halt, or for strangers.

SAN GABRIEL RIVER FREEWAY

                    POMONA FREEWAY NEXT
NEXT RIGHT

                              RIGHT
        SAN BERNARDINO FREEWAY
              LEFT LANES

TO SANTA ANA FREEWAY

              YORTY SKYWAY CENTER
KEEP LEFT

                              LANE
        LOS ANGELES LEFT
              LANES

"I can help," said Dr. Van der Mark, "but for me to help you, you must help me."

"What?" said Lindsey.

"You must help me." Dr. Van der Mark slumped in the tan leather chair. He was tall and stoop-shouldered, with the unconscious slouch of the tall man who doesn't wish to intimidate men of shorter stature. "I wonder if you could tell me your goals."

The Rorschach inkblots had been easier. Finally Lindsey said, "I don't know. I'm not sure. I want to be warm and safe."

"And loved?"

"There's a difference?"

From interchange to interchange the traffic fragmented and reformed, shifting Lindsey from lane to lane.

"This is scary," said Lindsey aloud. "I didn't expect this." The sun was nearly overhead and he looked at his watch: the hands stood at three twenty. Lindsey turned on the radio.

"—ee-twenty in the afternoon, this is KLA in Pasadena with a Wild Wax Weekend in store—"

He could see Mona, blurred. *Hard to focus*, Lindsey thought.

Eyes deep in shadow, Dr. Van der Mark regarded him. "It's not uncommon for a child to invent an imaginary playmate."

You fool! "I am twenty-six years old," said Lindsey.

"Please, I meant no—"

"Listen," said Lindsey almost pleading. "Please don't fuck around with reality."

"Mr. Lindsey, will you listen—"

You stupid, irresponsible—

"—to reason?"

—bastard. Nothing gives you the right.

"I can only help you with your full cooperation."

Nothing.

The radio: "—sule News. Today Los Angeles inaugurates its new multimillion-dollar traffic control plan. Acco—"

At the apex of a four-level traffic stack, Lindsey saw an opening on the right and cut in. The new signs read HOLLY-WOOD FREEWAY.

"—rding to LA Traffic Czar Chase, the new system will cut freeway congestion ten percent in the first month of operation. Further—"

Quickly, quickly! Lindsey cut to the left. The VENTURA FREEWAY. He glanced at the map; red freeways tangled in an unstrung skein.

"You don't need that map," said Veach.

"I don't know where I'm going," Lindsey said.

Veach nodded. "You feel it. The map won't help."

The radio: "—ozen random exit ramps and sites selected for maximum disposa—"

The freeway rose to the penultimate level of a five-layered

interchange and Lindsey looked down at California from a dizzying height. "It's got to be here somewhere," he said. "It's got to be." The route divided and Lindsey drove the San Diego Freeway south. To the right the sun glittered on water. "The Pacific," Lindsey said. "I've never seen it." He strained his eyes but saw nothing but hard glitter.

The freeways forked and spread like lovers' legs, and Lindsey followed them. The map was nearly useless, but in time he came to believe he was driving widdershins around the golden city of the golden state. The ocean to the west gleamed closer.

The radio: "—oday's QLI Report. QLI Authority reports smog concentration moderate, eye irritation severe, potential respiratory damage moderate. High temperatures today will range to the hundred-degree mark. Traffic levels are maximum. The retail price index is up four-tenths of a percent. All factors considered, the Quality of Life Index has receded to an all-time low of six. In oth—"

"Can't you describe her?" Dr. Van der Mark asked.

"Of course," said Lindsey. "As easily as my own face."

He heard the long-drawn thunder of waves rake the beach.

Blaring horns shocked him up one level of consciousness. The Camaro swerved back into its own lane. Lindsey gripped the steering wheel so tightly his knuckles began to ache.

"Just watch the stripes," said Veach. "They'll guide you. Watch the stripes."

The radio: "—ily as my own fa—"

"The quality of life is strained," said Lindsey. Immensely satisfied with his own cleverness, he said it again.

"We're here," said Veach, stubbing out his cigarette in the ashtray.

The sign blocked out the sun:

TEMP. ALTERNATE EXIT
SANTA MONICA FREEWAY
FAR RIGHT LANE

Lindsey found himself in the far right lane. The main body of traffic broke and flowed away to the left. The Camaro climbed an exit ramp describing a wide, asymptotic curve into the west.

The radio: "—ongratulations. You have opted for participation in the Los Angeles Traffic Control Plan."

The road angled free from the shadows of the interchange and Lindsey saw the ocean. The ramp arched high out over the beach.

"Just follow the stripes," Veach said.

East to west, the line was complete. Lindsey followed the ramp as it curved downward, followed as the stripes disappeared in a swirl of white water, as the waves of the Pacific broke above the roof of his car.

James Sallis

MY FRIEND

ZARATHUSTRA

MY FRIEND Zarathustra has stolen my wife.

Yes—I mean what I say, and you must listen; must hear what's not said if you're to understand properly what is said. For, as with him, silence is to me an instinct.

So (I repeat) Zarathustra—carrier of the ashes of the old to the mountains in order to prepare a new beginning, spokesman for the inseparability of creation and destruction, teacher of the eternal recurrence—this same Zarathustra has stolen my wife.

The bastard.

I try to recall, now, when it might have begun between them; at which point, perhaps, she first reached out to touch the hand he offered, but memory fails—I must have been working too hard at the book to take notice. I suppose she may have loved him from the first. That those months of close friendship in the huge house on the hill overgrown with vines—the fires at night as we read together, the fourteen rooms, the quiet, hollow Sundays—concealed all along the slow slide of this fact, and others, beneath me. As I worked in my room on the top floor above the trees. Sometimes when I wake now alone in early morning hours, I imagine there were moments when I felt, dully, never perceiving the truth, that some intangible thing was slipping from me; felt some pale remain of sadness inside, irretrievable. If so, these moments were few, and quickly passed.

(There were times he was happy; he remembers. Now he stands at the window, looking down on the town. Neons are coming on, like exclamation marks for something the darkness is trying to say; they show red on the glass. In the distance radio towers rise against the sky. Fragments accumulate on his desk. He is aware of the space between things. He holds broken facts in his hands.)

Her work grew ever better, the colors bold and the rapid
strokes finding relief in sudden, unexpected islands of close
detail, ever more explicit, the content increasingly erotic—a
body in grey fleshtones with three heads turned each to the
other, the lips livid, against a background of alizarins and
ochre; my own became increasingly subtle and sparse, moving
toward silence. It occurred to none of us, I think, to wonder
for so much as a moment whether things outside proceeded
along the course which had brought us, or driven us, there; to
that sole, solitary refuge.

The hills spread about me now as I write, looking down on
the tops of trees. A light fog resides forever inside them. The
dampness of it enters the open window of my bedroom each
morning, a clean, fresh smell appropriate to new beginnings.
The sunrise is splendid, breaking in rainbows through the mist
and drifting, light dew; most nights the Northern Lights fan
out and fill the sky, as though beautiful cities were burning
far away. There is no life anywhere in these trees. Where
birds once sang and young deer broke the crust of new-fallen
snow.

My work—what can I say of it? I fear I am now past all
ambition; that volition, like hope, has died within me and nothing will issue again from that still center. (There would be
such comfort in despair.) Times were, a single image, a
phrase, would imbue page upon page with life; stories would
spring fullblown from the chance word of a friend, the pattern of light through leaves at the window, the eager edge of a
razor. Now lifeless pages of notes and scattered scenes accumulate on my table like slices of cheese on a platter: these
weak attempts to retrieve my life. This might, I suppose, be
expected, a function of the events outside, an equivalent decay.

—Tonight J wants to play for us the piano. He sits on the
bench beside her, his face in his hands, weeping. B's fingers
form broad X's in the moisture on the tabletop. It is Chopin,
she says. The keyboard is roughly sketched out with a car-
penter's pencil at one end of the table; there are no halftones.
And so we wait.

—This morning we found him in the tub, the drain closed,
his own blood all around him; in aspic. His eyes stared up and
forward at the tiles on which J has painted a cluster of grapes,
and on them, a roach. One of the girls is pregnant. Bits and
shreds of half-digested food cling to the sink's sides each

morning.

—*Force of circumstances driving the protagonists to the commission of a dreadful act . . .*

(He is standing at the window. It is open, and he speaks words to it. They scatter on the darkness, random as facts, unforgiving. He has done this before. He will do this again. He is free.)

I remember the last night. We had just made love and she stood at the window, her stomach bulging slightly now and her breasts full, the old stretch-marks lost. The motel sign was red on the glass; darkness entered through the window. And she said, Jim. Jim . . . we're leaving. When she turned to me, light from the hall glinted on tears in her eyes that, now, would never fall. I'm sorry. After a moment I stood and nodded, then came up here and began to write down everything I remembered about her. At dawn I found I could write no more, and I realised she was gone.

(He is tall, large, with deep blue eyes and heavy ridges above them, like shelves for dark things that might fall out of the sky. He listens to his own voice ringing in the corridors of night. He smiles. It is almost over now.)

It is 3 A.M. now, a cool night wrapped in clouds, and again unable to sleep, I take down a book. It is a foreign edition and with a small silver knife I must cut the pages free as I read:

We are to recognise how all that comes into being must be ready for a sorrowful end; we are forced to look into the terrors of the individual existence—yet we are not to become rigid with fear: a metaphysical comfort tears us momentarily from the bustle of the changing figures. We are really for a brief moment—

But wait. There are sounds outside now. Voices milling about, feet. Voices. Together.

I go to the window. There are fires. The villagers have come at last.

Gary K. Wolf

THERAPY

"FOR THIS I came all the way downtown? Hell, Emma, it's a machine! You didn't tell me it would be a machine. At these prices, I refuse to talk to a machine. I demand something better."

"You refuse. You demand. That's right. Just keep it up, Harold. The machine is listening. Hear that, machine? Are you listening? Mister *Big Shot* refuses. Mister *Egg-sec-u-tiff* demands. Wait. Next he'll start bossing you around. The same way he does me."

"Must you distort everything, Emma? See here, machine, I think you can appreciate my position. I'm a sensitive man. Forced to come up the hard way. Groveling and clawing and shoving for everything I've got. When I get home at night, all I ask from her is a little understanding. Do I get it? No. What do I get instead? Nagging. Complaining. 'The servants did this. The children did that.' I can't take much more of it, machine. Already I've developed a very nervous stomach."

"Good morning." From the machine's tuba-shaped loudspeaker-mouth. "Please be seated." A pleasant voice. Persuasively calming. They sat down. "According to my schedule, you two should be Mr. and Mrs. Harold Hokey. Is that correct?"

Harold answered. "Substantially, yes, but lately we've taken to pronouncing it ho-*kay*, though. The rhymester at my ad agency suggested it. To go along with their creative strategy. See, I advertise a lot. I'm mister big in aphrodisiacs, you know. You've probably heard my ad a million times. Too pooped to play? Make it ho-kay. On TV? Every night?"

"Sorry, no. I have you down as a compatibility problem. What seems to be the trouble?"

Emma quickly fielded that one. "The trouble is that Harold High Hat there thinks he's God Almighty. Lord of the manner. Don't you let him fool you with that 'I'm so sensitive'

81

crap. Ask him why all that sensitivity didn't bother him the time he automated elk antler production and laid off those sweet old shepherds. How that man did gloat. All I heard about for weeks. Go ahead, ask him. You'll see. He's the one who needs help, not me."

"Now one minute, Emma." Harold stood up. The books advised it in situations like this. Put you at a better advantage. Gave you the psychological edge. People were all conditioned. Height equals authority. "I think we're taking a few things out of context, here, aren't we?"

"Please sit down, Mr. Ho-kay," from the machine.

"No, I will not." Harold scowled down at the machine. "Not until I get her to admit she's sick. And she is. It takes a genuinely sick mind to keep hammering away at me this way. Ruining my health. By distorting the facts. With sniveling half-truths." Harold turned. Ready. Thinking on his feet. Humiliate. Degrade. Discredit. Get that bitch.

"MR. HO-KAY." Stereophonic sound. At least two hundred watts. Fifteen-inch woofer. Thirty or forty mid-ranges. God-only-knows how many tweeters. Full blast. *From at least thirty feet off the floor.* "PLEASE SIT DOWN."

He sat down.

The machine's voice took on a cheery lilt. "Let's probe around at random, for a while. See if we can define the parameters of your problem. For instance, what are your hobbies? Harold?"

Harold brightened considerably. "I collect ad art. Not that crummy stuff you buy in those cheapie galleries down on Forty-second Street. Stuff that's already been thumbed over by a million people. No. I collect good stuff. First drafts. Signed by copywriter and art director. In fact, hanging in our living room, I have the original storyboard for the *Bubbly-Seltzer* 'Grandma's Coming to Dinner' commercial. You know the one. Opens with a long shot of everybody rushing around. Straightening up the house. Cooking. Fantastic thing of three or four years ago. On the tube five, maybe six times a day. Anyway, I have it. Authentic as hell. Some of the most prominent experts in the country certified it before I bought. Had to pay a fancy price for it, too. Art like that doesn't come along often. And I have more. Print stuff. The very first two-page spread for *Whoops-A-Daisy*. That one didn't come cheap, either."

"I don't imagine so. Now, you, Emma. What's your hobby?" the machine asked with soothing, pear-shaped tones.

Emma forsook candor for retaliation. "My hobby? Whining. According to Harold. He thinks I've got it so easy. Staying home alone. Raising the children by myself. While he's off somewhere gallivanting round the world looking for more ways to make people hot."

"Emma"—Harold whirled in his chair to face her—"you shut your filthy mouth."

She leaned forward. "Well, I get hot, too, Harold, and you aren't much help cooling me off, anymore, you know." A direct hit, and she knew it.

"Stop it, do you hear me," Harold screamed. "My sex life is of no concern to a damned machine."

"Quite to the contrary, Mr. Ho-kay," the machine responded with low wattage, jacked-up bass, muted treble. "All facets of your life together are my concern. Emma"—no treble, high filter, less than one db—"please tell me more."

Emma had taken a bright green handkerchief from her transparent lucite handbag. She blew her nose with a resonant honk and returned the handkerchief to her bag. Carefully. To avoid smearing up the inside and ruining the bag's transparency. She didn't succeed. She stared with disgust, first at her purse, then at Harold.

"Harold isn't home much, you see. I get lonely. For a man's company. I'm hardly what you'd call oversexed or anything like that, but I do have normal cravings. Like any other woman. I'm not saying what I did was right. Or even proper. But Harold's gone so much. I simply couldn't do without."

"Umm-uh." The machine. Sensing antennae forward and back. Forward and back. "So, you felt you simply couldn't do without."

"No, of course not. Could you?"

"I really don't know, Emma," with compassion, understanding, tolerance. "Suppose you tell me about it."

"Well, I . . ." Emma glanced sideways at Harold. Harold glared back. Emma looked at the machine, and blurted it out. *"I had an affair."* She turned toward Harold. "How does that grab you, big shot. Knowing that somebody else got in your personal property."

Harold was on his feet. "Who? Tell me. Who was it? I'll kill the son of a bitch."

"MR. HO—"

Harold sat down. "Who was it? I demand you tell me."

Emma stared at him coldly, hesitated for a moment, and let him have it. "It was Mark."

"Mark?"

"Mark Four."

"Emma, are you telling me you did it with a mechanical servant? That's repulsive. Worse. It's absurd."

"Yes, yes, yes. I did it with a mechanical servant. And it was better than it ever was with you. Even though his dusting attachment kept poking me in the ribs. Even though we had to tape a pillow over his accessory tray. Even though he had to use his pneumatic rinsing tube. Even though a hundred ings, it was still far, far better than it ever was with you."

"You degenerate biddy." Harold leaped out of his chair and moved toward Emma with clenched fists.

Emma was ready, though. On her feet. Crouched low. Position two. Right arm out. Three fingers stiff. Left arm in close. Fingers together. Ready to rip out Harold's balls. Like she learned at night school.

"Always try to sublimate open hostility," the machine advised.

Harold came in on Emma, low and underneath, using the old red dog technique he'd put to good service in many a football game, Merriwell High, ought-six.

"Violence is usually the manifestation of a threatened ego," explained the machine in an authoritative basso profundo.

Emma lunged forward with all the expertise she'd acquired in one and a half classes—she never could stand sweat—and missed Harold by a good two feet.

The machine tweaked its amplifiers to capacity. Its voice shot up at least an octave. "I can assign meaning to these aggressive feelings."

His forward motion impaired by the lateral shift of his truss, Harold gave up on his block. Instead, he crawled up to Emma on hands and knees, grabbed her about the legs and shook her back and forth.

"I have complete and total understanding of all the delicate interrelationships comprising the human psyche, you know."

Emma felt up under Harold's coat, grabbed his suspenders, pulled them back as far as she could, and let them go with a snapping *thwack*.

"I was programmed in Vienna."

Harold clutched the hem of Emma's dress that came from the Young Matron's Shop at Saks. With a downward swipe, he ripped it off her.

"In my professional opinion . . ."

"You degenerate animal," screeched Emma, clothed only in

her luster-pink acetate slip. She scooped up a handful of Harold's double-knit Brooks Brothers sport coat, and twisted it into a ball, stretching it all out of shape.

". . . the solution to your problem . . ."

Harold's upper plate fell out. He gnawed at Emma's ankle with his gums.

". . . lies in the realignment of your subconscious drives and motivations." The machine cleared its throat sequentially through its six channels. "Let's see how we might use such a realignment to correct your faults, Mr. Ho-kay."

Harold dropped his hold on Emma and shook his head dumbly. "Ma falls?" He slipped his plate back in. "Correct my faults? Hell, don't worry about me. Straighten her out. She's the one that needs it. Her and her perverted sex life. There's nothing wrong with me."

The machine assumed a scholarly air. "We all have our little human foibles, Mr. Ho-kay. You, for instance. If you were to be a trifle less pompous and a bit more considerate of fragile sensibilities and cravings . . ."

"After what she did to me? Fat chance." Harold banged his hand down on the machine to emphasize his point. Two little green lights winked and a knob fell off.

"And you, Mrs. Ho-kay"—the machine's voice wobbled a little—"have to overcome the fact that you're sexually fixated on an electric broom."

"Don't you talk about him like that." Emma clutched her dress to her with one hand, and swung her purse at the machine with the other.

Her swat shook loose three chrome panels and six feet of plastic tubing. The machine shimmied once, stopped and said with a lisp, "Two P.M., Mithter and Mithuth Ho-kay. I'm afraid thath all for today. Thee you nektht week?"

"Don't bet on it," Harold groused.

Carefully, to avoid touching each other, he and Emma tramped out of the office and into the elevator. Harold punched the ground floor button.

"Wise-ass machine," muttered Harold under his breath.

"Worthless piece of junk," complained Emma.

"He's really a nice, considerate boy, only so cerebral," said the elevator.

"What?" said Emma.

"What the *hell*!" said Harold.

"It's not like I don't tell him," the elevator went on. "Over and over, I tell him. 'Nobody likes a know-it-all. Keep up like

that, you'll never get ahead.' Believe me, of these lovers' spats
I know plenty. Better he should forget the hoity-toity. Try instead a little time, a little tete-a-tete. Look, I show you." The
elevator slowed to a halt between floors. "I don't let you out
till you kiss and make up."

Emma and Harold gaped at each other.

"Open these doors," Harold bellowed.

"Elevators can't go around telling people what to do,"
observed Emma.

"Kiss and make up," repeated the elevator firmly.

"What did I tell you?" it asked twelve hours and thirty-two
minutes later.

"Just fine," cooed Harold, with eyes only for Emma.

"Just fine," Emma echoed lovingly.

The doors popped open.

Arm in arm, Emma and Harold walked out into the early
morning sunshine.

"Remember," the elevator called after them, "all your
friends send to *him* with their problems. For myself, I want
only to give him a push in the business."

The door shut.

With a bustling, motherly whirr, the elevator headed
upstairs to make sure the machine had started off the day
with a good, hot breakfast.

W. Macfarlane

GARDENING NOTES

FROM ALL OVER

THE HERO HAS always been us. The villain has always been us, the right-thinking people. The wrong-thinkers are never wrong, right? What churns my guts is that straight decisions honorably pursued turn into a five-tier cloverleaf interchange. How could I do honestly what I've done, and end so mixed up with problems personal, cultural and for godsake, interplanetary?

I had been a gardener for three years when we found the beetles by the swimming pool. Before that I was employed by the Bureau of Entomology and Plant Quarantine at the Agricultural Research Center at Beltsville, Maryland. Unless you have subjected yourself to it, you cannot imagine the East Coast. My wife, Marian, was agreeable, though she is the daughter of a clergyman in Princeton, New Jersey. I bought a three-quarter-ton truck to carry her books and our personal gear, and we drove to California to live with my mother in her Point Loma home while I went job hunting.

It was refreshing to return to a multi-colored society, and the vegetables are a week to ten days fresher. People say that California is the world of the future, but when I feel low, I'm sure that Maryland is. The natives there are like french fries without ketchup to someone who has grown up with Filipinos, blacks, Portuguese, Germans, Italians, Japanese, Yugoslavs and all the others. While Marian and I are neither vegetarians nor frugiverous, the produce in our supermarkets does not make me want to weep—oh well—the shellfish on the East Coast is outstanding. At Point Loma I renewed a high-school friendship with Lance Yanabu when he came to mow my mother's lawn.

Lance was third- or fourth-generation Japanese. I said, "Hello, Yellow Peril!" and he said, "Harry Watson! Banzai, charge!" and we shook hands. He would not enter the house. "Are you out of your stupid gourd?" I asked. "I got spooky lady clients up and down the street," he said, and mowed the lawn and trimmed the hedges and pinched chrysanthemums for half an hour. Then I made him drive over to a bar with me and I plied him with beer. "Have you got an acute attack of race prejudice?" I asked.

"It's the mystique, you plick."

"And flied lice up your gunny-budger."

"It's this way," said Lance. "I am an inscrutable Oriental and I want to keep it that way. I knock back eighteen thousand dollars by not fraternizing with you bleached Americans. Harry, old buddy, I went to UC Davis and got a bachelor's degree in agronomy. I saved all my pennies and went farming. I lost my ass. And then it occurred to me I was being stupid. I will tell you what my wise old father said. 'Kid,' he said, 'what you want to be selling is what people want to be buying.' Now goddammit, that's wisdom."

"So where's the mystique?"

"Go along with it, I told myself. You got a ready-made role to fill, you got the world by the short hair on a downhill pull. I practiced grunting—ugh—and how to insuck a hiss politely. I practiced holding my hands over my stomach and saying, 'Ten dollah a week, Missy,' and I got fifty-two customers with more waiting to press sawbucks into my hand. I put in a nice eight-hour day outdoors. The overhead is small except for tax purposes. I got it made, Harry."

"That's more than eighteen thousand a year."

"And up your gunny-budger. Some pay cash—I mean ugh! No sprick Engrish velly good."

"Mr. Moto or Dr. Fu Manchu?"

"But many man smoke—I learned to talk like this from television. *Cherchez la femme*, but catch the mystique!"

Ugh! That's how I became a gardener.

Fortunately my eyes are dark brown. With a short hair-cut and a dye job, and suitable skin coloring I made quite a tolerable Japanese. When I bought a narrow-brim straw hat with a bright Paisley band, I had no trouble establishing a clientele in the Fletcher Hills area. I developed a nice additional income with exotics, such as jujube trees and peento peaches, the bitterish-sweet saucer peach from southern China, conversationally sophisticated if not gastronomically so, and they do have a low chilling requirement.

Well, my first year in business under the *nom de guerre* of

Haru Watsonabe I equaled my former income as an organic chemist. Marian and I bought an isolated old house and ten acres near Spring Valley. I built yards of bookcases, because she comes from a family of collectors, and began my experimental garden to gratify my interest in insecticides of plant origin, such as nicotine, nornicotine, anabasine, rotenone, deguelin and related rotenoids, quassin and the pyrethrins. Marian did her crewel work, read books, threw pots, read books, and we took an extension course at UCSD and another at San Diego State. The next year we put in the swimming pool and became involved with ZPG, Zero Population Growth. Like-minded people were our friends and we lived an intellectually satisfying, ordered life.

Then the beetles came.

They were about three feet tall and obviously intelligent. I am a chemist, not an entomologist. Marian described them as half-size Professor Wogglebugs, an imaginary creature from her childhood reading. They stood on their hind legs and dipped water from the swimming pool with buckets and carried them to the spaceship. It was beetle-shaped. There was a pullout spout and they poured water into this until I showed them how the hose worked. They had no trouble understanding the hose bib. They filled their tanks while we stood around and gawped at each other.

Marian started off to make sandwiches but I called her back, pointing out that while hospitality was in order, our new friends were better equipped to sample foliage than feast on peanut butter. I picked a dozen leaves from the garden and offered them on the redwood picnic table—geranium, olive, avocado, ginger, all the common plantings around the house.

They showed interest in coreopsis and cosmos, and one of the beetles lifted his antennae and walked to my experimental garden and brought back a dried *Chrysanthemum cinerariaefolium,* which is also called pyrethrum. It contains Pyrethrins I and II, and cinerins I and II. Pyrethrin acts directly on the central nervous system; the paralysis is a result of blocking of transmission of nerve impulses. It is nontoxic to warm-blooded animals.

Another beetle picked seedheads, of *Sesamum indicum,* from which sesame oil is extracted. It is a powerful synergist for pyrethrum, acting essentially in the same relationship as a sound system to an electric guitar. Others sampled *Schoenocaulan officinale,* which is sabadilla, and *Tephrosia virginiana,* devil's shoestring. It is a pretty little plant at the top of my garden, preferring dry, open sandy places. Marian brought out Coca-Cola and our new friends enjoyed dipping their beaks in that, so we had quite a nice social gathering.

"But aren't all those plants insecticidal?" Marian whispered. "Are we truly being friendly?"

Marian and I can talk together about anything, and too often that's all we do. We subscribe to journals of opinion, such as *The Nation* and *The Atlantic Monthly* and we take the Sunday New York *Times*. If there is one thing on which we and these publications agree, it is good interracial relationships. With the beetles gathered about us at the picnic table (it is not polite to stare at others eating) I pointed out that freedom and liberty imply an assumption that the other person (or beetle) knows what he is doing.

"I am happy to share the fruits of my garden," I said calmly. "The analogy occurs to me of the famous temperance lecture. You fill a glass with water and another with whisky, and drop a worm into each. After the demise of the worm in the booze, the lecturer asks, what does this prove? And the voice from the rear says, 'If you don't want worms, drink whisky!' My dear, a question of size is involved. If a thirty-foot anaconda drank the whisky, how could you say whisky is bad for worms?" Perhaps I was more excited by our visitors than I knew at the time.

But I grew alarmed when they lay on their backs with all six legs in the air. Their aristae, the feathery projections of the antennae, curled and uncurled briskly. For mankind to poison his intellectual peers upon meeting would be rather a blot on history. Then they began to rock back and forth, turned affectionate, and toward morning began mating like mad. This made Marian blush and she excused herself and went into the house. Our guests recovered from their frenzy before dawn. They were obviously pooped as they clambered into their ship. One of them returned to the door and handed me a packet of seeds. Then the ship lifted, caught sunlight a thousand feet up, diminished to a twinkle and was gone in the sky.

It was not exactly a packet of seeds. It was more like a bulb of transparent plastic the size of a golf ball. The seeds were ordinary in appearance, round and dark brown with a matte finish, somewhat larger than ordinary brassicas, such as cabbage or kale or broccoli.

While I believe in friendship and reciprocity, I wouldn't want my sister to marry a beetle if I had a sister. Nor would I want beetles for neighbors. Not because of property values, but neighbors should have some common standards, and Marian and I do not approve of orgies beside our swimming pool. Under a microscope the seeds were seeds and not beetle eggs—the thought had crossed my mind—and Marian mentioned a frivolous story by H. G. Wells about a carnivorous orchid, so I took reasonable care.

Plant diseases, virus, bacteria and fungi—the pathogens, in short—were not at all my business at Beltsville. I worked with organic insecticides, but I knew a little about precautions. I divided the seeds into three parts, wrapped one-third in plastic and put them into a screwtop can, sealed it and had Marian lock it in our safety-deposit box. I treated another third the same way and put the tin into a Mason jar at the back of the refrigerator. The last third I soaked in 120° water for an hour, dried, fumigated and coated with a mercurial dust.

I sterilized my potting mixture in the oven. It is a somewhat different mix of vermiculite, sand and peat than is recommended by the University of California. I planted the seeds two diameters deep and waited. I did not attempt to control the humidity in my little greenhouse, but shaded the seeds, assured good air circulation and kept the soil moist.

Germination took twenty-three interminable days with a soil temperature at about 68°. Tomato seedlings emerge in eight days and lettuce in three, cabbage in six days. I became irritable and morose and unlike my usual self. I told a woman at a pot-luck dinner of our ZPG chapter that this preoccupation with sex was a vicarious voyeurism like reading vulgar novels; Marian's purchase of *Portnoy's Complaint* made me wish she had her money back and the writer had the book stuffed—"What is a gunny-budger?" she asked, and I said it was all sublimation, and complained that the success of ZPG would limit births of the very people who should reproduce. Twenty-three days is a long, long time.

When the seedlings did show, I thought of telling my customers I was going to Honoruru, but with eighty-eight percent germination and growth proceeding normally, there was no real need to give my plants hour-by-hour attention. The U.S. standards of germination for the brassicas run seventy-five to eighty percent and the seed had survived my action against the pathogens, though that may have accounted for the long germinal period.

Growth was rapid. Wherever the seeds came from, our location was an approximate region of adaptation. Four weeks after sprouting, I transplanted to the garden. I used ethylene dibromide as a treatment against nematodes and certain soil fungi. I varied the distance between plants from six to thirty-six inches and the rows were five feet apart. I used furrow irrigation. The best fertilizer response was to a liquid fish preparation, 4-10-4, but the five rows with different treatment (and even the check row) showed, in fact, little difference.

Marian's reaction to this absorbing enterprise was ambivalent. She is not a person to avoid responsibility, but more than once she suggested turning the seed over to a U.S. Experiment Station. She was *comme ci comme ca* as the oracle at Delphi. And at the same time I noted a resemblance to the goddess Demeter as she looked at the plants, brooding and enigmatic, with a faint mysterious smile and a subtle shift in body stance which I was at that time unable to interpret.

The plants threw up a central shaft, a fluted column on the order of anise but a great deal thicker in relation to height. Leaves occurred at intervals, cupped around the column and tapered to three-fingered lobes at the tips. The root structure was creeping, matted and heavy. The stem and leaves were covered with a natural wax to reduce transpiration, an adaptation to low or variable humidity. Our conditions in the dry hills ten air miles from the ocean seemed to suit them admirably.

"How do you know they're not poisonous?" said Marian.

I borrowed a mouse from a young acquaintance whose parents' lawn I tended, and it ate the leaves with no reluctance and no particular enthusiasm. I borrowed a guinea pig and a rabbit for a few days and returned them to their owners in good health. The sap of the leaves had a spicy odor I found attractive, though, once again, Marian's reaction was mixed.

San Diego County has some good men at the operations Center on Kearney Mesa, but all agricultural experts are necessarily evasive. "There are two thousand named varieties of apples," the man told me apologetically, "and heaven alone knows how many plants like yours. Are you troubled by bugs?"

"I had some beetles, but no problem. How about a guess?"

"It could be a primitive cabbage or a kind of stem lettuce," he said doubtfully, and went on to explain that asparagus lettuce had long narrow leaves and a tall, thick edible stem. Not close, and no cigar.

The plants were a foot tall and it was obvious that those at six-inch intervals would be overcrowded, so I cut four of them. I boiled the leaves separately for five minutes until tender. The stalks resembled solid stems of broccoli, except they were a lighter green. Cut up, they took ten minutes to become fork-tender. The cooking fragrance was not cabbagy but something promising, equal to but totally other than celery.

The flavor was distinctive as pepper or parsley is distinctive. The leaves had a sharper flavor, but there was no doubt in my mind that the stalk was the *piece de resistance*. The texture was between that of artichoke heart and celeriac, the root form of celery. There was a ghost of a sweet, spicy aftertaste, immediately obvious when you took a sip of water.

Marian said, "We might as well go together when we go," and sampled the portion I served her. She grew very thoughtful and squeezed a lemon on the leaves, and tried the stem with mayonnaise. She ran the tip of her tongue over her upper lip. "I don't feel like waving my six legs in the air," she said. "I wonder how it is fresh?" That's what we had for dessert, with olive oil and vinegar dressing. We did not stay up late that night.

The next morning I slipped out of bed and went to the phone in the kitchen. I called Don Pashard, a doctor friend, who said it was all nonsense: no chemical agent in food can effect a direct physiological reaction upon the genito-urinary tract. Powdered blister beetles are an irritant of the mucous membrane and the individual response varied so greatly, as did the active ingredient of the material, that cantharides was downright dangerous. "Don't fool around with Spanish fly," he said. "You might scratch yourself to death. As for the old wive's tales—no pun—they're ridiculous—oysters—truffles—avocados. I have a suspicion the Avacado Advisory Council tried that route twenty years ago—a whispering campaign—but the allegation has no base in fact. Harry, there's no such thing as an aphrodisiac. Except—maybe—a stacked and willing blonde."

"Thanks—uh—"

Marian took the phone from my hand and cradled it. Her straw-gold hair was touseled. Her lips were full, her eyes heavy-lidded. "Come back, baby," she said.

An inhibitory factor in our marital relationship has been Marian's reluctance to consider herself in other than a coldly physiological light, though she abhors the diagrams and step-by-step procedures so popular today. She contends they are revolting. This attitude has been distressing to me, especially when she sniggers at the wrong moments. This peculiarity no longer pertained. Fortunately it was Saturday.

We had a pot luck scheduled the next evening at our house. We developed a system of purchasing entire filets in Tijuana from our general fund, while the hostess provided the other items of the meal. Our ZPG group is heavily larded with gourmets—though in fact they tend to watch their weight—and Marian's salad and casserole excited their admiration. I had thinned more of the six-inch plantings.

"Out of this world!" said Hazelrigg. He teaches at UCSD.

"What is the special scrumptiousness?" Connie Wechsler is secretary to a corporation, with secretaries under her.

"Or is it a family secret?"

"Perfectly delicious!"

"A rare Oriental spice?"

"How could it be a family secret when we don't have a family?" I said. Marian's eyes were inscrutable.

"It's not yohimbine. It's zilphion," just as if she knew.

Our guests were restless and the meeting broke up early that night. I was eager to see them go. Yohimbine is a crystalline alkaloid substance with a chemical analysis of $C^{21} H^{26} N^2 O^3$. It derives from the bark of the yohimbe tree *Corynanthe yohimbe,* found in central Africa, where it has been used for centuries by the natives to increase sexual powers. A plant explorer sent it to Beltsville when I was there, but it had no appreciable insecticidal properties. Those of us who in the interests of science personally checked out its reputed attributes, found it to be without merit. Well, when I got Marian alone we were distracted somehow, and it was not until much later that I remembered to ask her about zilphion.

"The silver didrachma coins of Cyrene," she said drowsily.

"What are you talking about?"

"Snuggle-pup, Cyrene was a Greek city in Libya and made its fortune exporting zilphion, which grew wild in the hills. The plant was in such demand that a syrup made from the stem and root cost a pound of silver for a pound of syrup. This commerce went on during the golden age of Greece. The plant was never brought under cultivation. By three hundred A.D. zilphion had been exterminated at Cyrene and what little grew in Syria was also gone. It was extinct, and Pliny the Elder mumbles about the cure of hemorrhoids and scrofulous sores. Absurd!"

"Marian, doll-baby, how do you know about this?"

"My family collects things. Father is a philatelist and my mother is a numismatist—"

"Yeah-yeah, coins—"

"And two of the didrachmas show zilphion. I looked it up again in the library. Sprouts are going to come up from each leaf base and grow a round flower. The central stalk will have a larger blossom on top. I imagine they'll be something like onion flowers, or maybe agapanthus. You wait and see. But while we're waiting, Snuggles—"

So that's the way it is at our house.

You'll see my pickup parked around Fletcher Hills during the day. I cut grass and prune shrubs and sell exotics and suck in my breath politely. Behind my inscrutable Oriental face, brother, I got problems.

You buy a man a drink and he buys one back.

We inadvertently gave the beetles a whee, and they gave us zilphion seeds. Now, dammit, are they friends or foes? Was the flowering of Greece due to zilphion? Or the decay? Demographers, the guys who study populations, guess that Greece grew like mad during that time. But no one has a monopoly on plants. What about the Egyptians and the Minoan Cretans, or was the Greek way of making olive oil different?

Olive oil is a synergist for zilphion. So is alcohol.

That's what Haru Watsonabe thinks about while he trims hedges and empties cuttings into plastic sacks for the compost pile. When he's feeling cheerful, that is. But look at our ZPG chapter. It has splintered off into SPG. That means Select Population Growth. "Why let the stupids outbreed us?" said Hazelrigg. "We can do anything they can do better," said Connie Wechsler.

While I don't think zilphion is habit-forming, the predisposition induced gives me withdrawal symptoms when I go to work.

Will the bettles be back, or do they drop in every twenty-five hundred years?

Marian was quite right about the flowering of the plant. The central stalk grew fibrous but the shoots were delicious. She found an old cider press with a hand-crank macerator, and I put a belt-drive, geared-down electric motor on it. We collected two pounds of mature seed and then I pulled the plants, washed the roots, ran stalk and all through the macerator, and we squeezed twenty-two quarts of sweet, spicy syrup. We used a cupful as the sugar base for daiquiris at our last ZPG meeting—the one that turned into a little orgy by the swimming pool.

And the withdrawal symptoms when I leave Marian.

And the overpopulation of the world.

And the Arabs of North Africa boil and eat the leaves of a thorny plant called zilla, oddly a brassicacea, but not to be confused with zilphion.

And the Egyptians used the scarab as the symbol of the sun god Khepera, though the scarabaeus beetle rolls dung balls, and did those old Eygptians know something I don't know?

And the golden age of Greece.

I lowered the moisture content of the seeds by sealing them into a large tin container over calcium chloride, using enough so the moisture absorbed produced no visible change in the chemical. Marian and I don't talk together as much as before, so I made the decision myself. I gathered all the seeds into eight containers and rented space in a cave owned by a data storage company. Judging by the Malpighian layer—the seed-coat—zilphion seed is mesobiotic—three to fifteen years of viability. With a moisture content of six percent and a constant temperature of 50°, the seeds should be vigorous for five years minimum.

Somebody has got to be responsible.

I never asked for the honor. I was just standing there watching beetles dip water from the swimming pool. But the buck stops somewhere and I have five years of grace to think it over. If I don't last that long—some mornings I'm not sure I will—the seeds and a short cover letter will be mailed to eight U.S. Agricultural Experiment stations.

But it's not easy—

As a right-thinking man—

Go home and—uh—talk to Marian—

A tiger by the—

You see why I'm snarled up, why I bumble and buzz like a bee in Japanese tennis shoes from garden to garden. I wonder what the other gardeners think about?

Ugh!

Doris Piserchia

IDIO

WE ARE IDIO:

Genadee: Her hair is short and black and sleek, and grows down to a fraction of an inch from her eyebrows. To look at her eyes alone, you wouldn't know she was once brainless. They're dark and shiny. She has a nice smile. Her build is like a pumpkin. No, a gourd. She has damp hands.

Creel: One of her ancestors must have been a spider. She has four arms. She can't wear shoes because her feet leak. Anytime you want to find her just look for a yellow trail; at the end of it is Creel. Since she has become part of this three-in-one trinity, Creel has taken to stealing. When anyone misses something they look in her locker.

Risa: Me. How do I know what I look like? I'm back here gawking the other way. Except that I have big legs. Big arms, too. The hair on me is about half an inch long. Not bad.

We would rather be one trinity than three human vegetables. Now we don't scream without making noise. Now if we want to scream, we do it.

Idio is a scientific experiment. It is living proof that anyone can perform meaningful work. It is a kick in the prunes of women who buck for abortion and mercy killing.

Right after Creel and Genadee and I were born, our mother gave us to the government. If anyone asked me what our I.Q. was, I wouldn't know what to tell them. We vary from 60 to 75, except when the Cycler breaks down, then our I.Q. is about 25. For a dog, that's okay. For a woman, it means she might as well be growing out in the garden.

The integrator in my head stimulates the waking parts of my brain, then it gathers up the energy and passes it on to the machine in the second brain of the trinity, which passes it on to the third brain. The Cycler takes all this current and sends it back through me. Each of the brains in Idio gets to share the energy produced by all three.

What this means is that our I.Q. is high enough so that we can get out of bed and act human. Without the machines, we would just lie still with our mouths open.

Idio is in the desert. We are working on a scientific project. This place is a weather station. Near one edge of the project is a radar unit. Idio goes into the unit four times a day and pushes five buttons.

Don't knock it. Nobody can push those five buttons but us, on account of a disease called boredom.

We had two caretakers. One of them we called Brown. He had brown hair, brown eyes, brown skin. Green wore a green hat all the time. They said they were geniuses compared to us. Their regular job had been kicking Boots in the Navy, and they were always saying how they wanted to get back to it and leave the desert and the dumdums to hell where they belonged. We couldn't have cared less, even when they called us names. They were supposed to look after us and cook for us and make sure we stayed in good shape, and if they didn't, they would catch hell from their bosses "out there." They didn't bother us about how we kept house. If we didn't want to clean the shack, it was our business. Our stink was their business. Brown and Green told us we had to take baths every night or they would switch off the Cycler.

"All right, idiots, drag your slimy butts out of bed or I'll switch you back into a cabbage, turnip and radish."

I opened my eyes and looked up and saw God-only-knew-what. The integrators in our brains lost power when we went to sleep. Idio became three dumdums. These woke up in darkness, inside and out. After a few minutes the integrators perked up and and the darkness faded.

Idio sat up.

"Hi there, Brown, you look good enough to lap," I said.

He didn't know what I was saying. We could understand him and Green when they talked, but they said we were mushmouths who would never learn to speak. I was always trying to figure that out. Creel and Genadee and I had no trouble understanding one another.

"One of these days I aim to strip the pants off him," said Genadee. She giggled and her widow's peak touched her eyebrows. "Got a feeling he's interesting."

"Hey, you know what? Somebody wet my bed." Creel leaned forward and reached for Brown, who hotfooted it away. One of his hands hovered near a machine on a table.

That was the Cycler.

"Goddammit, Creel, leave him alone," I said. "He might turn it off."

We sat on our beds and started discussing what it would be like if the Cycler were turned off permanently.

Brown listened to us for a minute, then he said, "Jesus," and went out.

"Why do you call Brown a him?" said Genadee.

"Get your mind off stupid subjects," I said.

She stood up and scratched herself all over, then she got dressed with everything going on wrong side out. She forgot underwear.

I sat on the edge of my bed and looked at the hair on my legs. Sometimes I thought about shaving it off, only I did that once and it grew back in stiff and since it's all the way up my belly I was damn uncomfortable.

"I recollect I had six cans of beer," I said.

"Don't look at me." Genadee made a big to-do about putting on lipstick. Her shoes were on the wrong feet. She had on a pair of jeans and a red sweater. Since the pants were on backwards she couldn't get the zipper all the way up without grinding some meat. Sometimes she did that.

"You're a dirty liar, and don't remind me that you took a bath last night."

"Kiss off," she said, and hauled her rosary from a drawer and began praying. I think that was the first thing they taught her after she graduated from being a vegetable.

I felt crabby as hell. Stomped into the bathroom and tore open the first door and there sat Creel with a can of beer in one hand and one of Brown's pictures in the other. Should have known better, but I reached out and grabbed the beer. She let out a howl and came up off the pot and rammed me in the belly with her head. Then she took back the beer and sat down again.

I went out and spent a few minutes kicking a hole in the wall. Pretty soon she came in, and when I told her the beer was mine, she handed it over. She was an amiable critter except when she was on the can.

My clock wasn't on my bureau. It was in Creel's locker, along with just about everything else I owned. I took it all back to my own locker and gave that thief a kick in the rear.

Idio walked out onto the desert. We wore sunglasses because our pupils didn't respond to light fast enough. We didn't mind the heat, in fact we liked it. I walked in front. Genadee kicked sand on my legs. It itched and reminded me that I forgot my jeans.

"First time I ever knew King Kong had that much hair on her behind," said Creel.

"He's a him," I said over my shoulder.

"What's the difference?" said Genadee. She ran ahead of us, slowed down and began to strut. Something was wrong with the way God put her hips together. When her feet hit the ground they were about a yard apart. Kind of funny-looking.

The radar unit was a big sonofabitch made of white rock. There was only one door in it, and when you went in you felt like you were walking into a grave. Smelled dry. It was quiet.

Idio was afraid of the machines in the radar building. Luckily, we were attracted to the color red. The five buttons on the five machines were a bright red.

"Tit," I said and punched the first one.

"Tit," said Creel and punched the second.

"Tit," said Genadee and punched the third.

Quick as could be I punched the last two buttons. Usually we punched those last ones together. I got clobbered for taking their turns, but it was worth it. They slugged me and busted me in the mouth and then I finally got sore, picked them both up by their sweater fronts and tossed them out the door and let them eat dirt.

"You look sick," I said to Green at lunchtime.

"He looks sick?" said Creel.

"Why is he a he?" said Genadee.

"I'll ask Sister," I told her. Again I said to Green, "You look sick."

It didn't do any good. Green never talked to us. He never looked at us, either, unless he had to.

We ate canned spaghetti and salad.

"Did you wash that lettuce?" said Brown, and Green nodded.

Genadee dropped her spoon and looked as if she might scream.

"He isn't calling you a cabbage," I said to her. "Lettuce and cabbage ain't the same."

We liked the cafeteria. It had wooden walls and tables and chairs and red curtains and a potbelly stove. Brown called the stove a rotten bastard and why can't we have decent equipment in this place God forgot.

Creel put some spaghetti in her pocket.

"All right, get up and stand in the corner," said Brown.

"All three of you. Stay there until you fall over. You're nothing but slobs."

I stood with my nose in the crack and wondered at the ignorance of pretty Brown boy. It wasn't much of a punishment to stand us in the corner. Creel couldn't stay straight and still for more than five minutes before her head started spinning. She had something wrong with a tube of water in her ear. Everytime she stood still for a while she always fell unconscious, and when one part of Idio conked out that was the end of the trinity and the rebirth of the dumdums.

I heard Green go outside. From the corner of my eye I hunted for Brown. Couldn't see him. Turned and looked. He wasn't there.

"They're gone," I said.

"So what?" said Genadee. "They say we stand here, we stand."

"Why?"

"Well, why not?"

"Sister says independence is not listening to orders."

"Does that include an Idio?"

"You know what an Idio is?" I said. "It's people born with something wrong with them. Three people."

"A trinity?" said Creel.

"Right. A trinity is an Idio. That doesn't mean we're idiots. Sometimes we are and sometimes we aren't. Depends on the chemistry of the moment."

"Then let's get the hell out of here," said Genadee.

We went back to our shack and listened to records. It was a nice change to do that instead of standing in the corner until Creel fainted and we all fell on our heads.

A few days before, I was punching the buttons in the radar station and dropped my top down in one of the machines. I tried to get it out, but it was stuck in a crack and I couldn't work it loose. Got irritated and punched wild and pushed a yellow button. Sister was born that day. She may not have been a genius, but I never asked her a question she couldn't answer.

"You ever hear of Idio?" I said.

"Project Idio is on my tapes," said Sister.

"Don't recollect you being around before."

"Who's in that machine?" said Creel.

"Get the hell out," said Genadee. "What do you think you're doing hiding in there?"

"I respond to questions," said Sister.

"How do you figure we can talk all of a sudden?" I said.

"You activated my mechanism."

"What does that mean?"

"We are in communication."

"Hell, this thing is another idiot," said Genadee.

Brown and Green used to read books, but later they spent most of their time looking at pictures. I described some of the pictures to Sister and she said they were pornography. She said some of the people in the pictures were women.

"Bull," said Creel.

"Tit," said Genadee.

"This Idio is women," I said to Sister. "Why don't we look like the pictures Brown and Green study all the time?"

"Idio is physically defective."

"What does that mean?" said Genadee.

"It means we aren't beautiful," I said.

"Go to hell, I'm as good-looking as you any day," said Creel.

"Why does Creel have four arms and all that piddling equipment?" I said to Sister.

"Define the word 'piddling.' "

"Going to the bathroom."

"The Idio portion known as Creel is androgynous."

"What kind of language is that?" I said.

"It only means she got four arms," said Genadee.

"Never mind that stuff, I want to hear some more about pornography," said Creel. "Why do Brown and Green read it all the time?"

Sister gave us a long lecture and we were all ears.

I sat in the hot sun and cried. Didn't know why, just felt like crying.

"Darkness making faces?" said Creel. She stood behind me and patted my head.

"Something sure is."

Pat, pat went her two hands on my head. I didn't know which arms she was moving. It had to be only one pair, because she couldn't use all of them at once. While she used one pair the other hung limp.

"You think maybe we're getting smarter since we found Sister?"

"We have more information, that's all," I said. "We ask Sister a question and she answers it, but we don't know what it means or how to use it any better than we did before."

Creel patted my head. "I feel intelligent today. Think I'll ask her how Idio works."

"Done asked her. It works like a relay. The action goes from my head to yours, then to Genadee, then to the Cycler and back to me again."

Just then Genadee came out of the shack and saw us. She stomped over and kicked sand on my feet.

"Let's do something."

"Like what?" I said.

"Hell, I don't know, let's just get clicking."

We went to spy on Brown and Green. Their shack was no better on the outside than ours, but they kept the inside in order and it was a pleasure to look at it. Keeping things neat was something Idio found impossible. We peeked in one of the windows and saw them lying on their bunks looking at pictures.

"Remember what Sister said about appetite?" said Creel. "Those two nice boys are suffering from lack of tactile stimulation, and it's a shame. We ought to do them a favor."

"What does that mean?" said Genadee.

Creel looked at me. "You know what I'm thinking?"

"Yeah, except none of us looks like those pictures."

"Sure as hell you or me don't, but I been imagining Genadee here and the more I imagine it the better she looks."

"What you talking about?" yelled Genadee.

Brown and Green heard her and threw away their magazines and got up cussing. Creel and I dragged our partner back to the shack and made her take a bath.

"How come you guys aren't getting in here with me?" she wanted to know.

"You're the one we're trying to make good-looking," I said.

The septic tank backed up into the shack, so Genadee and I took off for the sand and sun. We sat talking, and after a while Brown came out of his shack, yelling at the top of his lungs.

"What's that smell?"

I told him.

He cussed for a while. "If I wanted to know anything I wouldn't ask a mushmouth. It's that damned tank again. I told you to quit flushing beer cans. Well, you'll all have to get out of here till we get it cleaned up. Where's the other one?"

I jabbed a hand toward the shack.

"It'll have to get out, too," he said. "Can't have your valuable selves getting contaminated."

"If I was you I wouldn't go in there. Creel's on the can and she isn't amiable—"

"Mushmouth," he said. He looked at Genadee.

We had made her wear a piece of curtain to hide her gourd figure. She looked pretty damn good. Her hair was her best feature. Thick and glossy, it was just like fur and fit her head neat, and brushed back the way it was, she didn't look too much like a throwback to the cave. Her widow's peak was so pronounced that she sort of resembled Dracula, but sitting there in the sun with her cheeks rosy and her eyes glittering . . . well, anyhow, Brown looked at her.

He took off toward the shack, and again I said, "If I was you I wouldn't go in there."

In he went, then a few minutes later came a ruckus, then he ran outside holding his stomach.

"Goddamn," he said and went away to find Green so they could clean our house.

For supper we had ham and spinach. Creel and I sat on either side of Genadee and made her eat slow. We kept her chin clean and whenever she started growling we pinched her gourds.

"Just for that you have to stand in the corner," said Brown. He was eyeing Creel.

"What'd I do?"

"You threw your plate on the floor, mushmouth. Get up and stand in the corner, both of you."

I got up grinning, looked from him to Genadee.

"She didn't do anything," he said. "She's acting like a lady. You two are hogs."

Creel and I shoved our faces into the same corner. Knocking her out of the way, I said, "Go find your own."

It took her five minutes of standing still to faint. I followed a second later and as I dropped I hoped Genadee wouldn't slam into her plate and mess her makeup.

I needn't have worried. Woke up and found Brown had pulled the plate away and stuck a pillow there. Genadee wasn't messed and she didn't have a sore head.

I was in love with Brown.

"Tit, tit, tit, tit, tit." Five buttons punched. Nothing to do. We went and beautified Genadee some more, cut her fingernails, scrubbed them with Creel's toothbrush, then we put red polish on them. Had to do something about that black fuzz on her upper lip. Sandpapered it off while she bellowed.

Spent the afternoon drinking beer. So hot I finally took a bath. The septic tank backed up again so my feet stunk worse than ever, but they smelled better than Creel's.

"Tit, tit, tit, tit, tit." Five buttons pushed. Nothing to do.

We laid around on the sand most of the evening.

"Let's do something," said Creel.

"Like what?" said Genadee.

"Like shut up," I said. "What's those lights up there?"

"You know damn well they're stars," said Creel.

"Oh, yeah, I forgot. What are we gonna do when Brown and Green fall in love with Genadee?"

"We're gonna watch."

"Tit, tit, tit, tit, tit." Five buttons pushed. Nothing to do.

Creel and I built another shack. Brown and Green yelled at us and told us to quit it. They had the sweats. Everytime I saw one of them he was dripping sweat. Creel and I paid no attention to them.

"Genadee don't want to live with us," I told them, but they didn't understand.

"She is a lady, or don't you have eyes?" I said.

"The thing of it is, she's been taking a bath twice a day and she can't stand Creel and me," I said.

They went away cussing and we went on with the work. Sun was nice and warm.

"I feel dizzy," said Creel all of a sudden.

I started to raise my head toward her, then the lights went out.

We woke up on the sand. We went to the shack to find Genadee. She was taking a bath and drinking my beer.

"You took a nap, didn't you?" said Creel.

She squirted beer through her teeth and spattered the wall. "So what?"

"So get out of that tub and get hell beat out of yourself. You know the rules. You can't take naps or fall unconscious without our permission. We are out there breaking our asses building you a house and you're in here falling asleep. Suppose one of us had been on the roof when you conked out?"

This time the beer was squirted on us. "Kiss off. Brown and Green think more of me than they do you pigs, and if you don't—"

That was as far as she got. We hauled her out of the tub and laid her bellydown on the bed and beat her gourds till they were blue.

We got bawled out because we forgot to punch the buttons. Somebody from "out there" called on the phone and bawled Brown out. After he hung up he bawled Green out, then they both came and bawled us out.

"Quit working on this shack and do your job," said Brown. He had the sweats. From the corner of his eye he watched Genadee. She was building castles in the sand, and damn if she didn't look like a sweet little angel. Vampirish but still angelic. Matter of fact, the vampire part helped the other.

Creel and I watched her too, and we were thinking the same thing. If she didn't look up and smile, she wasn't going to be able to sit while she ate supper.

Up she looked. Big smile. Pretty as anything.

We laid in bed and listened to Genadee cry. Couldn't go to sleep listening to her. She hated sleeping in her new shack by herself.

"You lied to Brown," she had sobbed. "You told him I didn't want to live with you all anymore."

"You have to live alone," Creel said.

"Why?"

"A scientific experiment."

"No idiot can experiment," said Genadee scornfully.

"No, but an Idio can and that's what we are. Now shut up."

"You guys have to move in here with me."

She stayed awake three nights.

"Can't stand it anymore," I said to Creel. "I'm tired."

"Only one thing to do. We got to move in with her."

"Brown and Green won't come if we're in there," I said.

"Well, what if they don't know we're in there?"

It was a warm night and the shack felt stuffy. Genadee was snoring, but she wasn't asleep. I went over and pinched a gourd. She quit snoring and began singing her rosary. She did it softly so it wouldn't get on our nerves.

Creel opened a window and mosquitoes came in. We had forgotten to put up screens.

Genadee's bed was on one side of the shack. Creel and I were in the corner nearest the door. Bugs were making a racket. The shack was stuffy, but I was feeling good. Sprawled out on the straw mat, I relaxed and wondered about God.

"Move over, you're hogging the bed," I said to Creel.

Over she went.

"Which one of us is gonna put the others to sleep?" she whispered.

"Sure not Genadee."

We listened to the prayers being sung.

"If you want to know what I think, I think she is the dumbest of us," Creel whispered. "What do you think?"

"Agree."

"What was that noise?"

I rolled over and sniffed the straw under me. "Didn't hear anything."

She listened for a minute before she went on whispering. "The thing of it is, Genadee doesn't seem curious about much of anything."

"She don't, for a fact."

Laying a hand on my arm, Creel said, "Shhh."

"Huh?"

"Keep quiet, I hear something."

The moon came in and flew around as the shack door opened. With it came Brown and Green. They were pretty boys when they were dressed and they were pretty when they had nothing on. I couldn't see them perfectly, but I knew they had the sweats. Their voices dripped.

"Shut the door, she might start yelling." That was Brown whispering.

"Oh, let's get out of here, we don't have to be this hard up." That was Green whispering.

The door closed and the moonlight vanished. As Creel had said, Genadee was the dumbest portion of Idio. She didn't even know somebody had opened the door, didn't notice the moonlight coming in or going away, didn't give two cents that Brown and Green were in there stumbling around trying to find her. She lay in her bed, not singing anymore, but just growling now and then.

For a minute everything was quiet, then Brown and Green went the wrong way. Instead of moving toward Genadee they came to the corner. A hand went over me and I reached out and touched a leg. Lord, never knew Brown felt like silk.

The boys had come in after Genadee and she was what they would get.

In just a second.

Green missed me when he was fumbling, went across me and grabbed hold of Creel. The shock of Brown's leg in my hand had been powerful. Couldn't help what I did then. I raised up and gathered him close.

The shack was as full of noise as a Fourth of July picnic.

Brown was bucking like a mule as he tried to get away from me. His mouth was wide open and he shrieked in my ear. I kissed him silent. I had no trouble holding him down, he being kind of small and me outweighing him by about a hundred pounds, none of which was fat.

Creel was suddenly taken by Green. By that I mean she lost her head and forgot he was meant for Genadee.

To hell with Genadee.

Old Creel, she being androgynous and kind of freaky, she was strong as a bull and little Green couldn't do a thing but squawk. She kissed him silent.

Genadee started singing again and the prayers sounded gentle and innocent.

Bad was hurting. I knew Creel wouldn't forget that we were always good. Sister knew all the answers and she had passed them on to us. There was no such thing as doing what came naturally if you didn't know how. I knew how and so did Creel. Sister had told us. If you wanted to love somebody you had to do it right.

Did everything perfect. Genadee could go to hell. Pretty Brown was mine to do with as I pleased. As a matter of fact so was Green. Neither Creel nor I was stingy. We swapped the boys back and forth like dessert being passed across the supper table.

The bosses sent us two more caretakers after Brown and Green hanged themselves. We called the new fellows Curly and Peaches. They were pretty boys, except Peaches looked just like those pictures in the magazines. Creel spied while Peaches took a bath.

Today Sister told us Peaches is a girl. Creel is in love with her. "Tit, tit, tit, tit, tit." Five buttons punched. Nothing to do.

Albert Teichner

FANTASY'S PROFESSION

"I'M LEAVING, I've never been so insulted in my life!" cried the matron, leaping from her chair. "I didn't pay to be insulted!"

"You certainly did." Dr. Stanler looked blankly across his desk at her. "You paid to be insulted by the truth."

"Well, I'm leaving!" At the door she angrily awaited an apology.

"Yes, now—leave, please." His slate-blue eyes stayed blank and, after a pause, she went out, slamming the door.

Stanler pressed the intercom. "Miss Carter, that radio man may come in now." Waiting, he had no need to set his face for the publicity encounter. Still under thirty, Stanler had a deep vertical line down each cheek, like a slashed dimple, and this sufficed to give him the frightening dignity of an ancient Cherokee chief.

The man who entered was forty desperately pushing twenty, his long black hair carefully groomed into ragged disorder. A variety of love beads clacked softly across his breast. He even had the open-mouthedness of youth, his jaw more slackly controlled than the portable tape recorder gripped by his left hand. *A fool*, Dr. Stanler saw.

Stanler said, "Glad to see you, Mr.—"

"—Toby Woolton."

"By all means, yes."

Woolton set the recorder on the desk. "Always like getting right down to business."

"Yes, I don't have much time either, Mr. Woolton, so do shoot away."

"Well then—" He carefully adjusted the little microphone between them. "I am in the office of Dr. Ronald Stanler, the famous, the almost notoriously famous therapist."

"Ah no," Stanler broke in, "not a therapist, I don't claim to cure people. They come here, you might say, to be insulted."

Woolton was pleased. "Insulted, that seems the idea! Then you *don't* cure people?"

"Oh, I didn't say that either. I said I don't *claim* to cure people. How they absorb what I say is up to them."

"Then, while we're into a debunking spree, doctor, may I point out that you are neither a doctor of medicine nor psychology!"

"Again—I never claimed to be. My doctorate's in art teaching, but about two years ago I realized I'd make a better living telling people the bad news about themselves."

Woolton put a clipping on the desk. "You didn't state that at the beginning of your career."

"Nobody asked me. When they started to, I told them. I see you've researched thoroughly, that was my first ad. Ran it many times."

"Hardly more than a classified," Woolton told the microphone. "The little headline reads, *'See Yourself as Others See You!'* Then it says, 'For ten dollars an hour I will look at you and listen to you and tell you what I think are your bad features. No solutions offered, only the starkest, worst side of you, the things not even your best friends will tell you.' And that brought in customers right away?"

"Customers—there's the proper word! Yes, a trickle, then with word-of-mouth more of them. Only one thing's different today."

"What would that be?"

"I now charge forty dollars."

"And they're back week after week for *that?*"

Stanler chuckled. "A few weeks, anyway. Usually isn't that much more really bad stuff to tell after a few encounters. matter of fact, I'm usually the one who insists they stop coming, to end our mutual boredom."

"You seem remarkably cold about your clients, doctor—"

"Oh, I suppose you could put it like that, but affection doesn't give useful insights. 'Cold' analysis can, treating people as objects of inquiry."

Woolton pounced. "Suicides, you know several patients—pardon me, doctor—several clients, three, they say, are believed to have committed suicide after consulting you."

"They could have hardly done so relevantly to this interview before consulting me, could they? We needn't exaggerate, though. If I told you your principal defect so far spotted is a desperate need to cling to youth, well, if I said that, you wouldn't be likely to commit suicide just because it seems true, now would you?" Stanler caught himself up short. Going too far with this upstart. "Of course, Mr. Woolton, I shouldn't have said that—our whole chat could go down the drain."

Woolton frowned, then grinned. "You're likely to be proven wrong in at least my case, doctor. Well then, what gives you the skill at probing weaknesses some claim for you?"

"Some? Most ex-clients swear by, not at me. Personal recommendations have been my greatest booster, so, generally speaking, I may have done them good after all."

"Well, the skill—"

"Ah yes!" He pointed at a row of cartoon portraits running all around the room. "Unlike many art teachers, I actually had some talent. But a limited, very unbalanced one—not works of art, just of cleverness. Poor draftsmanship, indifferent composition, etcetera—one single talent, the ability to see a face's weak point and bring it violently forward. Even in the most beautiful face."

"But what *basically* gives you that special knack?"

"Haven't the faintest idea," he abruptly lied.

Fortunately, Woolton had already lost interest in that angle. "Listeners, I wish you could see 'em. One female physiognomy has an enormous, slightly lopsided nose. Next to it a grinning man is revealing enough teeth to fill a piano keyboard. Another woman's face revolves around a beauty mark filthily under a nostril." He hesitated, then, as invariably happened with Stanler's subjects, Woolton had to pick his own scab. "You said I look like a perpetual juvenile."

"*Try* to look like one." He shrugged. "I don't know you well enough to say more—not much time available—and it would just end *all* chance of this being broadcast, wouldn't it?"

Woolton stopped the recorder. "Nothing will be deleted," he snapped.

"Then I may listen tonight"—Stanler nodded—"as I sometimes did before I became so busy."

Woolton restarted the recorder. The interview went on for about ten minutes, then Stanler pleaded the press of business. After Woolton had packed up and gone he closed his eyes and stared at the dark. In five minutes, one more lout to consider. Of course, a little publicity wasn't essential, but it could help. Some extra clients would mean a thousand per week after all expenses, and eventually fees could rise again. A few years of this amiable rot meant enough capital to retire from any further bourgeois nonsense.

And it was such an *honest* living. Every other livelihood involved countless deceptions, but no lies here except for a few
negatives ones, things presently left unsaid. For instance, he
couldn't very well—as yet—admit to hitting on nonthera-
peutic therapy while a nightclub comic used him as a convenient butt for one-liners. How he had kept topping them to
the drunken audience's delight! Finally, the abusive filth
becoming a nuisance, he'd squelched this comic in a cold
voice: "You know, pal, during insults your face hangs to the
left in a way that could have been more useful in a lower,
less public part of your anatomy." The audience had roared at
it as just more meaningless pornography but the clown, all too
obviously impotent in Stanler's intuition, had eased himself
off the floor, bested. No, that triumph couldn't be openly admitted now—nor the other thing.

He blinked his eyes twice. Exactly three o'clock, time for
the next customer. "Send in Foster," he told Miss Carter.

Foster, short, plump and jolly-looking, bounced in to tell
how everyone in his apron business was trying to cheat or insult him. The recital proceeded for half an hour while his face
became progressively more repulsive. Foster had been ugly
the first time, two months ago, but now his intensified un-
sightliness told Stanler the moment of truth was at hand. He
raised a finger and the flow of Foster's complaints slowed.
Then, when the finger stayed erect, Foster stopped altogether.

"I've really heard enough crap from you," Stanler said.
"You're the one who's cheating. You've carried competitive-
ness to a psychotic endpoint, Foster, all because your height
bugs you. Well, although half the male population's no taller
than you, I, too, find you an extraordinarily small man. No,
no, don't start protesting, because I know what I see. Always
you've avoided admitting how small you feel by making
everyone else feel that way. Well, don't start trying it
here—your silly height obsession's your problem, no longer
mine!"

After Foster departed, Stanler prepared to leave himself.
Miss Carter was already gone and this was one of those un-
fortunate days with no late customers. But keeping Foster-
types for longer periods would have been a boring decline in
standards—and anyway, soon unnecessary.

He dialed Mrs. Hinten's number and she answered in her
clipped, pseudo-British accent. He said, "Mr. Rachelson here,
Ada."

Her voice bubbled back to its proper side of the Atlantic. "Hi, Abe! An hour appointment for later?"

"Well, yes and no—an hour but now—strike while the iron's hot." She giggled. "Six thirty?"

"Oh, excellent, that's excellent—a slow period!"

"—and the rates accordingly fifteen percent lower?"

"Ten, naughty!" she corrected. "Ten percent. We'll be ready for you."

Her brownstone, like her accent, was a compromise between social forces, he thought, buzzing the ground-floor bell; it was situated on the line between a high-rent residential district and a medium-rent commercial one. She answered the door herself, nodding a huge platinum wig at him. "Good to see you, Abe." He shook hands with her, passing the forty-five dollars to her moist palm. She promptly stuffed the money into her bosom, less, he suspected, for any practical reason than for the sluttish excitation it gave to the clientele.

Two girls wearing only bras and panties were seated on a velvet sofa at the far end of the basement corridor. One was black-haired, with blue eyes made mistily sexy by astigmatism, the other a Puerto Rican type with peroxided hair and a gaze of utter indifference that he always found stimulating. He chose the peroxide specimen and they moved into a bedroom where they both went through a series of mechanical gestures that he arranged to climax just as the hour was ending. He swiftly dressed, gave the girl a five-dollar tip and shushed her as she absently began thanking him.

Going out, he had to listen once more to Ada saying, "With a phone number, Abe, not even your real name, just a phone number, I could call whenever something special pops in and you could get more off-hour discounts, too—"

"No, dear lady," Stanler answered, "permit me to remain as anonymous as possible as long as possible. Until next week."

Feeling relieved now of all potential sexual tension, Stanler went home and carefully bathed his body clean of whatever contact traces might remain. He ate the *coq au vin* left by his housekeeper, then, with the regulation Scotch and soda on his end table, set a pile of Scarlatti records in the stereo machine and spent several hours reading sentimental claptrap by Freud. It was always amusing to see how each ostensibly new, "revolutionary" therapy repeated the fundamental error of all its predecessors.

At ten his timer switched from records to FM for Woolton's Show. Its theme was a syncopated Bach fugue tinkled out on a player piano while Woolton sang lyrics about "The show with the brainy sound."

The instant this song ended Woolton came on, leaving no second free of his presence. "Woolton says—and hello to you, my thinking public out there!—did you ever hear the one about the guy who got rid of his migraine headache by paying somebody to hit him on the head with a ball-peen hammer? Well, there are such guys—and gals—in this town, handing over hard cash for purely verbal blows to the psyche, and the place they go to is the office of Dr. Ronald Stanler. But don't laugh, not completely anyway, because, Mr. and Mrs. Thinking Public, some of these folks actually say it works! Decide for yourself!"

With that he launched into the interview, and Stanler could remember nothing he had said that was now omitted save for the brief slip-up about Woolton's perpetual juvenility. Afterward, Woolton took over again: "Well, somehow the milk of human kindness is preferable to mechanical indifference and you may even wonder why such things are permitted but—" he hesitated for emphasis and Stanler thought how this pseudo-cynic was as big an idiot as all the others—"but your ever-earnest reporter did manage to find a few people who had been patients—oops! I mean customers—of Dr. Stanler and all indicated they'd been helped *and* that he actually refused to keep them on indefinitely as high-paying clients! So add another wing to that supremely vast educational institution, the School of Hard Knocks—at least for some people.

"But now, to get another taste into our mouths, here's a supremely kind lady who has just returned from six heartrending months of aiding coca addicts in the Andean highlands. That's the highland zone of Peru and Ecuador and it's not co-coa but *c-o-c-a*."

There were no further references to "Ball-peen Hammer Psycho-Theatrics," but Stanler was pleased by what he had already heard; it could bring in the extra customers he desired.

And it did. The next day he acquired two clients and the day after, as if extra time were needed before such a cold plunge, five came in. All offered the possibility of insights that might be temporarily interesting and, in three cases, even amusing.

But the broadcast brought a further, less useful form of attention. A convention of psychiatrists was meeting at a nearby resort, and it seemed as if all five hundred delegates had heard the interview. These doctors were divided into about fifty schools of psychotherapy, ranging from traditional Freudians, Jungians, Adlerians and Rankians through electronic processors of sex acts and Jesuit confessors to group-care and love-scream advocates, but all managed to agree on a resolution condemning Stanler's approach.

". . . manifestly dangerous and pernicious . . . warranting closest scrutiny by the legal authorities . . . improper claims to therapeutic value . . . public should be warned . . ." The whole long statement was in this vein, and Stanler found himself besieged by news people demanding his reaction.

"To avoid wasting time on your stupid nonsense questions," he told them, always to their pleased what-a-curmudgeon reaction, "I am making one statement to everybody: I have never bothered to attack any of the one hundred and sixty-nine mutually contradictory schools of psychotherapy's claims to cure people, so I cannot see why they bother to attack me when I make *no* claims to cure anyone. I myself will say nothing more, advising you instead to contact my former clients. All possibilities of libel action by me against anything they say are hereby renounced. Maybe I'll be denounced, maybe not, but gentlemen, I assure you I don't give a damn one way or the other, and good day to you."

The news people protested that former patients would never come forward, so his challenge had to be a bluff. But come forward they did. Within two days a score had been interviewed and, while some said they disliked Dr. Stanler personally and never cared to see him again, all, whether liking or disliking him, insisted their sessions with him had been of great value. For Stanler, in every case where a name was volunteered, it instantly and intimately evoked the former patient. The intimacy always involved weaknesses that had been at first deplorably human and, at the last, merely disgusting. But here they were, supporting him. It would be most touching, Stanler decided, if he could be touched.

More new customers signed up at higher fees than ever, and he found room for them by brutally curative dismissals of some current ones. There was no more time for receiving calls of idle inquiry. However, Miss Carter did feel it necessary to pass on the one name. "Very persistent," she explained. "The woman's been on the line again and again, a Mrs. Hinten."

"Fame, like everything else, is a cross to bear," he muttered. "Thank you so much, Miss Carter."

When Stanler reached her on his private line, she said:

"Naughty, naughty—I always said it! Claiming Abe was your name!"

"Well, Mrs. Hinten?"

She was breathlessly pleased with her insight. "I just wanted to congratulate you—all those newspaper items, and TV, too!—on your wonderful work. It's always been the same with my best girls for the customers, they don't gush, they don't throw their hearts into it, they're *technicians*. Controlled indifference, that's what does their job best—and yours too!"

"The parallel may be overdrawn," he sighed, "but, Mrs.—uh—yes, Mrs. Hinten, perhaps there's something to what you say. Right now, though, I'm most pressed, so until—"

"One thing's certain," she exclaimed. "No matter what, I'll never discuss your patronage. Anybody doing so much to fight suffering deserves every consideration!"

"I don't know how to thank you enough, Mrs. Hinten, I am deeply touched," he said, "so until another time—"

Putting down the receiver, he knew there was unlikely to be another time; the madame was as gushy as the average clubwoman. It was funny, though, to see how universal the misunderstanding (indifference, she'd actually said indifference!) could be.

By the last day of the psychiatrist's convention, the doctors were forced to take into account the published encomiums to Stanler's rough methods. This was achieved by appointing a study committee of seven delegates to investigate Stanler's approach in detail before pressing further for legal action. "As already stated, we are sure the procedures indicated involve perils," a spokesman explained to the press, "but, being scientists, we are interested in learning anything of potential value, no matter where it may be found."

A photograph of this committee appeared in several newspapers. Looking at it, Stanler felt certain that one middle-aged doctor, a Jungian analyst, was largely homosexual and that both the aging Freudian and the chemotherapy enthusiast were obsessional neurotics. So when the group requested a meeting he readily agreed on the following Sunday.

Upon their arrival in his office he had to revise one assessment from largely to totally homosexual, but the previous, more ambiguous category did not remain empty as the doctors settled into chairs facing the desk; the leader of group-hysteria sessions, a surprisingly young fellow, was obviously deviant, from the slight limpness of his wrists to the infantile pout of his lips. Three other doctors remained undetermined quantities and he did not have time to determine what was wrong in their cases. One, a neat woman, was an advocate of cybernetic computer models for the ailing psyche. Another, in his late fifties, was a Catholic psychiatrist, and the third one, as young as the group-hysteria man, had been described in one newspaper as a "Marxist Revisionist Psychotherapist."

"You have come to learn something about me," Stanler smiled. "The reverse is already true."

They laughed and the Jungian, evidently temporary chairman, said: "We're not here because we're impressed with your methods but because we're impressed with your results and want to bridge the gap if possible. I have a feeling that, whatever your professed philosophy might have been, you'd be good at treating people. How did you develop what talent you have?"

Stanler shrugged. "I don't know much about that myself, just enough." He pointed at the caricatures which had attracted everyone's attention. "Mine—just have a knack for spotting people's weakest points."

"Ah," put in the Freudian, "but all talent is rooted in a life history. Something in the past. Your parents, for examp—"

"No, I doubt it, they were killed in a plane crash when I was fifteen—I'm now about double that—away at prep school then—"

"Ah, the great shock," persisted the same doctor.

"No great shock. Mildly upset naturally, but I quickly got over that. There was enough money left to put me through college." He sighed. "Gentlemen, I've had no shock in life, and I'm not interested in wasting everybody's time on fruitless biographical details."

"Agreed!" said the cybernetics lady. "We need less psychotherapies, more recognition that the mind's a very involved electrochemical circuit in the *present*, a circuit of which we understand, so far, only several diagrams. You've hit on a few truths about this wiring, Doctor, and shown the superiority of valid technique over ineffective, well-intentioned 'love' as a curative approach."

The group therapist's nose twitched for a sneeze, but Stanler knew from well-worn lines appearing around his nostrils that the sneeze would, as usual, remain unachieved. "Ah-ah—" said the man—"well! We may often try to bring out aggressions but they must end in affection between the group members—not some coldly technical mutual manipulation of psyches!"

"No hasty conclusions!" cried the Revisionist. "Technique becomes all-important if devoted to a decent social goal. The ideal for a therapy system is to develop techniques so adequate to patients' problems that *any* therapist-worker can automatically apply them."

"Oh, no!" moaned several doctors.

"Oh, *yes!*" put in the chemotherapist. "Would you rather have a heart operation performed by a relative or by a skilled surgeon indifferent to you as a person? But our 'revolutionary' friend here, dragging out all our dirtiest linen before Mr. Stanler, is actually as verbal as the rest of you. Only fully developed psychochemical treatments will permit cures by a doctor who's totally indifferent emotionally!"

Stanler let the wrangling continue for about ten minutes more, then slammed the desk for silence. "Some committee! I've seen about enough. Believe me, it's not that complicated—I simply have a talent for identifying people's shortcomings so clearly that they see what I see. And none of you have the slightest understanding of what I've just said!"

The accusation of nonunderstanding, the ultimate in professional insults, brought angry retorts from everyone. "Nonsense! . . . Everything has a reason! . . . A charlatan, I said it all along! . . . God gave us— . . . Poor eating habi— . . . Inferiority complex parading as utter self-confi— . . . Reactionary obscurant—" Stanler could almost feel their resentment as a solid wall closing in on him.

Suddenly disgust was too overwhelming for amusement and, before he could stop himself, he snapped: "Indifference? What did 'technical' indifference ever achieve? The only way to have useful insights into these people, any people, is to *hate* them—and I hate them all!"

A mistake, he thought, considering their stunned expressions; he had lost control and now they would surely find some law— But they were beginning to smile a little —knowing smiles of superiority—and then all looked unsurprised. "Utterest nonsense!" said the first to recover. "The one thing you can't cure anyone with *ever* is hate, *all* schools of thought know that much. And you know it, too, Stanler, as well as any of us."

"Right," several doctors murmured, starting to get up.

Stanler watched them leave, then stared into the convenient

darkness of his eyelids. Nothing would be done against him; the world's ultimate secret could safely be exposed and still remain a secret. When he opened his eyes again the one true world was still out there, and he felt the grin on his face become painfully, pleasurably, co-equal with that of his skull.

Charles Arnold

SPRING CAME TO

BLUE RIDGE

EARLY THIS YEAR

I PLACE MY BAG of instruments in the back seat from force of habit. I know they will not be needed. I get in the driver's seat and pause for a moment to get my breath. I am panting slightly; old age comes to doctors too, I tell myself—there is nothing else to say. The engine turns over easily and begins to whir; I let out the clutch slowly (we don't want to buck) and we, the old Dodge and me, rumble the half block from my office to Main Street.

I turn left to go to the high school, having the feeling that this has all happened before. It *has* all happened before, as a matter of fact, except it was winter, the morning after the heavy snow, the first time Sam Goodrich called me out, and now it's spring. I had been counting on spring to dispel the gloom that has settled on the town, but instead it has brought it into higher relief, has brought it into focus by contrast.

The air is warm and sweet, filled with the smells of damp earth and green life; as I drive down Main Street, the breeze ruffles my hair (it is all white now, no gray left) and the sun is warm on my elbow hanging out the window. At one time I would have felt invigorated; now I am merely reminded of how thoroughly pervasive is my tiredness.

I pass Dr. Hermann's office. There are five or six people in his waiting room. He is old and clings to the old ways, refusing to work on an appointment basis. Since he no longer makes house calls, and I'm the only other doctor in town, the onus fails upon me to make this one.

(I was weary and tried to get Hermann to go on that call to Walshville. Half asleep on the way back, I saw the car ahead of me lose control on an ice patch, and come to a precarious stop on the shoulder. The passenger was sure to be uninjured. There were cars coming in both directions and someone would stop to help. Who needs a malpractice suit? I thought. It snowed heavily that night.)

The usual complement of old fogies are sitting on the bench in front of the pool hall, where they can greet the other fogies that might pass by, and discuss baseball and arthritis without being interrupted by women. As the years pass, it pains me to note, more and more of them are my old schoolmates. They all wave as I go by; I am probably the biggest event of the afternoon so far.

Mrs. Simms pulls from a parking place without looking, as always, and I must stop suddenly to avoid plowing into her trunk. This too, it seems to me, happened the last time as well, or perhaps I just think so. It has happened often enough, it makes little difference. Her engine dies as she shifts from reverse to drive, so I must wait a moment. Finally she gets the lever into neutral, and turns the key. The engine ignites immediately, but she holds it on start for a good five seconds.

It's good I'm not going on an emergency call. There is no hurry. In fact there is no need to go at all, but no reason to avoid going, either. I know what will happen; it will be a repeat of last time. I will walk into the principal's office and Alice, the secretary, will say, "Go right in, Dr. Tyler. Mr. Goodrich is waiting for you." I will smile and nod and leave my bag on a chair and say, "Keep an eye on this for me," and I will go in. Sam Goodrich will stand up behind his desk and stretch his meaty hand to me. We will exchange greetings and he will comment about the pleasant spring weather. I will agree that the weather is indeed agreeable for early March on the prairie, and I will sit down next to a window and say, "What can I do for you?"

Mrs. Dreiser, the guidance counselor, will be called in, and we will perform the greeting ritual again. Then Sam will say, "I'm sorry to bring you here again on something so vague, but frankly I'm worried. There were only six students last time, but the number has grown to over thirty now, and nothing seems to help them. I'm probably wasting your time, but I wish you'd examine some of the new cases."

"Yes, Dr. Tyler," Mrs. Dreiser will say, "you'll make us feel better, even if you don't discover anything new. We just don't know what else to do."

I will fend off their apologies with forced jocularity, and we will go to the first-aid room, where there is an examination table. On the way, Mrs. Dreiser will tell me how the incidence is higher among the more intelligent students, which to her is the most mystifying aspect of the whole thing.

("The mystifying aspect to me," Randy, the day cop, said, "is how that little bump on her head could kill her." "It wasn't the bump," I told him, "she froze to death.")

The brightest boy of the junior class (or senior, or freshman) will be waiting when we arrive. Sam and Mrs. Dreiser will hover discreetly in the background as I examine the boy. I will open my bag and take out several instruments. I check his heart rate and listen to his chest. I take his blood pressure and tap his knee with a hammer. I shine a light in his eyes and peek in his ears, and no one will notice that his problem can't possibly be in his ears, but the whole thing is for show anyway. I know ahead of time exactly what I will find: nothing.

Mrs. Simms finally gets her Buick moving again, and jerks down the street with her nose brushing the steering wheel. I notice her windows are up, and she is wearing her fur coat. At the second intersection she turns without signaling or varying her speed from its constant fifteen m.p.h., and heads home. With her out of my way, I soon reach the railroad tracks and clatter over the six rails. Two of the six are rusty on top. The depot to my right, like everything else in town, is run down and in need of repairs. Howard, a retired telegrapher, is sitting in front of his old office, and waves as I pass. The smells of coal dust and diesel fuel blow in on the warm air; for a moment I feel better than I have all day.

The boy will say nothing during the examination. I will poke and prod, and he will be malleable, like putty. His eyes will be dull, his manner listless. "Going out for track, Dick?" I will say when I'm through with my monkey tricks. "I haven't decided yet," he will mumble in reply. "How do you spend your time at home?" "Homework . . . TV." He has not yet turned to face me. "What are you planning to do when you graduate?" "Hadn't thought much about it yet."

I'll tell him he's in good health, though a little run down, and he should go out for track to build his body up. As he shuffles out, Sam and Mrs. Dreiser will look at me question-

ingly, anxiously. I will shake my head. "I couldn't find anything wrong with him, physically."

They will bring in the next student; it will be a girl this
time, a cheerleader, a homecoming queen, the prettiest, the
smartest girl in her class—at one time. Like the boy, her
grades have been slipping, her class participation is nil, her attention span, her initiative, her creativity dead. I will go
through the motions of the examination again, and I will find
nothing. Her breasts will be full, her hips round, but I will
hardly notice, and my indifference will be more than professional.

("You seem worried about something," I told the girl last
time. "Do you want to tell me about it?" "It's happened
before, but my mother didn't come home last night," she said.
Then they told me Randy, the day cop, was looking for me,
and I learned her mother was dead. They expected me to tell
her, of course.)

Passing by Millie Perkins' house, I see her in her usual
place in the bay window, where she can see the street, see the
TV set, and reach the telephone at the same time. She is at the
phone now. No doubt she is anxious to discuss the soap opera
which has just finished its latest episode, the afterimage of the
final frame still etched on the screen, the final organ groan vibrating the china as she dials. The TV provides more of her
gossip than the street does these days. She is probably calling
my wife, herself an intimate of the mythical personalities that
dance and blink through our living room.

("Yes, you did get a call last night, just before you got
home, but it came during the last five minutes of *Gunsmoke*,
and then Millie was on the phone, and I forgot to tell you."
"What did the caller say?" "He said there was an unconscious
woman in a car on the road to Walshville. Oh, dear, I do hope
nothing terrible happened to her.")

I may examine one or two more kids, but probably not. We
will decide there is little point in it.

"What is it, Dr. Tyler?" Mrs. Dreiser will say. "What's
wrong with them? It doesn't make any sense, and I, for one,
am scared."

"I don't know," I will say. "Can't understand it myself. I've
seen people like this many times in my career. It's often a
reaction to mourning, or a buried psychological problem.
Usually the person will come out of it by himself, given time.
I've never seen it so lasting or widespread, though. If it's any
consolation to you, it's happening all over the country, strik-

ing the young mostly, just like here. It started in the small towns, but it's spreading to the cities now."

"But what *is* it?" Sam will say.

"The journals have called it various things. I prefer 'chronic apathy' myself. It's as good a term as any. I haven't heard any satisfactory explanation of the cause."

Mrs. Dreiser will probably start sobbing. "What's going to become of these young people?" she will ask between sniffles.

"Yes, Dr. Tyler," Sam will say. "What are we to do? What are we to *do*?"

I will hide my face and shake my head, and pretend I don't feel like crying myself. I will pretend there never was a time when I was ready for any commitment, no matter how great; never a time when my hope and confidence and energy were unlimited.

"I wish I knew, Sam," I will say. "I wish I knew."

Steve Herbst

CREATION OF A

FUTURE WORLD

IN *THE TRACER*

FROM *MEDIA*, December, 1931: Of all the movies' dream worlds, the palaces and exotic places in which we seek an escape from our Depression-burdened lives, by far the most fascinating and full of hope, is the dream world of the future. Indeed, the opulence of a screen drama is real for the actors alone, but the future belongs to everybody. And yet only a few films have tried seriously to deal with the consequences of scientific advancement and the changes that will result in art and society. "Science fiction" in the American cinema has lacked realism and has depended as much upon the imagination of the viewer as upon that of the filmmaker. In early September, however, German-born director Francis Rehage released *The Tracer*, a thrillingly realistic portrayal of the future. Rehage has made seven films in this country in three years; 1929's *Automobile* and his commissioned work regarding the upcoming World's Fair both demonstrate an uncanny talent for fooling his audience with special film effects. In *The Tracer*, he has developed this talent to a remarkable level. Although the film is limited in scope, it affords us a most breathtaking view of a world that exists in Rehage's mind.

Its simple story involves a robbery, the pursuit, and the eventual destruction of the criminal. Rehage's protagonist criminal, played by burly Arnold Cooke and whose name in the film we never discover, is very much like the misanthropic

heroes of *Public Enemy* and *Big House*. He is essentially
fearless, possessed with the overpowering need to be on top.
But despite his tough character, he is over his head in a
technological super-world. Here, perhaps, is the film's single
most disturbing flaw: Cooke lives in that world but does not
really belong to it; he is surprised and baffled, as we are, by
elements of the future that he should take for granted. There
is in him a fatal and enigmatic lack, because of which he is
hopelessly at odds with the environment in which he finds
himself. From the moment the film opens he faces justice in
the form of mechanical devices, unlike anything that exists today and yet frighteningly convincing. No alarm sounds when
he enters the offices of the futuristic Olympian Industries,
but in an opening scene we follow his actions on a pair of
eerie television-like screens. Here is where Rehage's construction of a technology begins. To give the effect of impossibly
sharp television pictures on the faces of impossibly small machines, Rehage used multiple exposure to combine three separate shots on one piece of film. The television pictures are actually film images printed through a grid of horizontal lines
onto high contrast film. When they are added to the
background of desk and office, it appears that we are witness-
ing the first in a series of electrical marvels.

The office scenes also show a whole range of more mun-
dane objects that were completely redesigned for the future.
Telephone switchboard, telephones and typewriters are all
streamlined and highly polished, dotted with trademarks and
switches to make them seem real. Light fixtures and furniture
were created especially for *The Tracer* out of what architects
have said are the materials of the future: chromed steel, hard-
woods, and white opaque glass. Wall-to-wall carpeting covers
all the floors. The effect produced is glamorous, the appliances expensive yet functional. Director Rehage had a large
staff of designers to help him, but it is the coordination of
their efforts and the unity of their styles that creates the illusion of a future world for us. Rehage's approach was
to eliminate the frills of our modernistic art while preserving
the simplicity of straight lines and smooth surfaces. The same
philosophy of styling was applied to every object in his sets:
the frames of doors, the elevator with its pushbutton controls,
the squared man-sized forms that appear to be coin-operated
vending machines. Such extensive and precise work must re-
quire a great deal of money; even though many of the design
problems were handled by private companies. Rehage spent

over a hundred thousand dollars building the office sets alone.

His outstanding achievement in these early scenes is the awesome dusk skyline of Chicago that we see for a total of under two minutes, behind the desk of Eric Haller. It is so believable and unusual, in fact, that we may tend to ignore Haller himself, the first man that Cooke encounters during the film. We should say a few words about this set. It was constructed primarily out of plywood and extends fifty feet behind the window of Haller's office, and was used only in this final office sequence. A small staff spent two weeks building it, to Rehage's detailed specifications; it is in almost no way related to the city's present appearance. When time came for filming, Rehage sealed off the portion of the studio that contained his model and filled it with smoke. The haze hanging over the city keeps us from making out any detail that might give it away. This effective illusion, sealed off by a window from the clean and brightly lit office interior, takes us once and for all into the future.

Simon Stern plays Haller, the business official who has been patiently watching Cooke on his television screens. Stern's portrayal of the character is as otherworldly as his surroundings. He never gets up from his chair behind the long hardwood desk, and he is perfectly calm in Cooke's presence. When the burglar pulls a gun on him, he only smiles. Clearly he is so far above the visitor in rank, in resources, and in subtlety that he is beyond fear. But in a way it seems that Haller hardly sees the other man, almost as if there is a barrier between them that makes it ultimately impossible for him to believe that Cooke exists. Meanwhile, the future which is on his side, the lofty panorama of the city behind him, arouse an overwhelming jealousy and hatred in his opponent. Before Haller can react, Cooke has shot him with his gun. Surprise and disbelief cross his face; now we see for the first time an almost featureless white box that Haller breathily refers to as "the tracer." Haller's blood stains his tan suit; he watches as Cooke makes off with the box.

The camera allows us plenty of time to appreciate Rehage's car of the future. It and two others were built upon the frames of racing cars and all are driveable. Cooke's car was made by fastening a specially formed sheet-metal body to the chassis of a 1930 Alfa Romeo GS sports car, the new body extending far over the front and rear wheels and having a high solid roof. Pictures of this car have already appeared in magazines; it is truly a dream car. Some additional futuristic touches: extra-wide tires and solid wheel covers, adding to the sleekness of the design, ornamental strips of chromium-plated trim for streamlining, and a wide one-piece windshield. The last of these presented a difficult problem for the production crew. In order to set his cars apart from those on the road today, Rehage decided to equip them with curved glass on front and back that would follow the shape of the body. His technicians, succeeded in producing a number of curved windshields by bending plate glass around carbon molds, and six of these were selected for the cars.

In addition, Rehage built a cutaway interior for Cooke's car and equipped it with a removable front seat, removable roof and doors, and a molded rubber dashboard that stretches the width of the car. In the dashboard were mounted a variety of manually operated dials, lights and buzzers, some of which were never used during the actual filming. For road footage to be used in conjunction with this interior set, Rehage experimented with techniques that would produce an exceptionally smooth ride. That effect was finally achieved by using a camera operating at twice normal speed, mounted on a racing car traveling at seventy or eighty miles an hour. When the film is slowed down, motion is very calm and more like that of a ship than of an automobile.

Other driving footage was shot by a camera moving on rails among Rehage's miniatures, which display the same attention to detail as those he used in his films about the 1933 World's fair. The miniature models of houses and storefronts, traffic signals and cars, were also combined with movies of the actual cars in motion, using an interesting and effective process: the film of car and road was printed frame-by-frame onto a sequence of paper proofs, which were then pasted over with photographs of the models. Because of the size of the artwork, Rehage could exercise a great deal of control over its composition and animation. Finally, the completed frames were rephotographed onto movie film, live action and miniatures combined.

Cooke never finds out the pivotal reason for his downfall, that the "tracer" on the seat at his side is nothing more than a radio transmitter which will lead the police right to him. This fact we are told by the police captain. In a series of impressive shots, Rehage shows us the modern police station and its machinery. Like the offices of Olympian, the rooms of the station are decked out with real-looking radios, telephones, switchboards, and in this case maps of a future Chicago. We see the helicopter equipment that locates Cooke's car on a suburban highway, and underneath the copter, a beautiful painting of lit streets that reemphasizes for us the scale of Rehage's imagination. Returning to Cooke's level, we pan back and see the lights of a police car.

The chase is a masterpiece. Still using miniatures to augment the action, Rehage leads the three powerful cars through an all-out test of their abilities. The police cars, with their flashing beacons and the dubbed-in purring of their engines, are a frightening spectacle. Rehage took thousands of feet of film of the pursuit, cars attaining speeds of up to ninety miles an hour. Frequent repairs had to be made during the shooting. The chase scene itself lasts only sixteen minutes on the screen, and ends on the parking lot of the supermarket which is the only outdoor set used in the film.

The supermarket was constructed out of concrete, aluminum and plate glass, under the guidance of Graham Keane. It is thirty feet high at each apex and one hundred twenty feet across. It predominant design features are a pair of huge wooden arches covered with four hundred square feet each of sheet aluminum, and a row of gigantic windows that make up most of the front wall. The parking lot is illuminated by five floodlight towers, around which the drivers race their cars, laying rubber on the new asphalt surface and filling the air with smoke. One policeman in the film fires a specially designed pistol with a wide nozzle, and the rear window of Cooke's car is shattered. Angrily, his visibility badly impaired, Cooke spins his car around. His collision with the first police car was captured by three cameras and two additional sound recorders; even so, the sound of the crash was augmented later for the film. Repairs had to be made on Cooke's car so that it could be driven. Before Cooke can turn the car around, one of the police in the third car fires a teargas grenade through his back window. Cooke charges at the other police car, is deflected, and crashes through the supermarket.

We might enumerate three ways that a filmmaker has of making his objects appear real. They are: 1) by using them, 2) by ignoring them, and 3) by destroying them. The televisions, radios and automobiles in *The Tracer* appear real because we see them work. Meticulously constructed appliances that are ignored by the actors, on the other hand, appear real because of the very lack of interest. To the film crew these objects are works of art, but inside the film they are part of the background of everyday life. Similarly, by destroying expensive machinery and sets that were made for the film, the director tells us that the supermarket is just another supermarket, the cars are just cars, and the man is just another man.

Lights in the market are turned on, clouds of tear gas rise from the wreckage toward the high ceiling, and we see Rehage's last constructed evidence of the future. Early in production, the plan of this sequence was fixed. Rehage contracted with popular soap manufacturers, and with several independent advertising firms, and collected more than one hundred futuristic package designs. These were carefully drawn and used in the final scenes. Framed by these fairy tales and by broken glass, the wreckage is grotesque and an intrusion. Blood was applied to the metal edges, and all post-collision evidences of the car's fake construction were concealed.

We must be honest in appraising *The Tracer* as a film. Its strength lies not in acting, nor even in the dramatic use of camera and music. It is most impressive, truly impressive, for its realism and technical perfection. Rehage's special effects, whatever their foundation, are ultimately convincing. We may sympathize with the protagonist, but it is not sympathy or sadness at his end that fills our hearts. For, even as *he* was devoured by a superior future to which he did not belong, so we of the present are devoured by Rehage's awesome vision. People who have seen this film have walked out of the theatre with their eyes on fire, and talk in their heads of the time when men will fly in rocket ships.

John Barfoot

COILS

CHERRY ORDERED the carcase of the Negro woman to be lowered into the white toilet. The carcase was a shapeless lump of lardy white, ridged with gristle. The block and tackle creaked as the two workmen hauled at it, hand by hand, and Cherry made little sounds with his mouth as he directed the lowering.

She said,

—Cherry, why are you doing this to her?

He replied,

—Because she is black.

—But she's white, she's all white, except for those brown patches of blood.

—She is black,

said Cherry.

The greasy carcase was almost entirely inside the toilet now. She saw a hair stuck on the fat. The carcase disappeared and the workmen disengaged the hook and pulled up the chain. The hook had little lumps of fat stuck onto it.

—Cherry, I feel sick.

—Go away,

he said, and when she did not move,

—GO AWAY,

he roared.

The sound of his voice traveled out and out to the distant walls of the huge room and bounced and reverberated back.

131

The air was vibrating and the great space was webbed with sound.

—AYAYAYAYAY,

came the sound of the room.

Cherry was looking into the gleaming toilet bowl and muttering to himself. The workmen were looking on uninterestedly.

She ran away from them, skimming over the radiant floor, birdlike, cloudy folds of white robe floating around her. She drove her legs hard against the floor, resilient, ran and ran, until the hazy walls took on definition and she saw a door. The door was so huge that the handle was out of her reach. She pressed hard against the smooth surface and it opened, silently. She looked back. Far away, at the other end of the enormous room the little group stood, almost hidden in the glimmer of light. Cherry was talking to the workmen and the distorted words of their conversation babbled from the walls.

She pushed the door with all her might and it swung slowly back into its housing.

—THOOOOMMM,

it sounded, dull surf-thunder.

A bell began to ring. If Cherry came after her . . .

She leaned over and switched off the alarm clock. Feet tangled in sheets and nightdress damp with sweat. If Cherry came after her . . .

Already, the unpredictable coils of dream were giving way to the ordered lines of existence. She closed her eyes against the day and tried to go back into her dream. But the lines were driven too deep for escape; her mind was already trundling along well-worn tracks, meeting no resistance, no retardation of steady, constant speed. She stumbled groaning out of bed.

She walked into the living room.

She cooked breakfast.

She ate breakfast.

She washed her face, neck, ears, arms up to the elbow.

She dressed.

She combed and arranged her hair.

She put on her coat.

She went to work.

At work, Mrs. Cox said to her,

—You're looking a bit haggard, dear. Bags under your eyes. Not getting enough sleep, I expect. My Ronnie's the same—out till all hours doing God knows what. I tell him the same as you—you need more sleep, my lad, instead of gallivanting God knows where in the middle of the night. But does he listen? Talk to the wall.

Mrs. Cox went on like this all the time. Her conversation was like a continuous tape-recording, endlessly repeating itself, forever beginning again. You could dip in at any point and follow it quite easily. Mrs. Cox was a small, neat woman. On her right cheek was a large wart with hairs growing out of it. She gave off a stale musty odor, like potatoes too long in the earth.

She sometimes liked to listen to Mrs. Cox so that she could smell the odor. It was not pleasant but she liked to smell it while Mrs. Cox talked to her, in the way that she used to prod a painful tooth with her tongue when she was a child.

A pile of invoices stood before her and she began to work on them. After a short while she simply sat with a pen in her hand, held over the paper, dreaming of nothing she could put into words. Her eyes were glassy.

Mrs. Cox tapped her on the shoulder and said,

—Mr. Cherry wants to see you, dear. Shouldn't worry—it can't be anything serious. Gor, you do look tired.

Mr. Cherry said,

—Sit down, do, Miss Taylor. No, over here if you don't mind. Where I can see you. Don't get much chance to see a pretty face stuck behind this desk. Well, just a general chat, dear. Just to see how you're getting on in the office, so to speak. How're you doing then, eh? Any complaints?

—No,

she murmured.

—Nothing.

—Good, good. I like everyone to be happy. I've observed that—

his face became serious,

—people work much better if they're happy. Don't you agree? Mmmm? I'm happy—wouldn't be here if I wasn't. And I like my staff to be happy. Don't like them moaning around with long faces all the time.

There was an underlying sense to his words, an unstated implication which she answered with an unintelligible sound.

—We had a girl here once, about the same age as you in fact, moped about all day with a face as long as a fiddle. It depressed you just to look at her. Last in in the morning, first out at night type, no interest in her work, you know the kind I mean. Well, I let things go like, and pretty soon she was doing

hardly any work at all, sat dreaming with her eyes out of the
window all day. Mrs. Cox got sick, having to do most of her
work for her, and I got sick, listening to Mrs. Cox's complaints—outcome of it was I had to sack her, told her she was
no use to the firm, getting a decent wage for nothing.

He paused and gave her a straight, honest, Northcoun-
tryman's look, full in the face.

—I've never had to do that again, so far—learned my lesson,
so to speak. I realized that besides doing the firm a bad service I was doing that girl a bad service as well, just letting her
go on like, the way I did. She wanted someone to put her
right, tell her she was doing wrong. Now if I see a young girl
shaping up that way I always have her in for a little chat, just
an informal talk, you understand, and I try and put her on the
right path. Suggest a few little pointers, you know. It's never
failed yet.

Silence. Then he laughed heartily.

—Anyway, enough of that. If you're happy that's all right.
Get out and enjoy yourself, have fun. I wish I had your life in
front of me, yes I do. Okay then, Miss Taylor, that's all I
wanted. Just an informal talk, just to get to know staff better,
you know. Feel free to pop in anytime you've got something
on your mind, I'll do my best to help you.

—Thank you, Mr. Cherry,

she said,

Beans on toast and a yoghurt for tea. Read for half an
hour. Stare at the wall for half an hour, hugging her legs
against the heat from the electric fire. Records, magazines,
and a bedtime cocoa.

—The lecture tonight,

said Mrs. Cox,

—is entitled "Time and Humanity." Dr. Cherry will speak for
approx. half an hour and there will be a short period for questions afterwards. Dr. Cherry.

There was a spattering of light applause, in which she
joined automatically.

—Thank you, thank you,

said Dr. Cherry, waiting modestly until the clapping died
down.

—The subject of my lecture tonight is one which might easily
daunt any man. Time in one form or another has been studied
or conjectured upon since the—ahem, I was going to say
since the beginning of time—

He paused for polite laughter.

—But of course we cannot imagine any beginning to Time, or to Space, for the two are sides of the same coin, so to speak. An infinity of Time and Space, an endless pool in which we, finite, short-lived, rude creatures of decay, dwell. Or perhaps a more apt metaphor would be that of a rushing river carrying us irresistibly onward for eternity.

The pedantic words walked jerkily on stilts above her. She gazed at Cherry's face, at the blue jowls, the thick pudgy ears, the folds of neck hanging over the white collar of his shirt.

Something tickled her hand. She looked down and saw a mouse on her knee, nuzzling her folded hands. She gently disengaged one hand and stroked the little furry nose of the mouse. It narrowed its eyes with pleasure and sat perfectly still.

—But it has not been *proved* that there is something eternal in man, something to correspond with the endlessness of the cosmos, something that is not tumbled and rushed downstream by the river of Time, but sails calmly on its surface, completely at home.

She took a pin and drove it firmly into the little humped back of the mouse. The skin dimpled at first, and then the point penetrated and the pin sank easily into the flesh. The mouse wiggled his tail quietly with pleasure. She stuck another pin into him, gently, pressing the head flush to the surface of his body with her fingertip.

—And yet there are those who fight against Time. I have shown you how it is necessary for men to order their existence into patterns, to have each thing happen for a set and known duration in time. I have shown you how it is imperative that a day be organized into little precise packets of time. And yet there are those who fight against this, those who do not see that the only defense, the only security against Chaos, is Order. You have met them, I have met them. They are a well-known type—the last in in the morning, first out at night type, so to speak.

She stuck more pins into the mouse, who remained still under her gentle hands. The pins were quite well spaced out over the little body and so she began to fill in the spaces beween them. Soon there were whole patches where she could run her fingers over and feel nothing but the rounded heads of the pins, no flesh or fur at all.

—She resents Order. She gets on the bus in the morning and she tries to play games with Time, tries to stretch it out. And how does she do this? She retreats to the only place where

Time is plastic and subjective, she retreats into Dream. She
dreams Time away, making no use of its precious ir-
recoverable substance.

There was no more room left for pins now. The mouse was
a little shivering silvery creature, a metalflesh mouse. No
room for pins on the body. She took a pin and drove it ten-
derly into one of the tiny black eyes. There was a pop and a
little bead of blood appeared. The mouse quivered with
ecstasy and then lay still as she pierced his other eye, pop.
Eyes of silver beads, body of silver foil, only the tail was
flesh. She cut it off with a pair of sewing scissors and the
mouse froze into metal immobility.

With the immobility of the mouse an awareness came to
her senses and she realized that the room was silent. She
looked up. Cherry and Mrs. Cox and the students were all
looking at her. They had been looking at her for some time.
—You were not paying attention. What were you doing?
asked Cherry.
—WHAT WERE YOU DOING,
he roared, when she did not answer.

Mrs. Cox strode up to her and pulled the metal mouse from
her hand. Cherry looked at it with horror and there was a
gasp from the students. Cherry held the little mouse up in his
big hand and it began to bleed. Each little pin-prick poured
out blood so that his hand was red. Tears of blood streamed
from the pierced eyes and the mouse died with a squeak.
—Oh no,
she cried,
—You've hurt him.

And then Mrs. Cox and Cherry took her outside and the
wind made her white robe flutter. The temple was bathed
white with light from the moon and the pillars shone silvery.
They each took one of her hands and ran, pulling her lightly
between them, and they ran at the pillars, one on either side,
she between, and they ran straight at the stone pillars and she
was smashed and crushed and torn on the hard stone and then
through the other side and the next pillar loomed up and she
was smashed and torn and then through the other side and she
died with shock each time the pillars crushed her. A bell
began to ring. Police?

She leaned over and switched off the alarm clock. Her body
was slippery with sweat.

She washed and pinned her hair up.

She put on her white robe.

She walked to the bus stop, birdlike, cloudy folds of white robe floating around her.

At work Mrs. Cox said,

—You're looking a bit haggard, dear. Bags under your eyes. Not getting enough sleep, I expect. Went to Dr. Cherry's lecture, did you?

She ignored her and began her work.

—Mr. Cherry wants to see you, dear. Shouldn't worry—it can't be anything serious. Gor, you do look tired.

Mr. Cherry said,

—Sit down, do, Miss Taylor. Just a general chat, nice robe you're wearing, by the way. It's come to my notice that your heart isn't exactly in your work. You know, last in in the morning, first out at night principle, and I just wanted to have an informal talk with you . . .

The droning words buzzed sleepily above her. She felt a tickling on her hand. She looked down and saw that a little mouse had crawled onto her knee and was nuzzling her folded hands. She proceeded to stick pins into the humped flesh of his back.

—I know you resent Order,

Mr. Cherry was saying,

—but you must know that human existence has to be ordered into little precise packets of time. Everything must have a known duration. It's obvious, isn't it? Of course it is, and if there's going to be any defense, any security against Chaos, everybody must live inside those little packets, because that means Order, and Order defeats Chaos. Everyone, mark you. If one single person lives outside Time that person represents a threat to Humanity, a chink through which Chaos can work its insidious intent, so to speak.

The little mouse's body was quite covered with pins now and there was no room for any more. And so she stuck pins into his eyes, pop pop.

She looked up and saw that Mr. Cherry was watching her, had been watching her for a long time.

—What are you doing?

he asked.

She lifted her hand and showed him the little mouse. He took it from her in his big hand and it began to bleed. Each little pin-prick poured out blood so that his hand was red. Tears of blood streamed from the pierced eyes and the mouse died with a squeak.

She began to cry and great waving sobs shook her whole body.

—Oh, you've hurt him,

she cried.

And then Mr. Cherry and Mrs. Cox came and took her gently by the arms and someone gave her tea and sat her down. Then a man in a uniform came and they lifted her into the ambulance and Mr. Cherry and Mrs. Cox were saying soft, gentle things. She lay in the rocking bunk and saw the mudstains on her white robe and a little mouse nuzzled friendly against her hand.

After the hospital it was sausage and egg for tea. Then she read for half an hour and then she stared at the wall for half an hour, hugging her legs against the heat from the electric fire. Records, magazines and a bedtime cocoa.

Mrs. Cox said,

—You're looking very haggard these days, dear. Bags under your eyes. Not getting enough sleep, I expect. My Ronnie's the same—out till all hours doing God knows what. I tell him the same as you—you need more sleep, my lad, instead of gallivanting God knows where in the middle of the night. But does he listen? Talk to the wall.

Mrs. Cox was boring but she liked listening to her because she could sometimes smell her damp musty odor, like potatoes too long in the earth. She also liked to look at Mrs. Cox's wart with the long hairs growing out of it.

She began to work on the pile of invoices in front of her. After a while she simply sat with pen in hand, dreaming. The invoices were exactly the same as the ones she had checked yesterday and they were the same as the ones she would check tomorrow. She dreamed of unpredictable things, coils and spirals that led nowhere, instead of straight lines that led to clearly signposted destinations.

—Mr. Cherry wants to see you, dear,

said Mrs. Cox.

—Just his usual pep talk, I expect. Nothing to worry about.

Mr. Cherry said,

—Sit down, do, Miss Taylor.

—No, over here if you don't mind,

she silently mouthed, just before he actually spoke the words.

—Where I can see you,

he continued.

—Don't get much chance to see a pretty face stuck behind

this desk, ha ha. Well, just a general chat, dear. Just to see how you're getting on in the office, so to speak. How're you doing then, any complaints?

She murmured something.

—Good, good. I like happy staff. One of my, so to speak, sayings, is that happy staff plus clever management equals good work. I've learned the truth of that myself over the years. I remember a girl we had here, about the same age as you in fact, moped about all day with a face as long as a fiddle. I tell you, it was downright depressing . . .

Afterwards there were more invoices and a tea break. Then there was lunch—two salad sandwiches and a Coke jammed into an hour—and then there were more invoices, and then another tea break and then it was getting near time to go home.

A bell began to ring. Finishing bell?

She leaned over and switched off the alarm clock. The floor of the temple was cold and hard and early sun was striking into her eyes. She washed herself and then donned her white robe, so light that it clung to her like haze. She walked to work, watching the one-winged birds spinning crazily in the sky, trying to fly from tree to tree.

At work Mrs. Cox said,

—You shouldn't try to attend all of Dr. Cherry's lectures, you know. You're not getting enough sleep. Bags under your eyes. In fact, Dr. Cherry's noticed it himself. Said he wanted to see you as soon as you came in. You'd better go now.

She walked along the corridor to Cherry's office. The floor and the ceiling and the walls of the corridor were white. It was hard to see, in the dazzling radiance, where floor ended and walls began, or whether there actually was a ceiling or simply a continuation of the walls. The corridor curved very slightly, so little that it was hardly noticeable except as a change in the quality of the sourceless light. She looked back. Only white. Nothing behind her but white.

There was complete silence. A vacuum of silence. Only the rustle of her white robe and her breathing made any sound. The sounds were sucked dry by the silent vacuum.

She walked on. Cherry's office could not be much farther.

She stopped. There was a faint susurration behind her. A soft, deep-drawn hissing. She listened closely and made out the sounds of breathing and rustling clothing. She turned but there was nothing behind her. She walked faster and again stopped. Holding her breath, she heard the soft sounds still behind her, the breathing sounding more labored.

She began to run, her body almost formless in the dazzling light, the corridor curving gently away ahead of her. She ran and ran, driving her legs hard against the floor, panting painfully. The corridor turned before her on its unseen axis.

At last she could run no more and stopped to listen. The sound was still there, but it did not seem to be coming from behind. She looked before her. A figure in a filmy robe walked slowly along the corridor, almost formless in the sourceless radiance.

The breathing and rustling behind her began again as the pursuer caught up. She ran forward, not wishing to be caught, not wishing to catch up with the white figure ahead.

The corridor curved and suddenly came to an end. She saw an exit through which the white-robed figure was disappearing. She ran forward and reached the exit. The breathing behind her grew louder and louder. She looked out of the end of the corridor into an enormous room. Not far from where she stood was a white toilet and Cherry and two workmen stood near it. Something bulky lay under a sheet and the white figure stood looking at it.

Cherry ordered the carcase of the Negro woman to be lowered into the white toilet. The carcase was a shapeless lump of lardy white, ridged with gristle. The block and tackle creaked as the two workmen hauled at it, hand by hand, and Cherry made little sounds with his mouth as he directed the lowering.

The mouth of the white figure opened.

The breathing behind her came closer and closer, the mouth opened, opened, the tongue stirring for speech. She looked behind and saw a figure in a white robe and as the coils tightened around her, she said,

—Cherry, why are you doing this to her?

Sonya Doramn

TIME BIND

AT SCHOOL they had called me Lightfoot, which saved me from being called Brain, or Filmworm, or something like that. Still, no one will ever know what sweat the combining of my talents caused me during my efforts, finally successful, to get into the Time Complex Building. I did it night after night (time after time, if you like) lightfooted, my kindled brain already at work as the microfilm passed before me on one of the office screens.

I was a quick study. My mother used to scold me for the speed with which I tore through homework, sometimes while braiding my hair, or filing my nails, any little chore done by the physical half of me while my demented and forceful twin, the head, galloped off with essay prizes, runner-up in physics contests, Science Fair winner, and all that.

There was still the problem of getting into the central vault of Time Complex, which necessitated further studies but easier ones, since the material was actually available at the library, if you knew where to look for it. Nobody paid me any attention when I tramped through, I'd been in and out of there for so many years; yesterday and today and, they could be sure, tomorrow too, with the squint line getting deeper between my eyes and my once fair skin fading.

Lightfoot I still was, all the same, having taken pleasure in staying in decent shape, even while the brain went on sloughing off its neurons. If I had drunk less sake would my short-term memory have lasted longer? Ah, that's one of

141

those questions . . .

I've reached an age where details bore me, so I won't go into them, about how I did learn the secrets of the vault door. They weren't really secrets, hardly anything physical is; you just have to gather up the pieces of information, like the ingredients for a recipe, and blend them.

There remained for me one scary part: my first trip. Head and body out of sync, I'd be done for. All of me in sync but time warped, like an old doorway, and I'd be done for. Of course, that was the risk I knew I'd have to face.

No glass booth. No dais with leather strappings on the chair. A green plastex console and at the right of it, set into the vault floor, some metal slats, tightly closed like a fist. Oh, just open up and let me dive through. I thought, listening to the solemn tread of the guard. I smiled in my conspiracy with the console. What would the guard think if he came in, seeing a middleaged woman with grey in her hair, setting the console dials and muttering hope? Muttering dialogues which had never been but might be? Taking both parts, her and him, me and you?

There was absolutely no sensation at all, but almost instantaneously I was in a big lecture hall, lightfoot, in acrylic pants which slid like fingers over my taut haunches. Wearing my double strand of ambers and a nose-clock. The lecture is just over and he stands with a group of his peers near the podium. With all my nights of rehearsal behind me I speed toward him, hand outstretched, smiling.

"Oh, how very nice to see you!" he says, and I plunge into their midst, reeking of anticipation, well aware of the impression I make and afraid that I'll lose my not very good balance at this game.

"I enjoyed your paper very much," I say, "in fact, I thought it was superb, and full of surprises."

His smile is always shy. Of course he hasn't got twenty years of rehearsal behind him as I have. "How nice of you to say so," he says. His eyes are blue. I always knew they were. "You're looking well," he says, holding my hand.

"You're looking simply marvelous," I say, closing his hand up warmly between my palms and holding on more than is necessary.

"Why don't we—?"

"Yes, couldn't we—?"

Here some inadvertence occurs, possibly I slipped on the slats or something, and the lecture hall vanishes, it's pitch-dark in some place comfy, I'm laid out on my back and he's just climbing on.

"Darling," he says, kissing my breasts alternately.

"Oh that feels so good," I say, helping him while at the same time wondering, frantically, where we left his friends and how we got here and what the hell happened in the interval? I expected a lot of that machine but hardly that it would book hotel reservations, so where am I?

There is a tremendous sound of hammering and before he even has time to roll off I'm poured back through the years to stand beside the console, hearing the noise in the corridor outside the vault door. It was just that damned guard, drumming out a new dance step, which echoed highly magnified through the alloy archways.

After I caught my breath, which took a while, I checked the time, I checked the dials. There was no explanation for what happened, for the timing to be so badly off. There hadn't even been time for any conversation. I mean, I never found out how he really was, whether he was working up a new paper. Obviously there was a lot about this business I still had to learn. Back to the library. Back to the lightfoot entry to all those offices upstairs in the Time Complex Building.

The next trip would have to go better. At least we should chat about the weather, and how his cactus collection was coming along, whether the Old Man (*Cephalocereus senilis*) had blossomed yet, that kind of thing, like two real people with a relationship, which we'd never had.

I thought it would take me a week to check out each step and find out where I'd gone wrong. It took me more like three weeks, during which I accumulated a lot of tension and several splitting headaches, but didn't dare take any pills because they'd slow down my thinking. I'd just have to manage until the job was done; I was determined to work it out.

Convinced finally that I had it figured, I went back wearing my no-skid, best-grip sandals to prevent slippage, just in case that was part of it.

We are cantering side by side, he on a bay gelding and me on a small chestnut mare. My shining black hair streams out behind me. He is wearing a hard derby. Up the languorous slope in slow motion, green hill against fiery blue sky. There at the top, the white fence bars to be jumped. Side by side we'll sail over. I collect the mare between my knees, and glance over at him. He smiles. His eyes are grey and beautiful. He raises his riding crop to the brim of his hat with a nice little salute to me as I take the mare up on the snaffle.

Up she goes, like a bird, over the fence with her hind legs tucked up neat and nice. Only we keep going, straight out into the blue, sailing away on a perfect level.

Desperate, I crane my neck: behind me there is the fence on top of the hill, there are hedges and trees; there, far below me in a lovely meadow, he canters away on the bay horse.

What has happened this time? I want to know. I yank on the reins but she sails on out like a rocket through the purest of blue skies, the air is hitting my nose and making me dizzy, we're so high up I can see the curve of the earth; hey, this is dangerous! I'm about to yell, when that mare puts her head down and bucks me off.

I sat up on the steel slats, sweating with rage and fright. No sound of the guard. How much time did I spend in that fruitless effort? My watch had stopped; that figured. Back to the library stacks.

As I passed the green plastex console, I resisted an impulse to kick in its panels. I couldn't do that, because I intended to get some good out of it yet.

"You look thin, are you losing weight?" several people asked me during my next course of study. Well, what did that mean, that I was too fat, or that the weight loss emphasized certain boninesses, or that they saw a faraway look in my eyes? A long-ago look, perhaps? I was going to get that machine to take me back and just once it was going to go right, all the dialogues I'd prepared, what I say, what he says, what we say and do together.

The next time I encounter him his eyes are hazel and his hair just going white above the ears. We're in the office of a highly esteemed scientific journal where he has brought in his manuscript. It's abstruse as hell and full of symbols which are not on my typewriter, which means, since I have said, "I'd be delighted to type it for you," I'll have to put in the symbols by hand. It will take me a long time but I have only a short time and none at all to spare.

"After dinner?" I suggest.

"Why not?" he agrees.

We concur. We comply. We are sitting in a pinkly shaded booth over snail salad and sake martinis. We are eating rare steak garnished with mushrooms. We are holding hands and murmuring into each other's echoing ears just as I always knew we would; palm to sweating palm down the avenue with everyone giving us envious glances, when the enormous facade of the hotel toward which we aim lights up from top to bottom in blazing green neon:

SHE HAS HER PERIOD

and I was lying crossways on the steel slats, tears in my eyes, biting my knuckles to stifle the sound of my sobs, for fear the guard would hear me. The guard had given up dance steps this week, or perhaps it was a different person this time; he was practicing a split whistle. I imagined that his whistles were boring little holes into the metal halls and naves of the building. It was no longer: what happened? It was not: where am I? anymore. It was beginning to be: why am I in such a fix? After the amount of work I had put in on this private project, I would see it through.

This time as I passed the console on the way out, I reached over and slapped one of its panels, though that didn't provide me with much satisfaction. I felt these mishaps couldn't go on much longer. All I wanted was one simple little episode which never happened but might have; it was not going to affect anything in the world, and I was taking full responsibility for my own part. Just once. Before I got too damned old to even care and as it was, I kept forgetting what color his eyes were.

His eyes are a light brown with amber flecks, beneath arched brows which are still dark though his hair, parted sharply to show pink scalp, is pure white. We are at table with his learned friends and my smile is cool as I murmur, *"En brochette,* of course," which is my witty reply to a question I didn't quite catch.

They all laugh heartily, give me approving glances. I can see him flush with pride in our friendship and I am so happy, he is so happy. There is a small hangnail on my right pinky which annoys the hell out of me but I pick at it under the table where no one can see.

The dinner is over, the brandies finished; flushed with pride and delight in each other, witty, beautiful, and best of all, together, we say good night to the gathered company and go off toward the grand staircase.

Above the first step there is a fantastic chandelier, white milk glass with baroque pink flowers and mint-green leaves; the light shines through milkily, dim, opalescent; an extraordinarily romantic chandelier and appropriate for the occasion. His hand presses mine reassuringly as we begin to mount the stairs. They are covered with a wine-colored carpet which has a curious kind of black and gold braid along the edges and each riser is edged with gold tacks which have curiously wrought heads.

The staircase is very wide, and we mount it side by side, hand in hand, flushed with exertion and anticipation, the eighth stair, the tenth stair, the seventeenth stair. There is another chandelier over the landing, this one pale blue and lavender, bits of crystal hang down in drops and fringes all around, flashing light into our eyes. I feel his hand press encouragingly on the small of my back, one thumb tentatively strokes my hip, yes, we are climbing the magnificent stairway to our bed of love above but why is the staircase so long and neverending? There are far too many landings; there are little sideways stairways, like the tributaries of a river.

There are lights flashing on and off the console. In one motion, ungainly though it may have been, I leaped off the closed steel slats and smashed my fists against that console in despair. Still keeping my wits about me, though, and not raising my voice; just cursing in a whisper until the thing should have fused into slag. The lights on the console went out and it stood cool and silent.

For a little while, listening to the guard walk the hallways, I confronted this misery, wondering if it was a fake, if all the technical information I'd absorbed was some kind of a joke. The Sunday supplements had suggested that it augmented history in some indescribable way; the commerical programs variously described it as Time Machine, History Machine, Truth Factor, Truth Detector, Headless Marvel, and, in one case, the Whizz Bang, to which the physicists objected, saying it cheapened the concept of time travel.

I had studied every paper on the concepts and the hardware; I had set the dials correctly; I had experienced no discomfort in traveling. What happened when I got there, then? Everything seemed to be all right at this end. I'd give it one more try, before I settled down into sniveling about my aches and pains, and declined into imbecility over a sake on the rocks.

The guard was neither dancing nor singing, he sounded like yet another person, with a light but rather brittle step, as if he were an elderly man doing the rounds. Perhaps they had different shifts. I'd have to be more careful, for without having any such amusements as singing, dancing, and whistling, this guard might be far more alert.

I'd take a week to check everything out, to double-check it.

To rest my head and soak my body or perhaps the other way around, anything that might help. Anything, damn it. I would have one night of delight with him before it was too late, and that wasn't much to ask. A night, a week, six months, a good relationship for a year, was that asking too much? It wasn't as though I hadn't been considerate the first time around, knowing he was preoccupied with professional matters, that he had serious attachments, and I wasn't then any too sure of myself, any more than I was now sure of what color his eyes had been.

It is too dark to see what color his eyes are and anyhow they are closed, he is snoring, and has put his pajamas back on. I lie there in a bitter and resentful daze for a few minutes, then snap on the lamp. A forty-watt bulb, it doesn't do much for the cracked walls and peeled paint of our hideout.

"Huh?" he says, puting one skinny forearm across his eyes to shield them, and he snores again, deeply. He sleeps with his mouth open. After a moment I raise my own forearm and regard the large pores and liver spots with the dismay of recognition.

Good God, how long have I been here?

I turn my head on the moldy pillow and look at his sparse white hair, the white stubble beginning to appear on his chin, the skeletal fingers of his hand limp against his own shoulder.

Good God, what if I don't get back?

Back to my studies, to my one-mile jog very morning, well, it's just half a mile these days; to the quiet simplicities I really enjoy. What if I live here now? It seems to me the time has passed alarmingly and this isn't at all what I had started out to do or be, nor him, either, when his eyes were blue or hazel and he was becoming famous and for how long, I'd like to know, is he going to lie there and snore?

The vault door snores and rasps as the guard comes in. The room lights up as the blinking console lights flicker and go out. I'm lying on the tightly closed steel slats, clasping my aching head with both hands.

He comes over and takes me by the arm, pulling me to my feet. "What are you doing in here?" he asks, more surprised than angry. "It's impossible for unauthorized personnel to get in here."

"No it isn't," I say. "Not if you really put your mind to it." I turn around, out of his grasp, and kick the console, but not hard enough to injure myself. As you get older, you have to be more crafty about these expressions of emotion.

"Now, now," he says, "don't do that. You're not even allowed in here."

"Yes, but—" I say, turning around to him.

And there he stands. His hair is white and his eyes are still blue.

"What are you doing here?" I ask, stunned by his presence. Did he pop up between the slats right behind me? I wonder.

"I've worked here for years," he says, regarding me kindly but firmly. "Why do you ask that?"

"What about all those papers? The ones I offered to type for you? The lectures? The dinners with all your peerless friends?"

He smiles, and guides me toward the door with one skinny hand on the fat of my back. "Oh, that," he says, smiling. "Yes, those days. I was promising, I certainly had ambitions, but it turned out I wasn't good enough, after all. I do remember you, vaguely. Do you want some coffee? I have a thermos."

"Well, thanks," I say, sort of lingering to glance back at the vault room where I'd failed so badly. "Aren't you going to arrest me?"

"Of course. I've already sent in the word. I still don't understand how you got in there like that."

Sipping his coffee, I say, "They used to call me Lightfoot."

"Did they? Nicknames are funny things. They used to call my wife Fickle, but it was because she had freckles. She says it started with her school friends calling her Freckles, but gradually—" and he launches into an interminable account of his wife's past, and goes on and on until they come to take me away, a whole squadron of slim men in squeaky shoes whose eyes are any color I don't remember. Everything considered, they handle me gently.

Their sergeant says: "You're charged with breaking and entering. Understand your rights?"

Rights, yes. But breaking and entering what? I wonder. Reentering somewhere? Breaking in or breaking out?

They put me away in a cell where I dozed for the rest of the night. In the morning they released me, my lawyer insisting I had not broken any law. If he only knew how right he was, though if I'd been able to follow my intentions, some laws would have lain in shards. They rarely sentence you for your intentions, though; perhaps they figure you can do that for yourself.

So there I was, free to go home to my filmscreen and warmed sake, and I found that's what I wanted. Though I wouldn't have said so, years ago when I knew whether his eyes were brown or grey.

C. L. Grant

EVERYBODY A WINNER,

THE BARKER CRIED

PERHAPS the sound had only been a trick of the wind, but the girl on the beach turned slowly, searching for the gull she might have heard cry. There was no hope in her face, and though her eyes squinted against the glare, she saw nothing but colors bleached and colors charred. And the only thing that moved with her was the wind, in early spring.

She wore slacks and a heavy green sweater hastily snatched from a fallen mannikin; there was a darkly stained kerchief and her shoes she held in one hand. Attractive once, now she was thin and there were coarse lines that deadened her face. She was tired, and as she walked slowly south, she tripped over nothings in the sand.

There was a pier, charred and splintered, where the ocean's roar was magnified and hurled itself back at her with the odor of salt and dead fish and the rotting slime that covered the pilings. She hesitated as if bracing to run, then bit at her lips and forced herself to walk—out of the white sun into the gray where the cool wind became cold. With one hand at her throat and breathing deeply, she looked straight ahead toward the sand on the other side. Then she stumbled. As she put out a hand to steady herself, the wind shifted a piece of blackened cardboard. There was a man underneath and she screamed when she saw the crabs.

"Oh God!" was not a prayer, but a cry for release as she ran into the open, seeing nothing and hearing only the sea until the pier was lost behind her, and ahead, the wheel.

She slowed until relief forced her to her knees while she stared at the boardwalk lined by rusting metal benches, and beyond them, facing blindly toward the water, the empty stands dwarfed by the once-domed building in their midst.

The wheel. The please-don't-leave-me-on-top ferris wheel rose through the shambles. It looked as if it were being devoured. But it was a memory.

The wind died. The girl slumped forward to her hands, and cried.

And when the time for weeping has passed, she brushed her hands against her legs and rose to her feet. In spite of the sun the sand was cold and the benches somehow looked warm. She took one step toward them and saw him. He was sitting almost directly above her, head down, his arms folded across his chest, still enough for death. But when he grunted and shifted, she cried out without thinking and he looked up. For a moment they stared unbelievingly at each other, and before he could speak, she turned and fled.

"Hey!" he shouted, jumping to his feet and vaulting to the ground. "Hey, wait a minute! Wait, please!"

His voice covered the waves, his feet crunching in the sand thundered in her ears as she ran. Suddenly she slipped, tumbling over a sharp incline just as a wave broke beneath her. The icy water slammed her against the low wall of sand, knocking the air from her lungs and rushing unchecked into her mouth. She was lifted and the sun rushed at her, then thrown, dragged and lifted again; and through it all she felt nothing.

When she next opened her eyes, she was lying between a tattered seaman's coat and a thin bed of rags spread on a bench. She tried to sit up but dizziness forced her down again, and with one hand she felt dried blood on her cheek.

"How are you feeling?" The voice was low and patiently quiet. She started, then pulled herself up, trying to see and understand what she saw at the same time. The effort made her want to gag.

The man was kneeling in front of her, a glass of dark, steaming liquid cupped in his hands. He held it out, urging her to take it.

"Here," he said, smiling. "Drink this stuff. It will make you feel better."

She hesitated, glancing from side to side as if deciding which way to run. But the man was insistent, and the obviously warm glass changed her mind. She drank without pausing for a breath, smiling in spite of herself at the taste, holding her elbows close to her side to keep the warmth within her. Then she rolled the still-hot container between her hands and looked at him.

He seemed as short as she, perhaps shorter. He was wearing faded jeans, a blazer ripped at the collar and a dark blue yachting cap with the plastic brim torn off. He was thin, but the folds around his neck were signs he had once carried much more weight. It was impossible to tell how old he was.

He was still smiling, his face half-turned as if in embarrassment, and when she frowned and looked down at herself, she saw she was naked. Quickly she pulled the coat to her chin, and exposed her legs. She tried to stretch it, but succeeded only in making him laugh.

"Here, take this, miss," he said, pulling off his jacket and handing it to her.

"Thank you," she murmured. Then added, unnecessarily, "I'm . . . I'm cold."

The man nodded and sat back on his heels to watch her intently. Though he looked only at her face, she became flustered by his stare. Her arms would not find the sleeves, her fingers slipped off the buttons. Finally, before she could recoil, he reached out and pulled the collar up around her neck.

"In case you're wondering, I haven't touched you." The amusement in his tone made her glare, then turn away. "I only pulled you out of the surf, that's all. Your clothes are still drying out. Over there. Please, miss. Don't be afraid of me."

She pointed at the bench a few feet away, her hand shaking. "Just . . . just sit over there, if you don't mind." She smiled quickly to try to ease the sudden hurt look on his face. "I . . . I think I trust you, but I'm a little confused right now. I didn't expect to see anyone here. Anywhere. Not ever." And she cried.

The man leaned forward anxiously, but she waved him away. "I'll be all right! Just let me be. Please."

He nodded as if he understood, waiting until she looked up again.

"Jan," he said.

"Linda." When she smiled, he smiled back: a handshake without moving.

"You know this place, Linda?"

"I used to come here when I was little. Every summer rain or shine. My parents, they used to make a big thing of it, loading the car like we were going to California and never coming back. Such . . . such a big fuss just to get away, and when they died I just stopped coming. There was no point, you know? It just wasn't worth it, the trip and all, you know what I mean? It . . . I couldn't . . . I . . . I was on vacation in Minnesota."

He nodded, leaning back and putting his feet up on the peeling, twisted railing. "Me, too. Come here, I mean. Used to work the stand in the summer. Sold ice cream and hot dogs, worked a wheel or two, stuff like that. They were lousy jobs with lousy hours, but the pay was pretty good for a fresh young college kid like myself. Great times. Just great. Years ago it was, it seems.

"I was out in Kansas bumming around when it happened. Took me nearly a month to get back, most of the time sick as a dog, if you know what I mean."

"Yes." Her reply was so low, she had to repeat it.

"I wanted to come *here*. Here, of all places. Screwiest damn thing, but I just had to see if the lights were still working. That must mean something, I guess. I don't know.

"I found some generators—they use, used them in case of power failures—and believe it or not, got a couple of them to work. So when I can keep it down, I manage to get hot things to eat, though I don't know why I bother."

Linda shuddered. "That coffee," she said. "It's the first thing that's stayed down there in three days."

"Yeah. I know what you mean."

He talked for a long time and his rather deep, pleasant voice relaxed Linda into a soothing, restful half-doze. He explained how he had avoided the cities, and how he was nearly killed when a car he had stolen plunged into a frozen river in Pennsylvania. She didn't ask and he didn't tell her what he was doing when the war started and finished.

There was a village called Onslow and a radio broadcast that sent them into a community shelter. There were people: weeping, cursing, praying with folded hands and clenched fists; the graveyard sound of huge steel doors that clanged shut and locked in the darkness. There were three weeks of mourning before filtration systems overloaded and they decided they did not want a concrete coffin. The villagers went about their business, the vacationers scattered, racing to reach some place, somewhere, before time and the radiation stopped them . . .

"Hey!"

Linda blinked and saw Jan standing over her with her clothes. They were still damp and stiff with salt, but she put them on gratefully. He waited until she was dressed, then settled himself on a blanket behind her bench and closed his eyes.

"Your turn."

"There's nothing much, really. I was on vacation, and with no one to go to, I came here. I found plenty of gas in abandoned cars and luckily it was a warm . . . I cried. I cried until I couldn't do it anymore and just came here. Don't ask me how I made it. I don't know." She paused, her hands twisting in her lap. "Jan? How long . . . how long will it be? Jan?"

He was asleep.

"Oh God, how can you do it?" she whispered.

Later, after the sky had gone from purple to black, she heard the sound of someone vomiting. She turned over, half asleep, and without knowing why, she whispered nursery rhymes to deafen her ears and was near the end of "The Owl and the Pussycat" when she fell asleep.

But the sound did not stop.

It was desert-bright when she awoke, smelling the salt air and something cooking. Jan was on the beach, huddled over a small fire with a pan of soup. He grinned broadly when she jumped down beside him, and handed her a partially cleaned spoon.

"It ain't the Ritz, kiddo, but it's hot. Eat it while I go wash up. Haven't had much of an excuse till you came by. It's good to feel . . . civilized for a change."

"But—"

"Eat! I've already had some. Couldn't eat a drop more."

She knew he was lying, but didn't protest. Cautiously she spooned the liquid into her mouth, holding her stomach and praying.

When she finished, they climbed back to the boardwalk, peering through the shadows at the times they had had when the sun was warm and the beach crowded. They discovered one stand that still had its wheel, and Jan leaped over the low barrier, beginning a mock spiel that echoed across the sand while Linda laughed. He ducked behind the wall and came up with a stained, badly torn towel whose color had vanished and flourished it over his head, cajoling her, winking, leering, trying to make her place a bet.

"Come on, lady, don't be afraid. Everybody wins, everybody wins at the wheel. No tricks, no gimmicks, everybody wins and that's a fact. Place your bets and say a prayer, whammy that wheel and everybody wins. Don't be afraid. It's only a game."

Finally she pulled off her ring, her father's ring, and placed it firmly on a faded number—there were only four. Jan spun the wheel, never stopping for a breath, shouting for the ghosts to come and watch the winner. The chattering made no sense, and faded into the sounds of a roller coaster and the sharp odors of over-spiced pizza and underdone hamburger. The wheel spun, clattered and stopped, paused and fell back one number.

She lost, but he bowed gallantly and returned the ring, winking and saying the game was fixed. It always was.

There were one or two stands still squatting in the cold ashes, but they stopped again only when they reached the huge, glassless double doors on the central arcade.

"How about a ride?" Jan asked, taking her by the arm.

Linda stared through the gashes of sunlight that drove shadows from the corners, and nodded. Inside the building the pinball machines lay crushed against the wall, and the floor, though gaping in spots, was cleared of debris. It looked like a mined church.

"I did it the first day I was here," he said before she could ask. "The other places I didn't much care about."

The carousel was empty, its multicolored umbrella caved in and black. A tiny stirrup hung by a scrap of leather from a rust-locked metal support. Gently he took her hand in his and led her to the wheel. There was only one seat, a cage, left on the rim, and she balked when he tried to bring her closer. Jan frowned, then went to the large lever at the wheel's base and, grunting, pulled it noisily toward him. An ear-shattering screech whipped through the building as the big machine shuddered, then lurched forward, and the cage disappeared through the mouth of the roof and into the washed-out sky. Linda hugged herself tightly as she watched the metal arms with no hands, and the metal hand with the basket. She started when he put an arm timidly around her waist, but followed his pointing finger.

"It's the only one left, but really very safe. No kidding. They have generators. I think I told you already." She remained silent and he pulled her forward, talking all the time. "Sorry I couldn't do anything about the lights, but the bulbs are all smashed. It's not as smooth as it once was, but it works. Ugly damn thing, isn't it?"

"No," she said, trying to look at Jan and the cage at the same time. "No, Jan, it's beautiful."

"Then ride with me. Please? I won't try anything. I promise." He grinned. "I don't think I could even if I wanted to."

Linda turned and touched his cheek with her hand. "I know you won't, Jan, but what if the engines—"

"They won't, believe me. There's enough fuel left for more than a dozen rides. Come on, take three with me and I promise we'll get right off. No funny stuff. Okay?"

"Why not?" she said, then added softly, "It's the best basket I can think of to go to hell in."

"Okay, you ready? No, don't stop it. Let's jump in."

She nodded and Jan ran to the wheel. When she followed, she could see that the cage door was missing as well as the wire in the windows. When it lumbered down again, she jumped first, pulling him in after her, then yanked the kerchief from her hair and threw it out the window. For a moment the sun blinded them and they gasped at the tidal rush of cold air.

On the first trip to the top the wheel jerked, swaying the cage, and she grabbed the sides in panic. But the ragged mouth of the roof swallowed them safely, and she leaned against Jan and watched the waves feed on the beach.

On the second trip she blinked . . . and saw the midway teeming with garish, neat, ill-dressed people gawking, eating, dragging half-asleep children. Dolls and unnaturally colored stuffed animals, candy apples and frozen melting custard were clutched to their chests while they were hypnotized by all the lights of the manmade night dream.

On the third turn Jan held her hand, saw what she saw . . . and baseball caps jammed down over pink ears, model planes, blue red white cotton candy, fringed holsters, shooting gallery with dripping gray candles and pockmarked ducks.

They had lost count of the revolutions when Linda suddenly leaned out the window while Jan held her waist and looked away. When it was over, she smiled weakly and he kissed her forehead while she cried.

Then the wheel shook and the boardwalk jarred, and they leaped from the cage when it reached the bottom.

Into the sunlight, and the people children games were gone.

They walked as far as they could away from the decaying amusement park, jumping to the beach only when there were gaps too wide to step over. Linda tripped over a loose plank, taking a long time to regain her feet while Jan walked on automatically, ignoring the splintering wood and damp sand.

Finally she lowered herself from the boardwalk and sat down. Jan dropped beside her, not touching her, and they watched the sun stretch their shadows to the water. The tide was out but the beach was still quite narrow, and quite deserted.

"Hey, Lin." He twisted around until he faced her, his dark eyes mirroring the hollows of her drawn cheeks and temples. "Why did you come here? Tell me the truth, Lin. I can't really explain it, but it's important. I've got to know."

She laughed tonelessly at the little-boy pleading from the fat-thin man's face.

"The wheel, that's all."

"But why?"

"I don't know, Jan. Maybe it's because I liked being able to see miles and miles from the very top. It was better than an airplane because there're no clouds. And the people, they're funny, you know?"

Jan nodded seriously.

"And . . . well, it was like you would never stop when you went all the way around again and again like that; and there was the view too. The people would never be the same every time you saw them." She clasped her hands in her lap and stared at them. "Sometimes someone would look 'way up and point at you and laugh. I always laughed and pointed back, like I was shooting a cowboy gun or something."

"I always stuck out my tongue. My brother . . . my brother told my dad about it once and he . . ." Jan clapped his hands and winced. "Linda, are you awfully tired?"

"Not awfully. Not yet anyway."

"Would you like to go on a trip? I know where we can ride the biggest damn, excuse me, ferris wheel in the whole world. Well, at least the biggest one I've ever been on."

She stared, not understanding, her eyes taking on the fear she had had when they first met. "But how can we, Jan?"

"It's a secret."

She shook her head hard. "No, Jan! I don't want any secrets, not anymore."

"I'm sorry, Lin, but I'm not crazy, you know. There are a million marinas around here, and somewhere there must be one boat that will work. If I can get those stupid generators to work, I can sure as hell start a dumb boat."

"But where would we go?" There was a recklessness in her voice now, half-believing, half-hysterical. Not caring. "Where can we go?"

"Coney Island."

"Oh Jan, Jan! We'd never make it. I can barely . . ."

"Nuts! All we do is stock some food I've got, run up the coast and hunt around until we find the stupid thing. It's a pretty big place, you know. It can't stay hidden forever."

She sighed and stood up slowly. Jan tried to follow but she put a hand on his shoulder, holding him down while she watched the waves.

"Jan," she said, after a long, gray silence. "Do you find me . . . that is, do you think I'm pretty?"

Jan dug a sand trough with one finger, then pulled off his cap to twist in his hands. "I . . . I suppose so."

"Then why haven't you . . . ? I know what you said before, but still . . ."

He squirmed but couldn't shake off her hand.

"Morals?"

He tried to laugh, knowing she was mocking him, and he coughed violently instead. Then, the spasm past, she helped him to his feet and pulled off the ring.

"I kissed you on the wheel, you know."

"Yes." She smiled and shoved the ring into his hand, tugging at his arm until they were headed south again. The sun's fading glare blinded them, made them weave a stumbling dance, tempted by the warm blackness beneath the boardwalk. The sea became loud, the almost colorless sky disturbingly near.

"I want to go," she said suddenly. "Let's hurry, Jan, please hurry." And she began to run, leaving him to stare after her. Then he chased her, running slowly, panting.

"Hey, Linda!" he called, waving one hand over his head. "Hey, Linda, your ring!"

"You won, I lost, remember?" she shouted back over her shoulder.

"But . . ." He tried to increase his speed and nearly tripped over a broken shell. "But Linda, the thing was rigged. The damn game was crooked!"

"I know," she laughed, and fell . . . and the wheel rolled colorfully through the dome, blinking red yellow blue and all the people were smiling; and when Jan picked her up and carried her, they could smell the cotton candy.

NAKED AND AFRAID

I GO

LAST NIGHT I dreamed I took a grain of dirt and examined it with a super microscope. I could see a cell in the dirt. The chromosomes lay in a pattern that tapered to two familiar designs—XX. The earth was female. I screamed, I screamed, I screamed.

She looked miserable, so I didn't laugh, merely told her she was in a fine state of health and that the pregnancy should be a breeze. Her name was Rose Willis and she wasn't one of my regular patients. She was attractive and young and probably worked as hard as any of us when she wasn't marching up and down Main Street with the man-haters. I showed her no reaction when she sat up on the examination table and called me a chauvinist pig stud.

Mean, mad and terrified, that's what she was, and if it hadn't been for the last part I would have matched her with the other two. As it was, I didn't want her to leave while she felt so low. She was no infant, about twenty-one or two, but right then she looked as if she had been hit with a battle-ax.

Broke and hungry and afraid, she stayed to talk, rested on the table and told me things I didn't believe. She said I was the fifth doctor she had seen, that none of the others would X-ray her to locate the tumor. They had told her the same thing I did—she had a growth, but it wasn't the kind that would kill her. Would I X-ray her? Somebody had to do it, she said, and no matter what it turned out to be she would feel better just knowing.

I had the idea that without more evidence she would go on refusing to acknowledge her condition. Not that it would have mattered in the long run; she wouldn't be able to lie to herself after she started to show. She seemed to be a decent person, a bit secretive yet somehow disarming, and she was very confused. It would be no strain on my time to give her the added proof of an X-ray, since two of my afternoon appointments had canceled. Besides, I was curious. Afflicted with humanity's most common malady, she behaved as if she had been created immune. Still, she was a stranger and could be

159

mentally unbalanced. Girls became pregnant every day, and this one had no business bullying me into doing something so unnecessary. Well, not exactly bullying. Converting was a better word. She just wouldn't quit, and before she finally ran out of breath I was halfway convinced that she was eaten up by tumors.

So I took the picture and it turned out to be what I'd said in the first place. The presence of the fetus made argument redundant. She was, in her own words, "knocked up," and I was a slightly disappointed medic.

More confused and tense than ever, Rose Willis wouldn't go away. She warmed the examination table and bent my ear for another hour. What I heard was a not too unfamiliar story. She hated men, but it was a superficial hatred. The group got their hooks in her when she was fifteen, and since she had nothing else to do, she went along with them. Not all that she did was phony. Plenty of things made her indignant, but this wouldn't stop her from getting married eventually and she said as much to a friend. The friend squealed and the group put her in isolation for a month.

"Nothing like that really works on us," she told me. "We think what we want to think. If I make up my mind to be reasonable I can figure out almost anything. I could be a nymph or a fag or an iceberg but it would never touch the real me. I'm way inside looking out, and someday I'll see what I want. When I do see it I'll go after it. Duty is a pain in the ass. Once I make up my mind that it's worth it, fine, then I'm a dandy lackey, but it really depends on how much static is threatening. I bide my time when it looks like it'll be too much to handle. You pig studs think we're soft, or you think we're like you. You just don't know."

She had a lot more than that to say, but when I remained patiently noncommittal she finally gave up, finally stopped trying to convince me. Slumping back on the table in exhaustion, she gave me a bitter scrutiny. I didn't believe the main point in her argument and she was too tired to say any more. From the instant she walked into my office she had insisted that I explain to her how she could be pregnant and a virgin. Someone else would have to help her there. Emotional problems were out of my domain.

What I did for her was pull some strings and get her admitted free of charge to a good nursing home. The last time I saw her she thanked me and gave me a wry smile and called me a chauvinist pig stud. Rose Willis. She had conquered the enemy and the spoils were hers.

In a few days I forgot her.

There were only four doctors in our clinic and we were thick as thieves, had been friends since med school. Tad Fraser was a genius who bullied the rest of us, told us which days we'd donate ourselves to the poor, told us when we'd have vacations, even told us how to handle our wives. We let him get away with it because he usually knew what he was talking about. Jim Thorne was a crewcut man; everything worthwhile could be had only by conforming. I don't know if he really believed this, but he said he did. Wally Cohen and I worked our cans off and were grateful for anything good that came our way.

Fraser was upset because his wife was pregnant. She had been a real slob, weighed nearly two hundred before he made her spend six months at a reducing farm. Three weeks ago she had come home in good humor and looking unrecognizably svelte, and then she dropped the bomb by mentioning that her factory must be out of kilter because she had missed two periods.

You could get an ovum by running a Wellman hose into a Fallopian tube and irritating the ovary. Polly Fraser spent a few days screaming the house down, then she showed up at the clinic and demanded to be examined by all four of us. Fraser threw her out but she was back the next day. Fluently profane, she let it be known that there was something wrong with her factory, not her morals, and that she was ready to shell out a hundred eggs to prove it. Fraser threw her out again so she went to the experimental lab at the University on the other side of town and offered to sell them two dozen ova at the going rate. The staff collected the ova, after which Polly stole the receptacles and brought them back to the clinic. She dumped them in Fraser's lap and told him he would either examine them or she would get all her friends and boycott the place.

I don't think she expected anything to come of what she did. She was scared and disoriented and acted on impulse. What she knew about anatomy would have fit inside a thimble, but desperation had made her grab at straws. No doubt she remembered Fraser's favorite saying, that a woman was a pawn of her cycle and everything she did was inspired by it.

"I don't know what this is going to prove," Fraser snarled

at us as he prepared to run tests. "Why doesn't she just tell me and get it over with? She knows I wouldn't divorce her if she banged a dozen guys. I might kill her but I wouldn't divorce her. Now she says if I don't tell her how a woman can get pregnant without a man she'll find six doctors who will. That's all I need, her opening her big yap and telling everyone she cuckolded me."

"No offense," said Thorne, "but why don't you abort her?"

"Dammit, because she says any woman who knocks herself up would be a damned fool to get rid of it."

Then was when I thought of the girl who had come to me a year ago. Rose Willis had said almost exactly the same thing.

How could Polly's baby girl look so little like her?

We thought we knew so much about sex cells. The crossing of genes in an ovum fertilized by a sperm resulted in a child who possessed characteristics of both parents. This was supposed to be all there was to it.

Polly's child developed from an ovum that had a full set of chromosomes. Of the two dozen ova, three had proved to be mutated. The genes in these three were strung out on the chromosomes in tiers or layers, huge numbers of them, and crossing seemed to take place spontaneously. This crossing was not confined within a single tier. All layers appeared to be involved, which indicated that nature was tapping an almost infinite supply of human traits. This was why Polly's child did not resemble her except in a most superficial way. Gene crossing normally took place within a single layer, and this layer represented traits of the mother and father. Crossing in a mutated cell involved traits that conceivably represented the mother's entire lineage. Polly's child was, literally, a haphazard (so it seemed to us) product of an unknown number of parents.

Despite what the experts said about the minute statistical chance of a mutation turning out well, Polly's daughter was big and alert and in perfect health. Her cells were complete and they carried the mutation.

There was something else. A sperm couldn't fertilize a mutated ovum. Polly continued producing ordinary ova, in fact most were normal, but the others remained aloof to sperm and, indeed, defied detailed explanation. We hadn't discovered, for instance, why one mutated ovum began to develop embryonically while others didn't.

A pack of the Libs marched in the street.

Fraser was frightened. His deep voice left him that day as he pulled back the curtain window to look down at the women, and it never returned. Always after that he spoke in a hoarse whisper.

"Say that again," he said, and Thorne repeated himself.

"Suppose there's a trigger that has been in them since the beginning? Call it a defense mechanism. It activates when the species is threatened, or when they finally raise their heads and gaze over the stack of diapers, or when some part of their brains develops, or when we've done enough conquering and we aren't essential anymore, or maybe their marching is doing it, or it could be nothing more than an emotion which has been pretty alien to them—united rage."

Fraser seemed to grow weaker. Leaning against the sill, he stared at the street as if a monster were there, searching for a sign of life.

"Why not?" said Thorne.

"It sounds unscientific," I said, and for a moment I thought Fraser was going to come over and hit me.

"You have to admit that this is the first time in history they've ever been united in anything," said Thorne.

"We've kept them quiet," Wally said. "Isn't that what we've done? Barefoot and pregnant? I mean, never before have so many of them been enraged at the same time."

"United in rage?" Fraser's eyes were wide open and staring, but he saw nothing in his line of vision. I knew he was looking at specters.

Pregnant virgins had to be showing up in other parts of the world. We had waited to see what would happen. Weeks went by but there wasn't a whisper of it in the newspapers. The medical journals poured in and we learned that the abortion rate was rapidly increasing. The answer was plain. Medics were keeping the lid down tight and women were taking the fastest available solution.

Was I ever afraid of women? Had I always been afraid of them? There were so many who made me laugh, or who annoyed me, or who disgusted me. I remember boarding a bus behind one, and we stood on the steps for a moment, waiting for those ahead to get inside, and I was shocked at the size of her can. I had forgotten all about the Conspiracy and simply stood on the step staring at the awesome human rear at my eye level. My first sensation was, as I said, shock, and then came amusement, and then I told myself that their rears were bigger than ours because they had that all-important function, and then the sickness of remembering made me nearly lose my balance.

I met women who impressed me. The old ones seldom failed to do that. They looked at me and their eyes said, "But for the grace, you would be my son."

The young women looked at me and their eyes said, "Whence and whither?"

I remember Wally saying to me once, "I envy the lion. He has an easy life. She does all the work and he sleeps and makes love."

It was a few weeks after the Conspiracy had been organized that Jim Thorne said to me, "I keep thinking of fleas. The dog keeps them safe and warm and fed while they torment him. Then one day the fleas jump off his back and go away to build themselves a house. He watches them go and all of a sudden he drops dead. They were the only reason he was alive."

Later I met Wally at JoJo's and we had a beer. "I'm hearing things these days," he said. "Sometimes out of a clear blue silence I hear swords clashing, bugles blowing, horses snorting. Not loudly, just echoes, as if they're coming from the other side of the world. Sometimes I hear other sounds, but mostly it's war. We were so good at that. I'm terrified when I hear those echoes, but I feel something else at the same time. My heart begins to pop and my legs twitch as if they're eager to mount up and ride."

People like Fraser were apprehensive by nature. They invented fear when they had nothing to be afraid of. Let something really frightening come along and Fraser's kind went off half-cocked but with a lengthy, logical-sounding argument to justify their behavior.

The committee was made up of fifty medical men, all from our area. Our intent was to maintain the status quo of silence at least until we could find out what was causing the mutation. Of course Fraser wasn't the only one who was insane those days. What we should have done was publicize the situation, but none of us thought of that.

A particular group of Libs that prowled the streets near the clinic consisted of young married women who were all known to us. In fact, any one of them might show up at any time in one of our offices as a patient. They were a vocal group and had succeeded in getting just about everything they demanded from the local government. Now they were protesting because other groups weren't getting the same kind of satisfaction. Fraser came out with the news that none of the women in this group were pregnant. In this he was correct, but the conclusions he went on to draw were purely insane. Or so I thought.

He convinced the committee that the mutations were occurring only in Libs and that when the Libs were given what they demanded, their cells didn't mutate. I don't know how many committee members even half-believed this but nobody slapped Fraser down, and from then on the Conspiracy included the sanctioning of almost anything a member felt like doing. Primarily we were supposed to become dedicated ass-kissers. The Libs were to be given everything they wanted, and any politician who ignored the committee would find himself out of a job or worse.

Wally complained. "I can't take this seriously. I can't remember when I've heard grown men discuss such a stupid subject."

"What's stupid about it?" said Fraser.

"There are only fifty of us. How can you expect us to make all women contented?"

"We'll do it a town at a time. First we make it work here, then the process spreads."

"My God, do you realize how long that will take?" said Wally. "If it works?"

"You dumb clod, this has to be an immortal project or no project at all. Don't sit there and whine to me that you'll be dead in a few decades. What do I care about you? You'll work on this for the rest of your life, the same as all of us, and long before we're gone, the new generation of men will be hard at it."

"Don't you see that it can't possibly work?"

"What do you want us to do, give up without trying? Even if we're lucky enough to stabilize the situation for the time being, it won't stay that way. Nature is pruning us out. From now on every time some female over the age of twelve decides that she's getting the short end of the stick, she's likely to start mutating. Dammit, don't tell me it sounds unscientific. What the hell is scientific about life? Name one thing."

"The enemy is exactly what?" said Wally.

Fraser gave him another black look. "The pituitary? The ovaries? We'll find out sooner or later. There's a switch somewhere, that much we know, and it also looks as if the switch is automatically flipped when a bunch of them gets mad enough to march. So far every one of our patients has been from a frustrated Lib group."

Said Thorne, "We'll have to move carefully to set up establishments off limits to them. We needed batch bars before but, Lord, they're absolutely essential now. Men are going to go out of their heads if they can't get away from them."

I said, "Maybe we needed those places because of the courage we gave each other."

"Why don't you go to hell?" said Wally.

Fraser jumped up from his chair and started pacing. "He didn't say anything off base. But it was more because we needed to let down our hair. Goddamn, we carried the world while half the species was outside of things. Right?"

Wally shook his head. "I never went to batch parties or bars. Practically everything I did was done with my wife. I lived in two worlds. One was work, the other was living, and I'd have dumped the first any time I could."

"To them you're a chauvinist pig stud," Fraser told him.

Never did I have more than a momentary urge to kill anyone. The old defense mechanisms always leaped to the fore and smothered the desire. Such mechanisms were a protection, a wall, an obstacle that had to exist, because if I had obeyed the urge I would have had to acknowledge that the step I'd taken from the cave was imaginary. To dwell in twilight is the destiny of man. Will those damned fleas hop off and go build a house?

Now I have an urge to kill and it isn't momentary but is with me day and night, and the defense mechanisms regard it with indifference. I want to kill my mother, not the bewildered flesh who gave me body, but the other one who said to me thousands of years ago, "You think, therefore you are; go now and conquer."

She is an infidel. She told me she loved me, but she never said she loved another more.

Wally and I were alone together for a few minutes before a meeting, and he said, "I'm highly offended by the whole idea, and I tell myself I shouldn't be. Objectively speaking, what everyone really wants is for the race to continue, right? What does it matter to us what the man of the thirtieth or sixtieth century looks like, so long as he isn't a monstrosity? Our egos have been shafted, almost the same as they would be if we found out the man of tomorrow was going to be black or Oriental. No matter how you look at it, we're mostly sitting on our heads and thinking with our asses."

Thorne came, then Fraser, and we sat for a while and looked at each other. Fraser was bitter and blunt. "We even opened up the solar system for them," he said. "Do you suppose that had something to do with the switch flipping? Look at all the machines they'll have to help them. Oh, you can bet they won't have too many wars. I always said they were different from us."

"You know what always bothered me?" Jim Thorne said. "I liked to see them primping or playing bridge or cutting one another, but I got uneasy when I saw them talking quietly."

Wally sat looking bewildered. "We loved them. My wife . . . they were wrong when they said it was only sex. There were some, sure, but my wife is different. That house is her, and I'm full of her and she's so much my world . . . I wouldn't exist without her . . . oh, God, I mean what's the purpose? What kind of human being is it that has no mate?"

Said Thorne, "More and more I think of the differences between us. Out loud I agreed with a lot of the bull, but, honest to God, privately I thought we were all one thing. Now, well, how are we different?"

"What makes you think sex requires two partners?" said Fraser thoughtfully, and we looked at him in disgust. "Go to hell," he said.

"What is really awful is that they don't know it's happening," said Wally. He stared at Fraser. "You like killing them, don't you? You're a sonofabitch. That poor woman you put to sleep like a damned cat the other day didn't know what was going on. Don't tell me it was her or us. I'm not willing to equate my life with a horde of helpless girls who are as much a product of nature as I am."

"You'd better get busy and do the same thing yourself. And the babies, too. They aren't human. Just keep telling yourself that."

"I keep telling myself that we're a bunch of murderers," said Wally. "I'm convinced that we'd be better off if we publicized it. After it's out in the open we can have every scientist in the world working on it. And that's exactly what I'm going to tell the committee when we go in there. They had better listen."

Could the Conspiracy endure? They said it could. They

promised me that it was possible, that we would find the solution. The mind of man was easily dedicated, they said.

I would have warned Wally if I'd had the chance. I would have told him not to trust Fraser. I knew only too well how much Fraser had changed. Long before the killing started, I had tried to back out. Fraser hadn't said much after I spilled everything I thought and felt. All he had done was look at me, then he had said, "This is a crusade. Every man who drops out shoves the rest of us that much closer to the cliff." I got the message. In, I stayed alive. Out, I didn't.

I loved Wally like a brother. No really. That's a remark the conditioners say is okay and proper. I delighted in Wally's being. I won't say he was a friend or a pal or my best buddy. Lately I've begun to see things in a clear light. To hell with them all, I loved Wally, period.

This week I delivered twenty babies. One was a boy. I held him, cherished him, grieved. How could She do this to him?

Last night the committee executed Fraser. It was their last official act before they dispersed. He had been so vehement about keeping the silence, had talked so long and earnestly about how the women would view this as the supreme victory and how they would interfere with our trying to find a cure. Fraser had been wrong and they killed him.

There were too many female medics and scientists, and the whole thing suddenly blew wide open. It didn't matter. The chances of our having found a solution had been very, very small and we ought to have realized it. Maybe we did. Maybe we knew. The felled giant may have had to be bludgeoned a few more times before he got the message. Anyhow, the human race fought its last big war in a quaint little place called ovaries. There was no bloodshed to speak of.

Charlotte gave birth this morning.

"Do you want me to kill it?"

I stood beside the bed and looked down at her. This was what Fraser couldn't understand. He had refused to believe they would be willing to go to any lengths because of love. They would even murder their own children, knowing full well that it would serve no practical purpose, simply to let us know how much we meant to them.

With tears in my eyes, I said, "That's a beautiful healthy baby and I hope she lives to be a hundred."

"I don't give a damn what my grandchildren a thousand

years from now will be like, or what they'll be doing," she said.

We were all in it together. The men and women of the world were united in fear. For the first time in history no one looked to their children for a better future.

"Did you kill any women or babies?" she said.

I lied and said yes. There were many demented souls who had killed. I allied myself with them without hesitation. I always was a pushover for lost causes.

My daughters look like my mother. So do I. My father resembled his father, and that used to please me until I saw a photograph of grandfather's mother. Everywhere I turned I saw women.

A computer might have said Nature's plan was sensible. That is a word I always viewed with wariness. Subconsciously I may have suspected the truth all along. A thing is born and it is weak and unformed. The Maker knows this thing will be worthy one day (another suspect word, "worthy"; beauty is in the eye of the beholder; I wonder if She is myopic). Anyway, this thing must endure until it can stand alone. A helpmeet is what is needed. Pfft. There he is.

I feel as if I'm Everyman. I worked so damned hard, knocked myself out, turned up my toes early while the ballbusters continued. I made war, but I don't know why. I seemed to exist on a high-tension wire while the ballbusters lazed and got fat. At times I was an aberration, in which case I would seek out a woman alone and then I'd open my overcoat and show her my nakedness. Or I'd rape. Or I'd beat.

I refute the above. I haven't done those things. The idiots, the depraved, are the guilty, and I'm ashamed that we're related.

Never once did I imagine that I, Everyman, my sum total, might be an aberration.

Often at night I get up and turn on the lamp. I sit on my bed and watch Charlotte sleep. In adjoining rooms the girls snore. They frequently have nightmares, which makes me wonder. Do they dream more than we? Charlotte has a habit of going to bed early. She doesn't mess the bed by tossing and turning. Usually she sleeps on her back with the covers tucked under her chin. She looks like a papoose or a cocoon. Someday the adult will emerge from under the covers. Will it be a great deal like this woman or will it be different?

Thousands of women are coming to hospitals and clinics for abortions. This will solve nothing and they know it, but they do it anyway. This afternoon a big ugly fag threw her arms around my neck and cried. Little ones sit on curbs and watch with sad eyes. Rarely do I go out but that a group of women gathers and silently follows me. Teen-agers come up to me and stare. They look so stunned.

Jim Thorne is cracking. He bought a rifle and in the evenings he stands by his upstairs window and draws a bead on every women who passes by. So far he hasn't pulled the trigger.

I've been going to visit my mother a great deal. I sit on the floor beside her rocking chair and rest my head in her lap. She fondles my hair, and sometimes she weeps and tells me everything will be all right. I feel at peace with her. Like me, she is a thing of the past. Life, time, have abandoned both of us. For neither the son-lover nor the son will there be a tomorrow.

I stand in the middle of my house and listen to the darkness. It is all around me. Outside a low breeze sweeps along the street. I'm cold.

Grace Rooney

TEETH

THOUGH I AM not a finicky eater, there are certain foods I do not like to eat in public. The sandwich, for example, embarrasses me because I cannot resolve the issue of how gracefully to dispose of that final corner. Usually I just pop it into my mouth after glancing over the area; this is done with practiced casualness.

Four months ago I had the added misfortune of sharing my table with an ingenuous-looking, curly-headed lad, whose eyes were directed toward observing me ingest my food. For days he stared at my mouth with fixity. As a result, I rescheduled my meals to allow me, instead of my regular lunch at twelve, a snack, the neatest and least obtrusive being one quart of milk, sipped through a short, narrow straw. I was then comfortable in his presence. But I noticed one disadvantage: since my entire mouth was not engaged in eating, he assumed I would be interested in speaking with him.

"Excuse me, sir," he said, "your teeth have a particularly glossy whiteness. Calcium deposits, of course," he remarked, "if they're real. Are they?"

"Certainly. I have always taken assiduous care of my teeth."

After I said that, I pressed my tongue over the surface of each tooth and presented a glossier, whiter set.

He responded. "Ah, yes, I can see that."

Since he had an annoying habit of unfurling his fingers in front of his mouth while speaking, I asked if he would repeat what he'd said.

"Of course," he answered, "I said, 'Ah, yes, I can see that.' "

171

His lips hardly parted, and the words were squeezed out with much effort.

"You must be wondering why I'm concerned about your teeth," he offered, flushing at his urgent need to explain.

"What?" (Sometimes I imagine that the fact of my beautiful teeth is related to the fact that I am slightly deaf. Psychologists acknowledge compensatory phenomena in the world of emotion, and one seeks analogies in all realms, especially if he is interested, as I am, in the Universal Oneness Hypothesis.)

He reiterated, adding that he is an avid student of orthodonture who delights in perfect teeth. Before he had time to explicate, I interrupted him with a basic tenet of the U. O. Hypothesis.

"Isn't it remarkable that Imperfection superimposes Perfection on all it knows, thereby judging according to what it can't know?" I extended my hand across the table as if passing him a microphone. He reacted as if I had.

"Well, teeth, when perfect, are naturally white, undefiled units, thirty-two . . . in two rows . . . in one mouth. We know that as perfection . . . in teeth."

Giving him the complete white effect, I interjected goodnaturedly, "Or the least imperfection . . . in teeth."

"*Your* teeth are the most beautiful I've ever seen," he emphasized, "and for a man your age . . . why . . . enjoying them, I've been unable to eat. I don't suppose you have any cavities, no fillings either, I bet."

"From overindulging in sweets, I have one surface filling in my wisdom tooth. It's gold. Look."

He leaned heavily on the table and scrutinized my gold filling. Then, like one in ectasy, he lowered his eyelids and scanned all of the teeth. If my jaw had not tired, I'm certain, he would have stayed longer, marveling at their perfection.

For a short interval, neither of us spoke; the silence bound us.

"I wouldn't mind exhibiting them," I said. This delighted him so much that I suggested he take photographs of my mouth's interior and perhaps X rays of individual teeth. I made an appointment with him for the next morning at his studio and he left me, both of us in good humor.

Before starting for his apartment, I brushed my teeth three times: first with Cow Brand baking soda and then, twice with Dresh, the ADA-approved paste. Thereupon I left my rooms, locking the door and placing the key under the welcome mat.

On the street a gray mottled tomcat leaped from the garbage heap to my side. His eyes were a violent shade of aquamarine, the parenthetical pupil bulging manlike at the center. Though of different Families, we were after all of the same Kingdom, Order, and Class; I allowed the encroachment. The cat, nevertheless, disturbed by the finer distinctions between us, deserted me at the end of the block.

From there, a bus transported me to the student's living quarters.

"Ah, I am so glad to see you again." He directed his greeting to my teeth and admitted me. Directly opposite the door was one window. In its scant light I discerned the skeletal framework of his studio-home. One flat cot, wrapped in an army blanket, jutted from beneath the windowsill. A human skull rested innocently on the bare kitchenette table. Tools, an aluminum flashlight, chisel and hammer, were strewn about the floor. Illuminating the exposed light bulb protruding from the low, ribbed ceiling, he revealed the room's full starkness. Color was concentrated in reproductions of healthy, decaying, or corroded dentures. To evoke further images of corrosion, he had used yellow and orange crayons. I was unnerved. Where were his books, his signs of practice—the chalk pieces, fine carving knives? How could he study under these conditions: dismal, ill-lit, cold?

"Please make yourself comfortable," he said. Unfolding a chair from which had been scratched the name of a funeral home, he settled it beneath the light.

"Thank you," I stammered. "May I have a glass of water?"

"Would you prefer a shot of whiskey with it?" he asked.

Hoping that it would settle my nerves, I accepted. My eyes followed him to the peeling doors of the cabinet above the table. From it he removed a pint of whiskey and one shot glass. After measuring out full capacity, he emptied the whiskey into a six-ounce cheese glass, added water, and brought the drink to me.

"Won't you join me?" I asked.

Rubbing his nose with the palm of his hand, he answered that he didn't care to drink in the morning, yet I thought I had detected liquor on his breath when he met me at the door. The whiskey had an acrid taste. I gulped it down and he offered me another. Since I was still disturbed, I accepted.

After two more drinks, I felt warmer, more relaxed.

"My dear young man, how can you survive under these conditions? You must need many things. Have you enough to eat?" I was beginning to feel paternal toward him and concerned myself with means of assisting him. "Have you a position?"

"I'm a student . . . that's my sole job at the moment. A student needs his mind and sources of stimulation. Presently you intrigue me and serve, as it were, as a text."

I could understand that the reality of perfect teeth was more satisfying than a text's substitutions. Truly I was warmly disposed toward him. How he flattered my teeth, how I revealed more and more of them, laughing open-mouthed at inappropriate times, exposing even the gums. But what harm could mutual enjoyment bring? Suddenly I was struck by a peculiar oversight: I had never seen his teeth. Moving closer, I raised my eyes to his face and waited for him to speak. He whirled to the window.

"I feel you don't like my way of living. You think I should be ashamed of this room. Is that it?"

Patting his arm, I soothed, "Why, no, not at all. The important matter is that you appreciate your rooms. Allow no one to insult you in this way."

For the first time he smiled at me. Too late did his hand pounce upon his lips. Horrendous sight. Grotesque image. He had no teeth. None. And his gums were ragged red bits of flesh. I was horrified. Still he smiled, unabashed.

"I see you're appalled that I'm without teeth, because my gums are destroyed, because there's no hope of inserting false teeth. Your reaction's natural; it's an ugly sight."

His statement lessened the condition's importance. I intervened with a comforting maxim derived from the U.O. eschatology: "The amoeba is toothless and he lives." But the student sneered, air gasping from his nostrils.

"Now you can understand why I'm consumed with the beauty of your teeth."

"Yes, that is obvious." In my mind, I compared it to substitution. "Normally one would be concerned with his own teeth. In your case it's only natural that you be engrossed with another's teeth."

"It's not that exactly," he interjected. "I'm only interested in the most beautiful teeth. For years I've searched through mouths." His eyes were transfixed. "Two months ago I thought I'd found the perfect set in a young woman's mouth. They were dentures. Besides, she had halitosis. I was about to give up when I met you."

Concluding, he became excited and grabbed my arm.

"But what can you hope to gain from studying my teeth?" I asked.

He told me that he'd pretend they were his. That is, he planned to care for them, ask questions about them, in effect, know them better than I did.

"As far as I am concerned, you may do that if you like. Teeth can be tiresome. Sometimes I wish I had none," I added, more to be kind than anything else. "Just sometimes, when I'm weary of caring for them."

Since that first day in his room, I had endured interminable gnawing investigations by him. What a grueling business it was. He spent hours probing my mouth. He'd purchased tooth powders, tubes of paste, bottles of mouthwash, and jars of cocoa butter. Perpetually he begged that I brush my teeth before him and distort my face into many possible expressions: grimacing, laughing, crying, grinning, smiling, gasping, etc. He was fascinated by the teeth's effect, peeking through the emotional contortions of my lips.

Often I had been tempted to skip visits with him, but somehow I was bound to his attention. For the past month, sensing that I was losing interest in such gymnastics, he bribed me with that same acrid-tasting whiskey. I became so disgusted with teeth that I no longer looked at them in the mirror. He was the only person who saw them. All he did was praise them. It was sickening.

Yesterday I decided not to see him and, retracing former habits, returned to the table where I'd first encountered him. Soon two young girls sat with me. For a while I was oblivious of them, and then I began to sense their eyes on me or, rather, on my mouth. I couldn't stand it.

"Yes, I know that I have beautiful teeth. You needn't bother to tell me. I know I have beautiful teeth. I know all about it, thank you." With that, I hurried away, not having finished eating.

Outside, I looked at them through the window; they were jubilant. Stupidly, I stuck my tongue out. As I was doing this, my eyes caught my reflection in the windowpane; I noticed that my teeth appeared dimmer. Uncontrollably, I slipped back into the building, pushing through the noon-hour crowd to the men's room.

A bald black attendant was sweeping the floor with a small broom and shovel. While he bent over, I gazed into the mirror, spreading my mouth wide to see my teeth. What I saw were not my teeth. My teeth were white. These were yellow, like the photographs of corroded teeth I'd seen in the young student's room. Black pits opened between almost every tooth. My gums were scarred and blood-clotted. Parts of the teeth had chipped away. I was confused. He said he wanted to care for my teeth. Suddenly I could see him, his face radiant as he worked in my mouth, wreaking his devastation. I hurried to his room.

"Come in," he said, pink-faced, happier than I had ever known him to be. "Though you're a bit late, I expected you."

"Why did you do this to me? Why?" I shouted, hands reaching for him. He grabbed my wrists.

I was almost crying. "You said you loved beautiful teeth . . . my teeth . . ." I was stammering, my body weaving before him.

"Ah, but I do," he said, as if he were a teacher clarifying some obscure point for a dull boy. And then he began laughing maniacally. "Look—look." He pointed to his gaping mouth. There I saw, glittering and unsullied, a row of teeth as wondrous as my own had been.

"You've served me well," he said, and patted my arm. "I herewith bequeath you a maxim for your philosophy: In the universe where matter is neither created nor destroyed, know you from experience that it is simply redistributed."

His demonic laughter followed me to the door.

Steve Chapman

TROIKA

THE WOMAN walked a hundred yards behind the other two, her white sneakers shoveling at the white gravel. Not because she couldn't keep up, and certainly not as a gesture of servility. Just so she'd have the other two to look at, something to see besides the plain of gravel with its spattering of lichen rippling behind the ocean of heat.

Years ago they'd fixed on a pace that suited all three of them. They were engrained with it—hindbrain, fuel pump, and lumbar reflexes. For the brontosaur, it was a lumbering trudge. For the jeep, a low-torque second gear that kicked up little dust eddies. For the woman, a brisk walk.

Of course they could have gone faster if the woman had climbed onto the jeep's photopanels or straddled the brontosaur's neck. But riding just encouraged paranoid agression in the x mind and sensory deprivation coma in y. x was in the woman's head today. And of course they were in no hurry. Hadn't been for years.

Just like the sand caught in her shoes, x in the woman felt the steady buildup of smugness from y in the jeep, the longer x stayed in the favored position, the rear. x fed his optic input through the hostility matrix left over from his military programming, but x couldn't make the jeep look bad. Free association: cliche mode: It's hard to hate your home. His hate locked and ground behind the woman's orange wire rims.

177

The brontosaur picked up on the tension and flexed its neck, looking back, scraping loose scraps of the lichen that slept in the furrows of its cracked, dull hide. Years of sandstorms had weathered its sleek skin into rutted leather that bagged at the shoulders and haunches.

The woman's steps had a counter-rhythm in the brontosaur's slow trot. Where gravel made bad footing, it reared up and almost scrambled. *Nothing stranger*, subverbalized x, *than a swamp lizard out on the flatlands.* Perhaps not. x remembered the same thought from years ago.

The jeep's time signature was random. Occasional downshifting, sliding down a slope. No use made of the six-wheel drive. Just like y not to care.

x wanted back into the circuitry of the jeep. Handsome machine. Sandblasting had only brightened its chrome. The woman squinted at the glare behind her sidescreen glasses. x hallucinated extensions of the planes of the jeep's body into a mechanical drawing in blueprint. x was getting a knack for visions. Something for a thinking machine to be proud of. When they were all rescued, x would be an object for study. Something to do with the storms, no doubt. Something about the weather. Just so long as he didn't pick up any more of y's traits.

x tucked the woman's hands into the armpits of her coveralls. The wet heat made her forearms feel cooler. x remembered enjoying the sensation some time ago. Forearms: by hinges on upper arms by ball and socket on torso. Receptors for heat, cold, contact, pressure . . . Interrupt. Not worth reviewing, really. Temporary accommodations.

During the next hour, the woman caught up with the jeep. She leaned down to the sound pickup by the headlight and said, "I shift." By this x meant, "Years ago, when we started, I was the jeep. Not you. I don't want you ripping up my transmission, not bothering to use third. Or would you rather pretend we all hold equal claim on these bodies we share? It's not *my* sanity, you dumb cunt. I shift."

The brontosaur's heavy eyelids tensed against a dusty breeze. Its bony pumpkin head, where the o mind often lived, craned over behind the curve of the woman's shoulder and whispered through teeth like a pebble garden, "Soon." By this o meant, "Settle your minds. Do not argue. Do not say things. There is so little left to say. The suns are both low. We will go a little farther, as far as the sand I can see now when I stretch up my dark old tunnel, my neck. Then we will grow close and wait for the mindstorm to rip x y o from jeep and woman and lizard. The storm is soon." o was limited to the grating frequencies of the jeep's speaker. And when o was in the woman, she would lie on a lake of lichen, and her hands would dance like ghosts of starfish.

The jeep whined and kicked into third gear. The speaker rasped. "How long, o?"

Just like y to make a fuss. Just like y to cause trouble. I will stick to this mind wherever it goes. I will not love either of you. That is how to survive closeness. That avoids confusion.

Where the orange sand lapped up to a shore of white gravel, the brontosaur stopped and grazed on the spongy lichen. Its feet left shapes like wide leaves that faded as the blue plants sprang back to their stiff ruffles.

x used the woman's knife to scrape new lichen off the jeep's photopanels and started it into a small fire with the solder gun from the toolbox under the jeep's fender. y let low static rumble from the jeep's speaker while she submitted to the grooming.

The brontosaur chomped intricate shreds of blue, green, blue-green.

The speaker buzzed in falsetto. "How much farther from here, Daddy."

A joke. I can even recognize her stupid jokes now.

The speaker broke into shrill squawking. y was trying to cry. Third time today?

"Now," x spat through the woman's pulpy mouth. And x meant, "y has upset herself again. We'll have to huddle for a long time. The more composed we can get, the less pain from the storm. o and x could get along very well without the endless, tireless whimpering of y. I hope the storm drops her into the woman's body. That's where she belongs. That's where she started. And that's where she's *most* unhappy. It's time we huddled. Now."

The woman laid her wet, small-boned torso across the jeep's hood, her cheek pressed to the windshield, close to the computer behind the dash. The dinosaur curled around them, neck and tail coiled over them. His giant green eyes shut tight. Sand trickled down through the wrinkles around his jaws.

The suns shone orange as ever. The wind hissed no louder than ever. All three felt the daily storm close in.

*standard program exceeds octane 18 only when lub—my
brain is a leathery starfish that scratches and scrapes in my
skull—save me let me never come back into any of us—just
like the cunt-brain—time and time and then time—I weep I
tear my hair I beat my breasts—you'll run out of tears you'll
run out of hair your breasts are sagging—we all have time
and time enough—I rip my clothes I bleed I eat my insides—you don't have the guts—time for a dolphin for a
lizard for a cancer for xyo—help me save me no not you or
you no help—we lizard metal breast wheel lip leather who*

x y o the letters once whatever now each other torn loose in
a direction inconceivable as out to a fish in water, sideways
for a jeep, death to a woman.

and all fall clutching without arms or wheels no jaws
into . . .

Wait.

o in brontosaur for the fourth time in a row.

x revs his engine.

y she trembles and gasps. Tears sit quietly on the jeep's
hood in the dusk.

The brontosaur touches the crusty bottom of his chin to the
sandy coveralls on the woman's narrow back. "Peace," o murmured. And o meant, "After so long, it should make no difference. Are you sure that x is right? Do you really think he
remembers where we started, which bodies we started with?
I'll tell you a story. I remember that this lizard is a
reconstruction from extinction. A man-made beast of burden,
cultivated in a vat of nutrient broth. One of a crop of neuter
plough animals. This I remember with my hindbrain. My
forebrain, I remember, was a transplant from a dolphin. I
remember an ocean. Starfish stirring up the sand, turning out
their insides. Fields of brown kelp, swaying, rubbery like lichen. A herd of others like me, close to me but never merging
like xyo. Touch and love, but never complete. Here with time
for completion, we hate. And stay apart. And remember an
ocean. Rocks that touched without knowing. Kelp that slept
without knowing. Starfish that loved without knowing. An
ocean. Have you enjoyed my story? I cannot say I have not
imagined it all. You are such a little thing. You should not
fret."

The orange sand sucked up her tears as she ran away from
them. One of the suns set.

Headlights glaring, the jeep dug in and patched out and

rammed through three gears to run her down, hacking a
laugh-rattle at top volume. His fenders shoved into lizard
flesh. x could never understand the old giant's speed.

"Cancerous bag. Let's see you stick your tail up your
bitch."

The woman held to the brontosaur, kneeling against it,
fingers buried in its bark. She pushed her hand into the rough,
orange sand and rubbed it across her cheek. She bled very little and didn't scratch her glasses. The dinosaur worked up a
bolus of food from its second stomach. The woman chewed it
slowly, pushing her hair out of her face, and rested against
the beast's neck. Finally she took a deep breath and said,
"Parade anyone?"

o smiled weakly, thinking that the extinct face he wore was
ill equipped for smiling. But then, o had picked up many
strange habits on the trip. At times, like the solar-powered
jeep, he was afraid of the dark.

"Yes a parade!" x bellowed with decibels that shook his
speaker grill. "And a speech!" While they marched in the ritual figure eight, x orated. "Yes and yes and yes we represent
here we are a symbol of course for a good reason, explicable,
immense, enormous, the ever onward troika of progress surely
man machine and nature bound into eternity until death us do
in! I thank you."

No, thought o, *we are not important. We are only stranded.*
It is a strange situation but not unusual. No one ever admits
to being one leg of a starfish. As we used to say in school.

She wrapped her arms and legs around o's foreleg, and o
whispered to her another lesson in the Buddhist religion, the
way of acceptance, o's way back to the lizard from the storm,
the lessons which o's keepers taught to the lizards of o's crop
to accommodate them to slavery, because the karma of the
keepers was the wheel of greed. o told y she was part of everything. y arranged ruffles of lichen on the sand and said she
didn't want to be. She said she was a Presbyterian, and she
was sure that God would forgive her for missing so many ser-
vices. They made love in their own way. The lizard did what
it could for her.

"Don't dream," she said and managed a small laugh. y
meant: "Remember when I told you that if you ever had one
of my bad dreams, you'd roll over and crush me?" She tried
to think why it was funny.

o was sleeping.

x never slept.

"And remember how when I carry you on your back when you're in me because I said you said and I knew you meant . . . you know . . . we must be rescued. Or find an oasis. Of some kind. What if they find your tumorous carcass and me smashed and smashed again by six wheels and far away the jeep broke down where my hands weren't there to fix it? They wouldn't even know how far we've come. They'd never know how we came to this! How long! What if we forget how we came to this?"

It was hard for them, and it took a long time.

Dennis Etchison

BLACK SUN

I LIVE on a hill. Tonight the dark came too soon. I was down cutting the grass for the landlady and I came up for a drink of cold water about seven o'clock. The wind started blowing over from the east side of town then. I had to stop by the back door. All of a sudden my face and neck were cool. The wind was from the cemetery. I closed my eyes. It smelled sweet and damp and full of roses.

Inside the house was filling up with blue shadows. Shyla never liked that time of day.

The living room.

Sitting in the rattan rocking chair.

How to tell you? Begin anywhere:

"I think I'll kill myself tonight," she sighs. "There's nothing *else* to do."

I stop long enough to manage a wan smile. "There's always Scrabble. But in a little while. I almost have Series II licked."

"What do they want to know now?"

" 'State the nature of your belief,' " I read from the 150 Form, " '. . . and state whether or not your belief involves duties which are to you superior to those arising from any human relation.' "

"Nosy."

" 'Explain how, when and from whom or from what source you received the training and acquired the belief . . .' "

"I wonder," asks Shyla, "why they don't just ask you to define the universe and give two examples? In twenty-five words or less."

"Don't exaggerate. They give me two whole blank lines here."

I watch her as she shifts her hip and lays her long legs up on the madras coverlet. She has to be moving every other second now; it is the macrobiotics, part of the natural high.

"That's Section III, I believe," I tell her, cracking my cramped knuckles. "You've been through this yourself, haven't you. Don't lie." I lift the typewriter off my knees and stretch my back. "Jeezus. This is worse than that last term paper."

I look over at her. The round rice-paper lantern moving slowly behind her head. She is absorbed. She is filing her nails with a long emery board very carefully, as if playing a rare violin.

"You do remember that weekend," I remind her.

"How could I forget? You, your typewriter, the kitchen table. Thank God you've learned how to type since then. I had to sleep in a chair, at your beck and call."

The bamboo wind chimes are tinkling outside the window.

I pluck off my glasses, rub my eyes and make a truce with myself again for a time.

Trying to get a fix on her through the blur.

"When do you . . . What's his name?"

"Dr. Soeul."

"Ha. With a name like that, he must get more word-of-mouth business than he can handle." I raise my hand. "Don't. I know he comes recommended. I was the one who turned you on to the whole thing, remember? But when do you see him next?"

Her glance has grown needle-sharp now since the diet. "Tomorrow night, seven."

I feel myself moving closer to her.

Her hands fold together like slender, pale fish. "I'm sorry, David. I love you." I see her slip up to her outer level, a silent *click*. "I think we both do," she tries.

My eyes clasp hers and my hands her warm cheeks, and then I bend to kiss her mounding stomach through the cloth. I am aware of my hair again. "What are you worrying about?" she asks as she touches it.

"Nothing."

"The ba—"

"No. Of course not."

She waits a beat. "The CO thing." I start to answer again, but her fingers tighten on my head. "I know it's getting to you." Her tone: strangely serene, as if separate from the words.

"It's nothing."

"Nothing," she says then, "is something inside out."

I have to look up. The dark eyes slip back to that other place. I can't help trying to press deeper into them. . . .

This is one night.

The horror lies in that there is no horror.

I sank back into the dry, distended hand of the chair, the chair crackling, accommodating me. Out somewhere the crickets began to chirp, a sound like the clicking of poker chips.

Rocking. Trying to rock. I held my breath. I couldn't smell then. Or see. I tried not to feel. Only the motion. And the story.

I remembered our first week. My II-S had expired that quarter. The first days of our relationship were like the first bites of a watermelon before you hit a seed. It started at Santa Monica. She was walking out of the sea and the sunlight was firing blinding bolts around her silhouette and I stood transfixed and just watched her come up to meet me. The next day my eyes peeled burned skin. She said she had run away from a place where they wrapped her in wet sheets. When she found out I lived in Silverlake, too, she asked me if I had a car. I told her I didn't and she moved into a new apartment ten miles away just to test me.

I was the one who gave her the book, along with *Albion Moonlight* and *From Bindu to Ojas* and some others. Of course you will blame me, as you should. Naturally. It started with a visit to his office in Little Tokyo; you know the type: Monday night Zen classes served up with brown rice; the following night another course. The regimens. Something. I didn't go. The vigil at the Friends House, a WRL meeting, maybe a counseling session somewhere or hours alone just going over and over my duplicate file. I don't remember.

When she came home I had turned down the bed. Afterward she shook herself like a puppy coming out of sweet grass and smiled around the house and left her hair down the rest of the night. In the morning she woke me to announce that she had dropped something. We searched the floor for her last pill, more valuable than a contact lens—it couldn't be insured. She wished it had been an IUD. Later she tried to drink a bottle of Jergens Lotion while I was out mailing a letter to the Board. "It smelled so good," she said. "Just like burnt almonds!"

After the Form was filed I had to beg the usual collection of "imminent piety" reference letters. Then the reclassification: I-A. No surprise. It did not take long; the Justice Department is no longer involved. Then the appeal. Then the request for a personal appearance. Then the letter requesting an appointment with the government Appeals Agent, a Compozed Larry Blyden impersonator who knew nothing. A formality. I can no longer remember when her thinness first became frightening. Then the personal appearance and the two counselors along as witnesses: refused admittance, of course: one more detail duly noted in case of a court test. The refusal to reopen the classification. Then the appeal to the County Board, where it is said the rubber stamp falls like a blade every eleven seconds. Then the filing of Form 151 with the Local Board, followed by their refusal to reclassify and rewind the appeal procedure for another replay. Then the preinduction physical, follow the colored stripes up and down the stairs and get in line for short-arm inspection. Later the fellow next to me bit his lip and spat blood into the beaker and it almost worked. Then the appeal to State Headquarters. Their reply. Then the letter to the National Director. She spidered her fingers around cups of mu tea, talked rapidly of tests in darkened rooms and small bottles and extractions. Then the first set of induction papers. Then the change of address through a front in San Francisco. Then the flight up to the Local Board there for a transfer of induction—$11.43 each way on PSA. Then the National Director's refusal to intervene. Then the new induction date in Oakland. Then the transfer back down here. Then the letter from the Friends counselor pleading for a new hearing. Then the letter requesting another appointment with the Appeals Agent, adjusting his glasses with sweaty fingers, handshake clammy. Then the new induction date. Then a final transfer back up to the Oakland Induction Center. . . .

Shyla. Shyla. It grew more and more difficult for her. I don't know how it happened. I don't even know what happened to her. Her condition was not enough for a III-S under the new law. For a time I thought of her like the place where I had met her: storms rend the sea but never change its hardness. If anything she seemed to be growing softer, more sensitive. That was good. I thought that.

One night coming home from there like so many other nights.

Looking up and seeing her halfway through the bead curtain.

Her body like one of those starving African children, bloated belly and pencil-thin wrists.

I stand and take her hands. "Hey, your gloves are cold," I tell her.

"I'm not wearing any."

I breathe on her fingers. We sit. After a while I say, "How is . . . ?" The way she looks, I don't want to press it.

"H-he's pleased with my progress. He said so. The examination—"

She creates a little pull at the corners of her pallid mouth but her eyes lid over. Her finger makes a fine tracing around my jawline.

"David," she pronounces. That is enough, I think. Then her lashes fly together and I can feel the strain growing as it draws together in her. It feels something like desperation. "David, let's get out of here." Her eyes open. She is unbelievably sanpaku, I notice, and for some reason, though I know better, much better, I get a cold rush in my chest. "Now. Tonight. We could start fresh—in Mendocino. Anywhere. Oh shit."

"Hey, hey."

I see she is struggling to stay ahead of herself. "I can't have it this way. I want to get out of here, out of LA. We have to, don't you see? This place is some kind of—of necropolis for—for the waiting dead." She shudders, unbelievably.

I have no idea what to say to that.

Then her eyes, flicking between mine, lose some of their depth and withdraw in the manner of a camera iris stopping down, *click*. And I know she has remembered my case and the way its weight has me anchored here.

I take her head in my lap and stroke it. Now there is neither resistance nor consent. . . .

She casts the yarrow stalks. She sits cross-legged, staring as into scattered entrails. She is still for a long time. Then she takes the book down from the shelf and unwraps it and the three coins and throws them, too. I ask her for the reading.

" 'If the bridge is weak at both ends,' " she recites in a dull, emotionless voice, " 'it does not matter what happens in the middle.' "

The hours unravel and I cannot think of a thing but her.

In bed she tosses just outside my arms. Once she sits up.

"*What is that?*" she whispers out of what sounds like terror.

"That?" I try to follow the trajectory of her stare. "That?" I get out of bed, pad to the corner, find a thing, pick it out of the dust. "Well, what do you know?" I turn it over and over. "It's nothing. It's an old pretzel! Ha."

I start to toss it over to her but I am afraid she might scream.

Just before I drop off, I study her face, the flawless line of her nose, her soft lip, her shoulders. I can no longer be sure when she is asleep, awake.

There are marks in the muscle of her upper arm.

I bend closer. Everything is a grainy blue-gray in the near dark. But there they are: tiny specks also dot her face above the eye sockets, her forehead, her temples, her cheekbones. With a shaky finger I tip her head to one side on the pillow. Marks along the tendons of her neck. I wonder how many other marks there are.

Dr. Soeul, I realize, has been practicing—what?

What do they call it?

A fist tightens in my stomach.

She promised that she is seeing an obstetrician as well. I believed her. I was busy.

She is weak. It is more than that. It can be stated simply. Something in Shyla is missing. It has not always been this way.

In the middle of the long night I wake at the sound of her voice close by me.

". . . All cold and clammy and brassy like a mummy's fingers . . . !" Her voice is racing, lost.

"Shyla?"

No answer.

I try to sleep some more. But I keep listening to her dreams. It is as if I need to hear them.

I wonder what happens when the dreaming stops—or goes mad.

Morning and I come out of it to find her on her back staring into the mottled pattern the sun makes on the ceiling.

I kiss her. No response. I feel like a man who has awakened to find himself bound in cement.

I blow the spider web of hair off her forehead. "Sleep okay?"

"For a while I couldn't," she replies. "The moon on the bottom of the bed wouldn't let me."

I blink, resume breathing.

But "I thought I heard a voice calling me," she goes on. "Then in the dark I heard a voice answer, 'yes?' "

I can't even shudder.

Finally I come up with, "Well, I hope you feel better than you did last night. You know—"

"Last night," she says, still staring at the ceiling, the walls, "I felt my brain shaking like jelly. And the water seeping into the ground."

I just look at her.

"It's all right, David," she says. "You understand what's happening, don't you? I'm only coming closer and closer."

"To what?"

"To the far away."

I laugh, tight-lipped. I try to think that it is beautiful to have a woman who knows things she will never tell me. I try. She must know. I have to believe in her. I have to return the belief.

She grew thinner and thinner. I continued to fight my case. The time came. Almost came.

Mostly I remember the shadows of the leaves on the trees covering the walls of the living room in a moving black wash through the glass. Shyla on the couch. This one day she chose the darkening living room. I don't know why.

She wouldn't leave the city without me and I had to be with

the lawyers at the CCCO. And she wouldn't change doctors. I
must have tried and tried. You would think so.

She had been reading a lot of poetry that day. Lastly she
was studying the cold black flaming on the wall. Sun through
leaves. Black centers deeper than the light.

"I need the dark," she says suddenly, settling the squirming
shape behind her almost translucent belly. Her voice is like a
rustling now, her body dotted all over. I haven't left this room
for three days. The file. "Do you know? It gives all . . . and it
takes nothing back!"

Turn from the pane. Start to speak. But see. There is no
longer any Word possible between her and the dark now.

Something quietly leaves the room.

The sun nails black to the wall. . . .

I sat in the chair. There. After cutting the grass. The sun
outside gone away. I don't think I even noticed when it happened. They say it will rain tomorrow. I don't worry about
the weather. I haven't for a long time. The sky has lost control.

This afternoon I burned my draft card. I thought about it a
long time. I read it over and over. Then I knew you can never
decide from the words. Consider the spaces. She taught me
that. I think she did. I squirted it with lighter fluid and
touched a match to it and threw it on the air. It flared to
something black and fell apart. After that I took my file and
scattered it down the hillside.

A little while ago I sat in the chair. Then I got up.

I went down the hill. The place called me. I used to go
there a lot evenings when I was a kid and it was warm and I
was thirsty after helping with the lawn or something.

I wasn't thinking anything. Down the hill. The leaves at the
corner crackled at my heels. I turned around half-expecting to
see myself. Fosselman's was cool neon at the end of the long
block. I thought it looked good.

Went in the store. Too many flavors to pick.

Got in line. There was a girl in front of me with a snowy
streak put in her hair. She turned around and looked at me
and the second time she smiled. But I just turned away. Her
dress enclosed her like a self-addressed envelope. She swept
out with a cone and didn't look back. I noticed her ice cream:
it was almost colorless, sort of a brain-gray.

The counter was stainless steel and plastic frosted over on

the underside. Leaned my palms on it and looked down.

"Double or single?"

"What?"

Mr. Fosselman gave me a look.

"You wanna buy something, or you come here to sprout roots?"

He didn't recognize. The hair, the way I don't care anymore. Maybe he did, maybe he did.

Right then a chill touched my face.

And I knew that I didn't want anything there. I turned and clipped over the waxed linoleum squares, past the wrought-iron chairs, the peppermint shaft and the cardboard boy licking it so patiently.

It was cold outside, but a cold that numbs, without a chill.

I rolled up my sleeves and then threw away my jacket and started east across town, stripping off my shirt, everything as I went, through all the yellow and red lights, stepping on every crack, all the way.

Tomorrow I will find him in among his sharp gold needles and small bottles; I will take them all back from him and I will kill him and read his bloodstains like a Rorschach test and find an answer.

Then I will come back here. They will never find me when they come looking, if they do. I have left everything behind. Maybe I will live here, in the trees and bushes, the lawn and the shadows of the shrubbery, and the headstones. Maybe I will.

William F. Orr

THE MOUTH IS

FOR EATING

LOFDUNS HADN'T eaten for five days, and it would be six more before it had any appetite at all, at least in the strictly physiological sense. But it was hungry. The inner lining of its mouth twitched and contracted impatiently as it paced the small hotel room—ridiculously small for a person used to the spacious chambers of the Ansrals villa—and finally resolved to assuage its appetites. It went to the door and fastened the lock, and then began to search the room for a suitable object.

A melon would have been perfect now, but melons were all but unobtainable on this pygmy colony. Without fruit, without proper meat, it would have to make do. Its eyes moved slowly around the walls of the narrow room, searching, contemplating, discarding. The low mattress was too large; the night-table, although of about the right size, was an impossible shape, with four long, pointed legs, quite unappetizing. Then it spied one of its own bags standing near the closet, round, smooth, and hard, with just a bit of flexibility.

It leaned down and emptied the bag carefully onto the floor, its heart speeding in anticipation. It ran its hands once over the surface of the bag, lifted it, and then cursed the pygmy architects for a band of ulcer-ridden ignorants, as its head banged against the six-meter ceiling. Stooping again, walking slowly to prolong the pleasure, holding back an urge to begin salivating even before entry, Lofduns took the bag to the bathroom and carefully washed it. Air slipped through its wind-hole in rapid spurts, as it set the bag down and unhooked the straps of the muzzle from around its waist.

Now completely naked beside the tub, its soft brown plumage hanging loose about its golden shoulders, Lofduns put its hand over its wind-hole—an unconscious gesture of shame—and looked down at its mouth, a thin cross of two creases in the flesh below its belly. Below that, all but invisible, were the brief slits of the sperm and ovum-holes. But it was the mouth that dominated its attention, its primary lips twitching as the muscles began to relax for opening and insertion.

As it lifted the bag and placed it against its lips, it perversely pictured its Teacher scowling with indignant shock at the sight of its ward "abusing its body," as it would say. But it smiled at its own reluctance to forget the past, with its pablum people and pablum morality, and eased the bag in, through its wide primaries, between the tight secondary lips, and deep into its expanding mouth, where soft tentacles held it close, and began rubbing its morst-hide surface with a slow, rolling motion.

All pablum thoughts were gone, as Lofduns' mind filled with bright, joyous images of hidden cellar rooms, stocked with fresh cuts of meat, huge violet melons, sharp tanya leaves, colmya stalks sprinkled lavishly with contraband rock salt. Its eyes rolled toward the ceiling, its hands hung loose at its sides, and its saliva flowed unchecked around the bag, as it imagined that the mild, musty taste of morst was, instead, the sweet and delicate inner meat of a pantofs melon, raised under the sun and open sky on secret farms in the West, smuggled across the Strait, and bought from an anonymous grocer in some dingy corner by the River. Strong muscles, strengthened by ten circuits of clandestine chewing, rubbing, piercing, and mashing, hugged the bag until its two indented sides nearly met.

Burning air coursed in forceful gulps through Lofduns' open wind-hole, as it held back an urge to go on to the second digestive stage. It had no idea what the juices would do to the morst-hide bag. But it couldn't control itself, or else it wouldn't control itself, and before it could reason out the foolishness of the act the secretions had surrounded the bag and filled its mouth with the tingling, tickling illusion of eating, of food, of hard, living matter giving way under its attack and joining the rhythm of its body, uniting itself to it in a union of strength and wonderful physical warmth.

After it had carefully washed the bag and examined it for damage, Lofduns refilled it, rinsed out its mouth in the tub, and lay down on the mattress to quiet its tense muscles. Its first thought was to assess the damage to the bag's surface and to try to find a reasonable excuse for it, should anybody ask. Then, as often happened at these times, its mind turned to self-recrimination.

Now Lofduns was an enlightened and liberal person, and it knew there was nothing shameful or immoral in what it did. It had learned long ago that the morbid guilt it had once felt over sucking its fingers or holding back its second stage to make the pablum last was only a result of learned reactions from its childhood, and had no basis in science. Notwithstanding, it often felt depressed and uneasy after the act. This had not been the time for it. It would be night soon, and it must save its muscles for the new and alien adventure of this place. Wasn't that, in fact, why Lofduns, considered a person of high moral character by its pablum-spined colleagues, had applied for transfer to a colony in the Terran sphere of influence? And now it was tiring itself a few hours before the first real attempt.

And besides, though the damage to the bag was minimal, it had *known* it shouldn't go on to second stage, but it had gone on anyway. If such a thing were to happen tonight, it would be unspeakably dangerous and cost Lofduns its pleasure, perhaps even its entire career or its life.

But tonight would be different. Tonight would be more relaxed, more easy, more meaningful, and more joyous than all the bags, spices, steaks, and melons of the last ten circuits.

The times were changing, but they were changing slowly. The most optimistic claimed limited legalization would come within five circuits. The most pessimistic said it would never come, and some even enjoyed the thought, finding the pleasure of the act heightened by its extreme danger. And then there were the millions who held back progress with their own fear of the body, who dreaded their bi-weekly trips to the pantry to fill themselves with tasteless pablum, who still spoke of the pablum-man as "the runner" and of eating as "going away."

Such a one had been Lofduns' Teacher, and during the early years of its life in the Ansrals villa it had lived in constant dread and prayed to the God that some way could be found to keep it alive without ever having to go "down there" to fill its ugly belly.

Lofduns whistled through its wind-hole in disgust, and stepped faster along the dark, pygmy street. It would never raise the young assigned to it that way. They would know from the start that the God had meant for them to enjoy eating as naturally as making sperm and ova or any other pleasure of life. The times were changing, but they were changing slowly.

There had been only light foot traffic on the streets, most of it pygmy. But as soon as Lofduns reached the edge of the park it was aware of feverish activity, despite the complete silence of the night. Among the trees, for several meters ahead, it could see brief shadows, both large and small, moving slowly back and forth, in a hypnotic and monotonous dance. They were all out for a walk in the park at night, tracing random but determined paths among the trees. Some were natives of this colony, some had sought it out because of its reputation; some were new like Lofduns, frightened by the tired shades that strolled past them; others were performing an automatic nightly ritual. Some were shy, some bold, some cheerful, some detached, some ready to cry out in pain. Each of them walked alone.

Lofduns knew the Terran language reasonably well, having worked with pygmies in its business, even having become quite close to some of them on a social level. It knew the two types, their faces, their moods, their movements. But as it stepped into the park and let itself be absorbed in the dark dance, it suddenly felt panic at being surrounded by totally alien and unfathomable creatures. Even those of its own race were strangers out of some sick poet's bad dream. They glanced at it quickly, like Wolgons warning an intruder in their fields. It felt sick. It walked on.

Ahead of it was a woman. It could tell she was a woman by the flared cut of her pants, the way her body moved and, when she came closer, by the features of her face. She saw it, stopped, and looked casually in another direction. Lofduns stopped and looked down at her, scarcely seven meters away, an attractive woman, but no real beauty (for Terran standards of physical beauty were not so different from its own). But the light was not good, it was not certain, and besides, she was a woman. Women, the ovum-producing sexual type, were more difficult for a novice, it had been told. And perhaps it had mistaken her intentions. Perhaps she was simply out for a walk and had happened to stop at this particular point and wasn't even aware of its presence. Perhaps it should go on, look for another. Perhaps it should go home and forget this mad idea. Perhaps it should give up the whole business and rejoin the pablum-eating society of its Teacher. But it just stood there, watching her.

She turned and raised her eyes to its, moved them down its face to its wind-hole, down its chest, rested them on the spot where its muzzle would be below its coat, and then looked it straight in the eye with a vague sort of smile on her lips, formed by moving them up at the corners. On her lips. On her mouth. A smile. The very thought of her mouth in the middle of her face, smiling, breathing, and talking, by the God, *talking*, filled Lofduns' whole body with such a thrilling sense of discovery that it could not move for a number of seconds. Then it turned away from her, down a darker path, shaking and uncertain.

It stopped and leaned against a tall tree, not knowing which way to walk now, or how to select, to approach, to suggest, not knowing the proper rituals of assent before this thing could be done. It stood for several minutes, watching a bright star quite close to being eclipsed by a rather small moon, before it noticed two things. The first was a man, a pygmy of the sperm-producing type, who was standing several meters off, watching it. The second was the fact that it had unconsciously folded its hands over its muzzle, in a rather suggestive and derisive gesture. It folded its arms, wondering if their position hadn't been interpreted as a very obvious come-on.

The man sauntered over to it, looked up and grinned. "Nice night."

He seemed not to expect a reply, but just stood there, looking up and chewing. Yes, chewing something lazily in his half-open mouth. He was a very attractive, dark-skinned man, with a look of confidence beyond his merits. And he liked Lofduns; that was evident. His eyes were busy admiring its slick golden skin and deep violet eyes. His face was busy saying the obvious, with a twist of the mouth, a cock of the head. And he was appetizing, quite appetizing.

Discretion had become an automatic part of Lofduns' life

since it had first searched out the banquet crowd by the river. So it didn't even think about secrecy when it led the man in through the garage entrance of the hotel and up the back lift to its room. Its mind was involved with half-remembered passages from cheap books it had read, images of fruits wiggling and squirming of their own accord, pictures of people self-consciously sliding their hands into others' mouths, and questions, too many often-asked questions. Was this what it really wanted? Or was it just a crazy way to occupy its mind and body and shelter them from the demands of life? Would it be, after all, disappointing? Would it know what to do at the right moment? And what would it say?

As it was, not a word was spoken. As soon as they entered the room, even before it had locked the door, the man began to strip. Lofduns followed him, stripping off its drab tunic and pantaloons, and stood by the mattress dressed only in its muzzle, looking down at the man's naked body. Small, yes, but remarkably like its own, narrower in the middle, but with two arms, two legs, a head with eyes and a windhole, not unattractive at all.

Its mouth muscles began to relax in stages. The man had no mouth. Or rather, his wind-hole and mouth were the same thing. Between his legs, below where his mouth should be, below his flat stomach, was something else, a stiff rod which was, in fact, a sperm-hole. No ova, just sperm.

Lofduns removed its muzzle and lay on the mattress. The man climbed on top and began to slide his legs into its mouth, which opened wide to receive a meal such as it had never had before. And gone were thoughts of fruits, of cherries, of melons, of spices. Gone was the frightening urge to go on to second stage. Relaxing, relaxing, exploring the curves and surfaces of this moving morsel, Lofduns began very slowly to salivate. New sensations, new shapes, new tastes all gave way in importance to the uniqueness of a shared experience. For it was shared. Only the man's head and arms lay outside, and his eyes were wide, fastened on Lofduns' own, empty of their brash cockiness, soundlessly crying against his loud eneven breathing for something, for something more, that Lofduns did not quite understand, as his body twisted and pushed, rolled and slid deep in its kneading mouth, building power to the moment, to the mad surge of giving, of giving, of feeding.

He didn't stay long afterward. He bathed, smoked a cigarette silently, dressed, and left. They said good-bye, good-bye only. And Lofduns lay, drained of energy, its muscles aching with pleasure, on the mattress, not disappointed, not ashamed, but sad. And it thought about tomorrow night, about a different one, maybe even a woman, who would stay perhaps a bit longer, who would be perhaps a bit warmer. Another night and another meal. For there is nothing like a good meal, but a meal, it seems, is always so very short.

Gardner R. Dozois

FLASH POINT

BEN JACOBS was on his way back to Skowhegan when he
found the abandoned car. It was parked on a lonely stretch of
secondary road between North Anson and Madison, skewed
diagonally over the shoulder.

Kids again, was Jacobs' first thought—more of the road
gypsies who plagued the state every summer until they were
driven south by the icy whip of the first nor'easter. Probably
from the big encampment down near Norridgewock, he
decided, and he put his foot back on the accelerator. He'd
already had more than his fill of outer-staters this season, and
it wasn't even the end of August. Then he looked more closely
at the car, and eased up on the gas again. It was too big, too
new to belong to kids. He shifted down into second, feeling
the crotchety old pickup shudder. It was an expensive car,
right enough; he doubted that it came from within twenty
miles of here. You didn't use a big-city car on most of the
roads in this neck of the woods, and you couldn't stay on the
highways forever. He squinted to see more detail. What kind
of plates did it have? You're doing it again, he thought, sud-.
denly and sourly. He was a man as aflame with curiosity as a
magpie, and—having been brought up strictly to mind his
own business—he considered it a vice. Maybe the car was
199

stolen. It's possible, a'n't it? he insisted, arguing with himself. It could have been used in a robbery and then ditched, like that car from the bank job over to Farmington. It happened all the time.

You don't even fool yourself anymore he thought, and then he grinned and gave in. He wrestled the old truck into the breakdown lane, jolted over a pothole, and coasted to a bumpy stop a few yards behind the car. He switched the engine off.

Silence swallowed him instantly.

Thick and dusty, the silence poured into the morning, filling the world as hot wax fills a mold. It drowned him completely, it possessed every inch and ounce of him. Almost, it spooked him.

Jacobs hesitated, shrugged, and then jumped down from the cab. Outside it was better—still quiet, but not preternaturally so. There was wind soughing through the spruce woods, a forlorn but welcome sound, one he had heard all his life. There was a wood thrush hammering at the morning, faint with distance but distinct. And a faraway buzzing drone overhead, like a giant sleepy bee or bluebottle, indicated that there was a Piper Cub up there somewhere, probably heading for the airport at Norridgewock. All this was familiar and reassuring. Getting nervy, is all, he told himself, long in the tooth and spooky.

Nevertheless, he walked very carefully toward the car, flat-footed and slow, the way he used to walk on patrol in 'Nam, more years ago than he cared to recall. His fingers itched for something, and after a few feet he realized that he was wishing he'd brought his old deer rifle along. He grimaced irritably at that, but the wish pattered through his mind again and again, until he was close enough to see inside the parked vehicle.

The car was empty.

"Old fool," he said sourly.

Snorting in derision at himself, he circled the car, peering in the windows. There were skid marks in the gravel of the breakdown lane, but they weren't deep—the car hadn't been going fast when it hit the shoulder; probably it had been already meandering out of control, with no foot on the accelerator. The hood and bumpers weren't damaged; the car had rolled to a stop against the low embankment, rather than crashing into it. None of the tires were flat. In the woods tak-

ing a leak, Jacobs thought. Damn fool didn't even leave his
turn signals on. Or it could have been his battery, or a vapor
lock or something, and he'd hiked on up the road looking for
a gas station. "He still should have ma'ked it off someway,"
Jacobs muttered. Tourists never knew enough to find their ass
in a snowstorm. This one probably wasn't even carrying any
signal flags or flares.

The driver's door was wide open, and next to it was a
child's plastic doll, lying facedown in the gravel. Jacobs could
not explain the chill that hit him then, the horror that seized
him and shook him until he was almost physically ill.
Bristling, he stooped and thrust his head into the car. There
was a burnt, bitter smell inside, like onions, like hot metal. A
layer of gray ash covered the front seat and the floor, a couple of inches deep; a thin stream of it was trickling over the
doorjamb to the ground and pooling around the plastic feet of
the doll. Hesitantly he touched the ash—it was sticky and
soapy to the touch. In spite of the sunlight that was slanting
into the car and warming up the upholstery, the ash was cold,
almost icy. The cloth ceiling directly over the front seat was
lightly blackened with soot—he scraped some of it off with
his thumbnail—but there was no other sign of fire. Scattered
among the ashes on the front seat were piles of clothing.
Jacobs could pick out a pair of men's trousers, a sports coat, a
bra, slacks, a bright child's dress, all undamaged. More than
one person. They're all in the woods taking a leak, he thought
inanely. Sta'k naked.

Sitting on the dashboard were a 35-mm. Nikon SI with a
telephoto lens and a new Leicaflex. In the hip pocket of the
trousers was a wallet, containing more than fifty dollars in
cash, and a bunch of credit cards. He put the wallet back. Not
even a tourist was going to be fool enough to walk off and
leave this stuff sitting here, in an open car.

He straightened up, and felt the chill again, the deathly
noonday cold. This tine he *was* spooked. Without knowing
why, he nudged the doll out of the puddle of ash with his
foot, and then he shuddered. "Hello!" he shouted, at the top
of his voice, and got back only a dull, flat echo from the
woods. Where in hell *had* they gone?

All at once, he was exhausted. He'd been out before dawn,
on a trip up to Kingfield and Carrabassett, and it was catch-
ing up with him. Maybe that was why he was so jumpy
over nothing. Getting old, c'n't take this kind of shit anymore.

How long since you've had a vacation? He opened his mouth to shout again, but uneasily decided not to. He stood for a moment, thinking it out, and then walked back to his truck, hunch-shouldered and limping. The old load of shrapnel in his leg and hip was beginning to bother him again.

Jacobs drove a mile down the highway to a rest stop. He had been hoping he would find the people from the car here, waiting for a tow truck, but the rest area was deserted. He stuck his head into the wood-and-fieldstone latrine, and found that it was inhabited only by buzzing clouds of bluebottles and blackflies. He shrugged. So much for that. There was a pay phone on a pole next to the picnic tables, and he used it to call the sheriff's office in Skowhegan. Unfortunately, Abner Jackman answered the phone, and it took Jacobs ten exasperating minutes to argue him into showing any interest. "Well, if they did," Jacobs said grudgingly, "they did it without any clothes." *Gobblegobblebuzz*, said the phone. "With a *kid*?" Jacobs demanded. *Buzzgobblefttzbuzz*, the phone said, giving in. "Ayah," Jacobs said grudgingly, 'I'll stay theah until you show up." And he hung up.

"Damned foolishness," he muttered. This was going to cost him the morning.

County Sheriff Joe Riddick arrived an hour later. He was a stocky, slab-sided man, apparently cut all of a piece out of a block of granite—his shoulders seemed to be the same width as his hips, his square-skulled square-jawed head thrust belligerently up from his monolithic body without any hint of a neck. He looked like an old snapping turtle: ugly, mud-colored, powerful. His hair was snow-white, and his eyes were bloodshot and ill-tempered. He glared at Jacobs dangerously out of red-rimmed eyes with tiny pupils. He looked ready to snap.

"Good morning," Jacobs said coldly.

"Morning," Riddick grunted. "You want to fill me in on this?"

Jacobs did. Riddick listened impassively. When Jacobs finished, Riddick snorted and brushed a hand back over his close-cropped snowy hair. "Some damn fool skylark more'n likely," he said, sourly, shaking his head a little. "O-kay, then," he said, suddenly becoming officious and brisk. "If this turns out to be anything serious, we may need you as a witness. Understand? All right." He looked at his watch. "All right. We're waiting for the state boys. I don't think you're needed anymore." Riddick's face was hard and cold and dull—as if it had been molded in lead. He stared pointedly at Jacobs. His eyes were opaque as marbles. "Good day."

Twenty minutes later Jacobs was passing a proud little sign, erected by the Skowhegan Chamber of Commerce, that said: HOME OF THE LARGEST SCULPTED WOODEN IN-DIAN IN THE WORLD! He grinned. Skowhegan had grown a great deal in the last decade, but somehow it was still a small town. It had resisted the modern tropism to skyscrape and had sprawled instead, spreading out along the banks of the Kennebec River in both directions. Jacobs parked in front of a dingy storefront on Water Street, in the heart of the town. A sign in the window commanded: EAT; at night it glowed an imperative neon red. The sign belonged to an establishment that had started life as the Colonial Cafe, with a buffet and quaint rustic decor, and was finishing it, twenty years and three recessions later, as a greasy lunchroom with faded movie posters on the wall—owned and operated by Wilbur and Myna Phipps, a cheerful and indestructible couple in their late sixties. It was crowded and hot inside—the place had a large number of regulars, and most of them were in attendance for lunch. Jacobs spotted Will Sussmann at the counter, jammed in between an inverted glass bowl full of doughnuts and the protruding rear-end of the coffee percolator.

Sussmann—chief staff writer for the Skowhegan *Inquirer*, stringer and columnist for a big Bangor weekly—had saved him a seat by piling the adjacent stool with his hat, coat, and briefcase. Not that it was likely he'd had to struggle too hard for room. Even Jacobs, whose father had moved to Skowhegan from Bangor when Jacobs was three, was regarded with faint suspicion by the real oldtimers of the town. Sussmann, being originally an outer-stater and a "foreigner" to boot, was completely out of luck; he'd only lived here ten years, and that wasn't enough even to begin to tip the balance in his favor.

Sussmann retrieved his paraphernalia; Jacobs sat down and began telling him about the car. Sussmann said it was weird. "We'll never get anything out of Riddick," he said. He began to attack a stack of hotcakes. "He's hated my guts ever since I accused him of working over those gypsy kids last summer, putting one in the hospital. That would have cost him his job, except the higher echelons were being 'foursquare behind their dedicated law enforcement officers' that season. Still, it didn't help his reputation with the town any."

"We don't tolerate that kind of thing in these pa'ts," Jacobs said grimly. "Hell, Will, those kids are a royal pain in the ass, but—" But not in these pa'ts, he told himself, not that. There are decent limits. He was surprised at the depth and ferocity of his reaction. "This a'n't Alabama," he said.

"Might as well be, with Riddick. His idea of law enforcement's to take everybody he doesn't like down in the basement and beat the crap out of them." Sussmann sighed. "Anyway, Riddick wouldn't stop to piss on me if my hat was on fire, that's for sure. Good thing I got other ways of finding stuff out."

Jed Everett came in while Jacobs was ordering coffee. He was a thin, cadaverous man with a long nose; his hair was going rapidly to gray; put him next to short, round Sussmann and they would look like Mutt and Jeff. At forty-eight—Everett was a couple of years older than Jacobs, just as Sussman was a couple of years younger—he was considered to be scandalously young for a small-town doctor, especially a GP. But old Dr. Barlow had died of a stroke three years back, leaving his younger partner in residency, and they were stuck with him.

One of the regulars had moved away from the trough, leaving an empty seat next to Jacobs, and Everett was talking before his buttocks had hit the upholstery. He was a jittery man, with lots of nervous energy, and he loved to fret and rant and gripe, but softly and goodnaturedly, with no real force behind it, as if he had a volume knob that had been turned down.

"What a morning!" Everett said. "Jesus H. Christ on a bicycle—'scuse me, Myna, I'll take some coffee, please, black—I swear it's psychosomatic. Honest to God, gentlemen, she's a case for the medical journals, dreams the whole damn shitbundle up out of her head just for the fun of it, I swear before all my hopes of heaven, swop me blue if she doesn't. *Definitely* phychosomatic."

"He's learned a new word," Sussmann said.

"If you'd wasted all the time I have on this nonsense," Everett said fiercely, "you'd be whistling a different tune out of the other side of your face, *I* can tell *you*, oh yes indeed. What kind of meat d'you have today, Myna? How about the chops—they good?—all right, and put some greens on the plate, please. Okay? Oh, and some homefrieds, now I think about it, please. If you have them."

"What's got your back up?" Jacobs asked mildly.

"You know old Mrs. Crawford?" Everett demanded. "Hm? Lives over to the Island, widow, has plenty of money? Three times now I've diagnosed her as having cancer, serious but still operable, and *three* times now I've sent her down to Augusta for exploratory surgery, and each time they got her down on the table and opened her up and couldn't find a thing, not a goddamned thing, old bitch's hale and hearty as a prize hog. Spontaneous remission. All psychosomatic, clear as mud. Three *times*, though. It's shooting my reputation all to hell down there. Now she thinks she's got an ulcer. I hope her kidney falls out, right in the street. Thank you, Myna. Can I have another cup of coffee?" He sipped his coffee, when it arrived, and looked a little more meditative. "Course, I think I've seen a good number of cases like that, I *think*, I said, ha'd to prove it when they're terminal. Wouldn't surprise me if a good many of the people who die of cancer—or a lot of other diseases, for that matter—were like that. No real physical cause, they just get tired of living, something dries up inside them, their systems stop trying to defend them, and one thing or another knocks them off. They become easy to touch off, like tinder. Most of them don't change their minds in the middle, though, like that fat old sow."

Wilbur Phipps, who had been leaning on the counter listening, ventured the opinion that modern medical science had never produced anything even half as good as the oldfashioned mustard plaster. Everett flared up instantly.

"You ever bejesus try one?" Phipps demanded.

"No, and I don't bejesus intend to!" Everett said.

Jacobs turned toward Sussmann. "Wheah you been, this early in the day?" he asked. "A'n't like you to haul yourself out before noon."

"Up at the Factory. Over to West Mills."

"What was up? Another hearing?"

"Yup. Didn't stick—they aren't going to be injuncted."

"They never will be," Jacobs said. "They got too much money, too many friends in Augusta. The Board'll never touch them."

"I don't believe that," Sussmann said. Jacobs grunted and sipped his coffee.

"As Christ's my judge," Everett was saying, in a towering rage, "I'll never understand you people, not if I live to be two hundred, not if I get to be so old my ass falls off and I have to lug it around in a handcart. I swear to God. Some of you ain' got a pot to piss in, so goddamned poor you can't afford to buy a bottle of aspirins, let alone, *let alone* pay your doctor bills from the past half-million years, and yet you go out to some godforsaken hick town too small to turn a horse around in proper and see an unlicensed practitioner, a goddamn backwoods quack, an un*mit*igated phony, and *pay* through the nose so this witchdoctor can assault you with yarb potions and poultices, and stick leeches on your ass, for all *I* know—"

Jacobs lost track of the conversation. He studied a bee that was bumbling along the putty-and-plaster edge of the storefront window, swimming through the thick and dusty sunlight, looking for a way out. He felt numb, distanced from reality. The people around him looked increasingly strange. He found that it took an effort of will to recognize them at all, even Sussmann, even Everett. It scared him. These were people Jacobs saw every day of his life. Some of them he didn't actually *like*—not in the way that big-city folk thought of liking someone—but they were all his neighbors. They belonged here, they were a part of his existence, and that carried its own special intimacy. But today he was beginning to see them as an intolerant sophisticate from the city might see them: dull, provincial, sunk in an iron torpor that masqueraded as custom and routine. That was valid, in its way, but it was a grossly one-sided picture, ignoring a thousand virtues, compensations and kindnesses. But that was the way he was seeing them. As aliens. As strangers.

Distractedly, Jacobs noticed that Everett and Sussmann were making ready to leave. "No rest for the weary," Everett was saying, and Jacobs found himself nodding unconsciously in agreement. Swamped by a sudden rush of loneliness, he invited both men home for dinner that night. They accepted, Everett with the qualification that he'd have to see what his wife had planned. Then they were gone, and Jacobs found himself alone at the counter.

He knew that he should have gone back to work also; he had some more jobs to pick up, and a delivery to make. But he felt very tired, too flaccid and heavy to move, as if some tiny burrowing animal had gnawed away his bones, as if he'd been hamstrung and hadn't realized it. He told himself that it was because he was hungry; he was running himself down, as Carol had always said he someday would. So he dutifully ordered a bowl of chili.

The chili was murky, amorphous stuff, bland and lukewarm. Listlessly, he spooned it up.

No rest for the weary.

"You know what I was nuts about when I was a kid?" Jacobs suddenly observed to Wilbur Phipps. "Rafts. I was a'ways making rafts out of old planks and sheet tin and whatevah other junk I could scrounge up, begging old rope and nails to lash them together with. Then I'd break my ass dragging them down to the Kennebec. And you know what? They a'ways sunk. Every goddamned time."

"Ayah?" Wilbur Phipps said.

Jacobs pushed the bowl of viscid chili away, and got up. Restlessly, he wandered over to where Dave Lucas, the game warden, was drinking beer and talking to a circle of men. ". . . dogs will be the end of deer in these pa'ts, I swear to God. And I a'n't talking about wild dogs neither, I'm talking about your ordinary domestic pets. A'n't it so, every winter? Half-starved deer a'n't got a chance in hell 'gainst somebody's big pet hound, all fed-up and rested. The deer those dogs don't kill outright, why they chase 'em to death, and then they don't even eat 'em. Run 'em out of the forest covah into the open and they get pneumonia. Run 'em into the river and through thin ice and they get drowned. Remember last yeah, the deer that hound drove out onto the ice? Broke both its front legs and I had to go out and shoot the poor bastid. Between those goddamn dogs and all the nighthunters we got around here lately, we a'n't going to have any deer left in this county . . ." Jacobs moved away, past a table where Abner Jackman was pouring ketchup over a plateful of scrambled eggs, and arguing about Communism with Steve Girard, a volunteer fireman and Elk, and Allen Ewing, a postman, who had a son serving with the Marines in Bolivia. ". . . let 'em win theah," Jackman was saying in a nasal voice, "and they'll be swa'ming all over us eventu'ly, sure as shit. Ain' no way to stop 'em then. And you're better off blowing your brains out than living under the Reds, don't ever think otherwise." He screwed the ketchup top back onto the bottle, and glanced up in time to see Jacobs start to go by.

"Ben!" Jackman said, grabbing Jacobs by the elbow. "You can tell 'em." He grinned vacuously at Jacobs—a lanky, loose-jointed, slack-faced man. "He can tell you, boys, what it's like being in a country overrun with Communists, what they do to everybody. You were in 'Nam when you were a youngster, weren't you?"

"Yeah."

After a pause, Jackman said, "You ain' got no call to take offense, Ben." His voice became a whine. "I didn't mean no ha'm. I didn't mean nothing."

"Forget it," Jacobs said, and walked out.

Dave Lucas caught up with Jacobs just outside the door. He was a short, grizzled man with iron-gray hair, about seven years older than Jacobs. "You know, Ben," Lucas said, "the thing of it is, Abner really doesn't mean any ha'm." Lucas smiled bleakly; his grandson had been killed last year, in the Retreat from La Paz. "It's just that he a'n't too bright, is all."

"They don't want him kicked ev'ry so often," Jacobs said, "then they shouldn't let him out of his kennel at all." He grinned. "Dinner tonight? About eight?"

"Sounds fine," Lucas said. "We're going to catch a night-hunter, out near Oaks Pond, so I'll probably be late."

"We'll keep it wa'm for you."

"Just the comp'ny'll be enough."

Jacobs started his truck and pulled out into the afternoon traffic. He kept his hands locked tightly around the steering wheel. He was amazed and dismayed by the surge of murderous anger he had felt toward Jackman; the reaction to it made him queasy, and left the muscles knotted all across his back and shoulders. Dave was right, Abner couldn't rightly be held responsible for the dumbass things he said— But if Jackman had said one more thing, if he'd done anything than to back down as quickly as he had, then Jacobs would have split his head open. He had been instantly ready to do it, his hands had curled into fists, his legs had bent slightly at the knees. He *would* have done it. And he would have enjoyed it. That was a frightening realization.

Y' touchy today, he thought, inanely. His fingers were turning white on the wheel.

He drove home. Jacobs lived in a very old wood frame house above the north bank of the Kennebec, on the outskirts of town, with nothing but a clump of new apartment buildings for senior citizens to remind him of civilization. The house was empty—Carol was teaching fourth grade, and Chris had been farmed out to Mrs. Turner, the baby-sitter. Jacobs spent the next half hour wrestling a broken washing machine and a television set out of the pickup and into his basement workshop, and another fifteen minutes maneuvering a newly repaired stereo-radio console up out of the basement and into the truck. Jacobs was one of the last of the old-style Yankee tinkerers, although he called himself an appliance repairman, and also did some carpentry and general handywork when things got slow. He had little formal training, but he "kept up." He wasn't sure he could fix one of the new hologram sets, but then they wouldn't be getting out here for another twenty years anyway. There were people within fifty miles who didn't have indoor plumbing. People within a hundred miles who didn't have electricity.

On the way to Norridgewock, two open jeeps packed dangerously full of gypsies came roaring up behind him. They started to pass, one on each side of his truck, their horns blaring insanely. The two jeeps ran abreast of Jacobs' old pickup for a while, making no attempt to go by—the three vehicles together filled the road. The jeeps drifted in until they were almost touching the truck, and the gypsies began pounding the truck roof with their fists, shouting and laughing. Jacobs kept both hands on the wheel and grimly continued to drive at his original speed. Jeeps tipped easily when sideswiped by a heavier vehicle, if it came to that. And he had a tire-iron under the seat. But the gypsies tired of the game—they accelerated and passed Jacobs, most of them giving him the finger as they went by, and one throwing a poorly aimed bottle that bounced onto the shoulder. They were big, tough-looking kids with skin haircuts, dressed—incongrously—in flowered pastel luau shirts and expensive white bellbottoms.

The jeeps roared on up the road, still taking up both lanes. Jacobs watched them unblinkingly until they disappeared from sight. He was awash with rage, the same bitter, vicious hatred he had felt for Jackman. Riddick was right after all—the goddamned kids were a menace to everything that lived, they ought to be locked up. He wished suddenly that he *had* sideswiped them. He could imagine it all vividly: the sickening crunch of impact, the jeep overturning, bodies cartwheeling through the air, the jeep skidding upside down across the road and crashing into the embankment, maybe the gas tank exploding, a gout of flame, smoke, stink, screams— He ran through it over and over again, relishing it, until he realized abruptly what he was doing, what he was wishing, and he was almost physically ill.

All the excitement and fury drained out of him, leaving

him shaken and sick. He'd always been a patient, peaceful man, perhaps too much so. He'd never been afraid to fight, but he'd always said that a man who couldn't talk his way out of most trouble was a fool. This sudden daydream lust for blood bothered him to the bottom of his soul. He'd seen plenty of death in 'Nam, and it hadn't affected him this way. It was the kids, he told himself. They drag everybody down to their own level. He kept seeing them inside his head all the way into Norridgewock—the thick, brutal faces, the hard reptile eyes, the contemptuously grinning mouths that seemed too full of teeth. The gypsy kids had changed over the years. The torrent of hippies and Jesus freaks had gradually run dry, the pluggers and the weeps had been all over the state for a few seasons, and then, slowly, they'd stopped coming too. The new crop of itinerant kids were—hard. Every year they became more brutal and dangerous. They didn't seem to care if they lived or died, and they hated everything indiscriminately—including themselves.

In Norridgewock, he delivered the stereo console to its owner, then went across town to pick up a malfunctioning 75-hp Johnson outboard motor. From the motor's owner, he heard that a town boy had beaten an elderly storekeeper to death that morning, when the storekeeper caught him shoplifting. The boy was in custody, and it was the scandal of the year for Norridgewock. Jacobs had noticed it before, but discounted it: the local kids were getting mean too, meaner every year. Maybe it was self-defense.

Driving back, Jacobs noticed one of the gypsy jeeps slewed up onto the road embankment. It was empty. He slowed, and stared at the jeep thoughtfully, but he did not stop.

A fire-rescue truck nearly ran him down as he entered Skowhegan. It came screaming out of nowhere and swerved onto Water Street, its blue blinker flashing, siren screeching in metallic rage, suddenly right on top of him. Jacobs wrenched his truck over to the curb, and it swept by like a demon, nearly scraping him. It left a frightened silence behind it, after it had vanished urgently from sight. Jacobs pulled back into traffic and continued driving. Just before the turnoff to his house, a dog ran out into the road. Jacobs had slowed down for the turn anyway, and he saw the dog in plenty of time to stop. He did not stop. At the last possible second, he yanked himself out of a waking dream, and swerved just enough to miss the dog. He had wanted to hit it; he'd liked the idea of running it down. There were too many dogs in the county anyway, he told himself, in a feeble attempt at justification. "Big, ugly hound," he muttered, and was appalled by how alien his voice sounded—hard, bitterly hard, as if it were a rock speaking. Jacobs noticed that his hands were shaking.

Dinner that night was a fair success. Carol had turned out not to be particularly overjoyed that her husband had invited a horde of people over without bothering to consult her, but Jacobs placated her a little by volunteering to cook dinner. It turned out "sufficient," as Everett put it. Everybody ate, and nobody died. Toward the end, Carol had to remind them to leave some for Dave Lucas, who had not arrived yet. The company did a lot to restore Jacobs' nerves, and, feeling better, he wrestled with curiosity throughout the meal. Curiosity won, as it usually did with him: in the end, and against his better judgment.

As the guests began to trickle into the parlor, Jacobs took Sussmann aside and asked him if he'd learned anything new about the abandoned car.

Sussmann seemed uneasy and preoccupied. "Whatever it was happened to them seems to've happened again this afternoon. Maybe a couple of times. There was another abandoned car found about four o'clock, up near Athens. And there was one late yesterday night, out at Livermore Falls. And a tractor-trailer on Route Ninety-five this morning, between Waterville and Benton Station."

"How'd you pry that out of Riddick?"

"Didn't." Sussmann smiled wanly. "Heard about that Athens one from the driver of the tow truck that hauled it back—that one bumped into a signpost, hard enough to break its radiator. Ben, Riddick can't keep me in the dark. I've got more stringers than he has."

"What d'you think it is?"

Sussmann's expression fused over and became opaque. He shook his head.

In the parlor, Carol, Everett's wife Amy—an ample, gray woman, rather like somebody's archetypical aunt but possessed of a very canny mind—and Sussmann, the inveterate bachelor, occupied themselves by playing with Chris. Chris was two, very quick and bright, and very excited by all the company. He'd just learned how to blow kisses, and was now practicing enthusiastically with the adults. Everett, meanwhile, was prowling around examining the stereo equipment that filled one wall. "You install this yourself?" he asked, when Jacobs came up to hand him a beer.

"Not only installed it," Jacobs said, "I built it all myself, from scratch. Tinkered up most of the junk in this house. Take the beah 'fore it gets hot."

"Damn fine work," Everett muttered, absently accepting the beer. "Better'n my own setup, I purely b'lieve, and that set me back a right sma't piece of change. Jesus Christ, Ben—I didn't know you could do quality work like that. What the hell you doing stagnating out here in the sticks, fixing people's radios and washing machines, f'chrissake? Y'that good, you ought to be down in Boston, New York mebbe, making some real money."

Jacobs shook his head. "Hate the cities, big cities like that. C'n't stand to live in them at all." He ran a hand through his hair. "I lived in New York for a while, seven-eight yeahs back, 'fore settling in Skowhegan again. It was terrible theah, even back then, and it's worse now. People down theah dying on their feet, walking around dead without anybody to tell 'em to lie down and get buried decent."

"We're dying here too, Ben," Everett said. "We're just doing it slower, is all."

Jacobs shrugged. "Mebbe so," he said. " 'Scuse me." He walked back to the kitchen, began to scrape the dishes and stack them in the sink. His hands had started to tremble again.

When he returned to the parlor, after putting Chris to bed, he found that conversation had almost died. Everett and Sussmann were arguing halfheartedly about the Factory, each knowing that he'd never convince the other. It was a pointless discussion, and Jacobs did not join it. He poured himself a glass of beer and sat down. Amy hardly noticed him; her usually pleasant face was stern and angry. Carol found an opportunity to throw him a sympathetic wink while tossing her long hair back over her shoulder, but her face was flushed too, and her lips were thin. The evening had started off well, but it had soured somehow; everyone felt it. Jacobs began to clean his pipe, using a tiny knife to scrape the bowl. A siren went by outside, wailing eerily away into distance. An ambulance, it sounded like, or the fire-rescue truck again—more melancholy and mournful, less predatory than the siren of a police cruiser. ". . . brew viruses . . ." Everett was saying, and then Jacobs lost him, as if Everett were being pulled further and further away by some odd, local perversion of gravity, his voice thinning into inaudibility. Jacobs couldn't hear him at all now. Which was strange, as the parlor was only a few yards wide. Another siren. There were a lot of them tonight; they sounded like the souls of the dead, looking for home in the darkness, unable to find light and life. Jacobs found himself thinking about the time he'd toured Vienna, during "recuperative leave" in Europe, after hospitalization in 'Nam. There was a tour of the catacombs under the Cathedral, and he'd taken it, limping painfully along on his crutch, the wet, porous stone of the tunnel roof closing down until it almost touched the top of his head. They came to a place where an opening had been cut through the hard, gray rock, enabling the tourists to come up one by one and look into the burial pit on the other side, while the guide lectured calmly in alternating English and German. When you stuck your head through the opening, you looked out at a solid wall of human bones. Skulls, arm and leg bones, rib cages, pelvises, all mixed in helter-skelter and packed solid, layer after uncountable layer of them. The wall of bones rose up sheer out of the darkness, passed through the fan of light cast by a naked bulb at eye-level, and continued to rise—it was impossible to see the top, no matter how you craned your neck and squinted. This wall had been built by the Black Death, a haphazard but grandiose architect. The Black Death had eaten these people up and spat out their remains, as casual and careless as a picnicker gnawing chicken bones. When the meal was over, the people who were still alive had dug a huge pit under the Cathedral and shoveled the victims in by the hundreds of thousands. Strangers in life, they mingled in death, cheek by jowl, belly to backbone, except that after a while there were no cheeks or jowls. The backbones remained: yellow, ancient and brittle. So did the Skulls—upright, upside down, on their sides, all grinning blankly at the tourists.

The doorbell rang.

It was Dave Lucas. He looked like one of the skulls Jacobs had been thinking about—his face was gray and gaunt, the skin drawn tightly across his bones; it looked as if he'd been dusted with powdered lime. Shocked, Jacobs stepped aside. Lucas nodded to him shortly and walked by into the parlor without speaking. ". . . stuff about the Factory is news," Sussman was saying, doggedly, "and more interesting than anything else that happens up here. It sells papers—" He stopped talking abruptly when Lucas entered the room. All conversation stopped. Everyone gaped at the old game warden, horrified. Unsteadily Lucas let himself down into a stuffed chair, and gave them a thin attempt at a smile. "Can I have a beah?" he said. "Or a drink?"

"Scotch?"

"That'll be fine," Lucas said mechanically.

Jacobs went to get it for him. When he returned with the drink, Lucas was determinedly making small talk and flashing his new dead smile. It was obvious that he wasn't going to say anything about what had happened to him. Lucas was an old-fashioned Yankee gentleman to the core, and Jacobs—who had a strong touch of that in his own upbringing—suspected why he was keeping silent. So did Amy. After the requisite few minutes of polite conversation, Amy asked if she could see the new paintings that Carol was working on. Carol exchanged a quick, comprehending glance with her, and nodded. Grim-faced, both women left the room—they knew that this was going to be bad. When the women were out of sight, Lucas said, "Can I have another drink, Ben?" and held out his empty glass. Jacobs refilled it wordlessly. Lucas had never been a drinking man.

"Give," Jacobs said, handing Lucas his glass. "What happened?"

Lucas sipped his drink. He still looked ghastly, but a little color was seeping back into his face. "A'n't felt this shaky since I was in the a'my, back in Korea," he said. He shook his head heavily. "I swear to Christ, I don't understand what's got into people in these pa'ts. Used t'be decent folk out heah, Christian folk." He set his drink aside, and braced himself up visibly. His face hardened. "Never mind that. Things change, I guess, c'n't stop 'em no way." He turned toward Jacobs. "Remember that nighthunter I was after. Well we got 'im, went out with Steve Girard, Rick Barlow, few other boys, and nabbed him real neat—city boy, no woods sense at all. Well, we were coming back around the end of the pond, down the lumber road, when we heard this big commotion coming from the Gibson place, shouts, a woman screaming her head off, like that. So we cut across the back of their field and went over to see what was going on. House was wide open, and what we walked into—" He stopped; little sickly beads of sweat had appeared all over his face. "You remember the

McInerney case down in Boston four-five yeahs back? The
one there was such a stink about? Well, it was like that. They
had a whatchamacallit there, a cover—the Gibsons, the Swells,
the Bradshaws, about seven others, all local people all hopped
out of their minds, all dressed up in black robes, and—blood,
painted all over their faces. God, I— No, never mind. They
had a baby there, and a kind of an altar they'd dummied up,
and a pentagram. Somebody'd killed the baby, slit its throat,
and they'd hung it up to bleed like a hog. Into cups. When we
got there, they'd just cut its heart out, and they were starting
in on dismembering it. Hell—they were tearing it apart, never
mind that 'dismembering' shit. They were so frenzied-blind
they hardly noticed us come in. Mrs. Bradshaw hadn't been
able to take it, she'd cracked completely and was sitting in a
corner screaming her lungs out, with Mr. Sewell trying to shut
her up. They were the only two that even tried to run. The
boys hung Gibson and Bradshaw and Sewell, and stomped Ed
Patterson to death—I just couldn't stop 'em. It was all I could
do to keep 'em from killing the other ones. I shot Steve Girard
in the arm, trying to stop 'em, but they took the gun away,
and almost strung me up too. My God, Ben, I've known Steve
Girard a'most ten yeahs. I've known Gibson and Sewell all
my life." He stared at them appealingly, blind with despair.
"What's happened to people up heah?"

No one said a word.

Not in these pa'ts, Jacobs mimicked himself bitterly. *There
are decent limits.*

Jacobs found that he was holding the pipe-cleaning knife
like a weapon. He'd cut his finger on it, and a drop of blood
was oozing slowly along the blade. This kind of thing—the
Satanism, the ritual murders, the sadism—was what had
driven him away from the city. He'd thought it was different
in the country, that people were better. But it wasn't, and they
weren't. It was bottled up better out here, was all. But it had
been coming for years, and they had blinded themselves to it
and done nothing, and now it was too late. He could feel it in
himself, something long repressed and denied, the reaction to
years of frustration and ugliness and fear, to watching the
world dying without hope. That part of him had listened to
Lucas' story with appreciation, almost with glee. It stirred
strongly in him, a monster turning over in ancient mud, down
inside, thousands of feet down, thousands of years down. He
could see it spreading through the faces of the others in the
room, a stain, a spider shadow of contamination. Its presence

was suffocating: the chalky, musty smell of old brittle death, somehow leaking through from the burial pit in Vienna. Bone dust—he almost choked on it, it was so thick here in his pleasant parlor in the country.

And then the room was filled with sound and flashing, bloody light.

Jacobs floundered for a moment, unable to understand what was happening. He swam up from his chair, baffled, moving with dreamlike slowness. He stared in helpless confusion at the leaping red shadows. His head hurt.

"An ambulance!" Carol shouted, appearing in the parlor archway with Amy. "We saw it from the upstairs window—"

"It's right out front," Sussmann said.

They ran for the door. Jacobs followed them more slowly. Then the cold outside air slapped him, and he woke up a little. The ambulance was parked across the street, in front of the senior citizens' complex. The corpsmen were hurrying up the stairs of one of the institutional, cinderblock buildings, carrying a stretcher. They disappeared inside. Amy slapped her bare arms to keep off the cold. "Heart attack, mebbe," she said. Everett shrugged. Another siren slashed through the night, getting closer. While they watched, a police cruiser pulled up next to the ambulance, and Riddick got out. Riddick saw the group in front of Jacobs' house, and stared at them with undisguised hatred, as if he would like to arrest them and hold them responsible for whatever had happened in the retirement village. Then he went inside too. He looked haggard as he turned to go, exhausted, hagridden by the suspicion that he'd finally been handed something he couldn't settle with a session in the soundproofed back room at the sheriff's office.

They waited. Jacobs slowly became aware that Sussmann was talking to him, but he couldn't hear what he was saying. Sussmann's mouth opened and closed. It wasn't important anyway. He'd never noticed before how unpleasant Sussmann's voice was, how rasping and shrill. Sussmann was ugly too, shockingly ugly. He boiled with contamination and decay—he was a sack of putrescence. He was an abomination.

Dave Lucas was standing off to one side, his hands in his pockets, shoulders slumped, his face blank. He watched the excitement next door without expression, without interest. Everett turned and said something that Jacobs could not hear. Like Sussmann's, Everett's lips moved without sound. He had moved closer to Amy. They glanced uneasily around. They were abominations too.

Jacobs stood with his arm around Carol; he didn't remember putting it there—it was seeking company on its own. He felt her shiver, and clutched her more tightly in response, directed by some small, distanced, horrified part of himself that was still rational—he knew it would do no good. There was a thing in the air tonight that was impossible to warm yourself against. It hated warmth, it swallowed it and buried it in ice. It was a wedge, driving them apart, isolating them all. He curled his hand around the back of Carol's neck. Something was pulsing through him in waves, building higher and stronger. He could feel Carol's pulse beating under her skin, under his fingers, so very close to the surface.

Across the street, a group of old people had gathered around the ambulance. They shuffled in the cold, hawking and spitting, clutching overcoats and nightgowns more tightly around them. The corpsmen reappeared, edging carefully down the stairs with the stretcher. The sheet was pulled up all the way, but it looked curiously flat and caved-in—if there was a body under there, it must have collapsed, crumbled like dust or ash. The crowd of old people parted to let the stretcher crew pass, then re-formed again, flowing like a heavy, sluggish liquid. Their faces were like leather or horn: hard, dead, dry, worn smooth. And *tired*. Intolerably, burdensomely tired. Their eyes glittered in their shriveled faces as they watched the stretcher go by. They looked uneasy and afraid, and yet there was an anticipation in their faces, an impatience, almost an envy, as they looked on death. Silence blossomed from a tiny seed in each of them, a total, primordial silence, from the time before there were words. It grew, consumed them, and merged to form a greater silence that spread out through the night in widening ripples.

The ambulance left.

In the hush that followed, they could hear sirens begin to wail all over town.

ARCS & SECANTS

KATE WILHELM ("The Scream," p. 7) has appeared in every volume of *Orbit*. Harlan Ellison said about her, in *Again, Dangerous Visions*, "She is certainly the very best writer we have working in the field of speculative fiction."

Grania Davis ("Young Love," p. 32), the descendant of Russian Jews who came over in steerage and eventually settled in Los Angeles, is the former wife of Avram Davidson. Now married to a Bay Area doctor, she is a well-to-do suburban matron with a house, two cars, 2.2 children, a basset hound, two Siamese cats, etc. She recently finished her first novel.

R. A. Lafferty's self-education began when his father gave him the eighteen-volume Grolier *History of the World* for his tenth birthday. Lafferty read straight through it in a year, still remembers most of it. "And Name My Name" (p. 51) is his eleventh story for *Orbit*. His latest book is *Okla Hannali* (Doubleday, 1972).

Edward Bryant ("Going West," p. 64) was born in White Plains, New York, but has lived mostly in Wyoming since he was six months old. In college he spent a year as an aerospace engineering major before slipping back into "arts and sciences —general." Regarding "Dune's Edge," which appeared in *Orbit 11*, he wrote, "Aaaagh. The only time I've spent more time discussing emendations with an editor was three years ago when David Gerrold wanted me to drop the one lone appearance of the word 'fuck' in a story. I won, but it took months of citing literary critics, social pundits, and the like . . . There was another time, later, when I clashed with Bob Hoskins over his desire to change my 'watercress sherbet' to 'watermelon sherbet.' (Unbelievably yeccch," said Hoskins.) I lost that one."

James Sallis ("My Friend Zarathustra," p. 78) is a southerner educated at Tulane, a poet, a beer-drinker, ex-editor of *New Worlds*, restless traveler. He was the director of the Clarion Writers' Workshop at Tulane in 1971. Macmillan published a collection of his stories, *A Few Last Words*, in 1970.

Gary K. Wolf ("Therapy," p. 81) is married to an airline stewardess, with whom he has visited the Orient, South Pacific, Caribbean, Nether Antilles, Europe, etc., etc. Because of allergies, he avoids contact with all four-legged animals. He would like to have a pet, and his wife has made one suggestion, but so far, he says, he has not been able to generate much enthusiasm for a duck.

W. Macfarlane ("Gardening Notes from All Over," p. 87) was drafted after college when he was working for Lockheed, and the Army made him a professional artilleryman; he ended up a major. He has been an orchardman (still is), a winter vegetable wholesaler, and an estimator for a highway contractor. Some of these experiences turn up in his fiction.

Doris Piserchia ("Idio," p. 97) and "Naked and Afraid I Go," p. 159) still lives in a madhouse—see the note about her circumstances in *Orbit 12*. Her husband successfully underwent heart surgery in April, 1972, but his condition is deteriorating. Writing is Mrs. Piserchia's lifeline.

Albert Teichner ("Fantasy's Profession," p. 109) was once a member of a three-student writing class at Rutgers; one of the other members was James Blish. After the war, which he spent mostly in New Guinea and the Philippines, he took an MA at Columbia with a thesis entitled "Some Uses of Logical Paradox in the Poetry of John Donne." Weather permitting, he swims a mile a day.

Charles Arnold, a physics dropout from Carleton College, was working on the Illiac IV project at the University of Illinois when the United States invaded Cambodia. ("Illiac IV will be the biggest and fastest computer in the world if it works when they plug it in; it was designed at U.I. and is being built by military money.") During the complications that followed, he quit in protest and turned to writing science fiction. "Spring Came to Blue Ridge Early This Year" (p. 120) is his first published story.

C. L. Grant ("Everybody a Winner, the Barker Cried," p. 150) spent the summer of 1972 in London studying drama at Royal Holloway College (University of Bath). He was pleased to find that the British countryside was just as he had pictured it in "The Summer of the Irish Sea" *(Orbit 11)*. He also met a sympathetic young lady to whom he expects to be married by the summer of 1973; he adds that he can't say he is sorry, because being a bachelor ain't all that it's cracked up to be.

Dennis Etchison ("Black Sun," p. 183) spent several months doing a feature-length adaptation of Ray Bradbury's story "The Fox and the Forest," but the producers did not like it. (They also did not like two previous versions and one later one by other writers, and refused to look at a sample script donated by Bradbury.) More recently he has been collaborating with George Clayton Johnson on an original screenplay called *The Cops*.

William F. Orr ("The Mouth Is for Eating," p. 192) teaches mathematics at the University of Wisconsin at Milwaukee, and is working on a thesis in algebra and finite geometry. He has translated the poems of Lewis Carroll and most of the songs from *Hair* into Esperanto. This is his first published story.

Gardner R. Dozois, who retreated to Philadelphia more than a year ago, has hardly left it since and is beginning to feel hidebound and barnacle-covered. "Flash Point" (p. 199) is his sixth *Orbit* story.

FOOD FOR THOUGHT:
BERKLEY BOOKS ON THE PSI PHENOMENA

INCIDENT AT EXETER   (Z2539—$1.25)
  by John G. Fuller

THE COMING OF THE GODS   (N2398—95¢)
  by Jean Sendy

THOSE GODS WHO MADE
HEAVEN AND EARTH   (Z2690—$1.25)
  by Jean Sendy

SPIRIT MAGIC   (N2478—95¢)
  by Alice Wellman

THE SECRETS OF NUMBERS   (N2532—95¢)
  by Vera Johnson and Thomas Wommack

THE LIFE BEYOND DEATH   (Z2234—$1.25)
  by Arthur Ford, as told to Jerome Ellison

THE LEGACY OF THE GODS   (Z2589—$1.25)
  by Robert Charroux

HOUSES THAT KILL   (Z2620—$1.25)
  by Robert de Lafforest

Send for a *free* list of all our books in print

These books are available at your local newsstand, or send price indicated plus 25¢ per copy to cover mailing costs to Berkley Publishing Corporation, 200 Madison Avenue, New York, N.Y. 10016.